BURNING EMERALD

Also by Jaime Reed

Living Violet

Published by Kensington Publishing Corporation

BURNING EMERALD

THE CAMBION CHRONICLES

JAIME REED

Dafina KTeen Books
KENSINGTON PUBLISHING CORP.
http://www.kensingtonbooks.com

DAFINA KTEEN BOOKS are published by

Kensington Publishing Corp.
119 West 40th Street
New York, NY 10018

All Kensington titles, imprints, and distributed lines are available at special quantity discounts for bulk purchases for sales promotion, premiums, fund-raising, educational, or institutional use.

Special book excerpts or customized printings can also be created to fit specific needs. For details, write or phone the office of the Kensington Special Sales Manager: Attn.: Special Sales Department. Kensington Publishing Corp., 119 West 40th Street, New York, NY 10018. Phone: 1-800-221-2647.

KTeen Reg. US Pat. & TM Off.
Sunburst logo Reg. US Pat. & TM Off.

ISBN-13: 978-0-7582-6925-6
ISBN-10: 0-7582-6925-0

First Printing: June 2012
10 9 8 7 6 5 4 3 2 1

Printed in the United States of America

To friends:
patient ears to listen,
wise mouths to counsel,
and generous hands to lend.

Priceless.

1

When you're a Cambion, balance is paramount.

Never lose control, never allow emotions to run wild, and never, ever forget who you are and what lives within you. Such discipline requires a sound mind, a thick skin, and a high tolerance for all things weird, because one wrong move and it's over. No matter how tempting it is at first, in the end there's nothing more tragic, more excruciating, than losing yourself.

Well, except maybe high school.

I swam against the rough current of swinging backpacks, sharp elbows, and whipping ponytails, all in hopes of reaching the auditorium in one piece. The corridors overflowed with foot traffic, disorganized chatter, and the rowdy boom of slamming lockers. The floor rumbled from the stampede fleeing the fourth class of the day.

The varsity team hooted victory chants to the trophy gods behind the glass case in front of the main office. Teenyboppers huddled together in tight clusters, sharing magazines and gushing over the latest fad. Straight ahead lay the obstacle course of shameless make-out bandits who needed to rent a hotel room and stop blocking the hallway. The only thing missing was the cheesy pop soundtrack and the CW logo in the bottom corner. TV high school looked a lot cleaner though, and I bet it didn't reek of bleach and dried ketchup.

I hid my face behind my compact mirror while trying to ignore the dagger stares aimed in my direction, especially if the owners of those eyes had a boyfriend nearby. Even Lilith, my "internal roommate," bristled at the laser beam of hate that shot my way.

My peers had dubbed me the freak of James City High School, not because of the red and white stripe in my hair or my butterball figure, but because of the avid attention from the males who crossed my path. 'Twas the curse of the dreaded possession, I'm afraid.

I wouldn't have been able to explain what a Cambion was three months ago, or known such a thing as human-demon hybrids existed. But now I knew from firsthand experience what it meant to have a soul of a succubus inside me, draining my energy, and luring unsuspecting males to their death to get more. Nothing much I could do about the long, hungry glances and the not-so-subtle whispers. All I could do was avoid eye contact, stay out of trouble, and pray for June to come quickly. I only had eight months to go.

Flashing lights attacked my retinas as soon as I entered the auditorium. Two murky gray backdrops were stationed in the center of the stage, where hired photographers captured our final year for posterity. Two lines ran at opposite ends of the platform steps and leaked into the aisles.

I trotted down the steep incline where teachers directed students to the photo table. I found my name on the list, grabbed my ticket and one of those cheap plastic combs nurses use to check head lice, and then got in line. A good number of students stood ahead of me, fixing their hair and retouching their makeup. The rest sat in the rows of seats, in no rush to go to class.

Not even a moment after I stood in line, my best friend rested her head on my shoulder, her whole body trembling with laughter. "Girl, did you see what Courtney G. is wearing? It's what you would call 'a piping-hot mess.' "

I blotted my nose and chin. "Now, now, Mia. Be nice. We all can't be a fashionista like you."

"Of course not, but I expect the basic principles of co-ordination. I mean, really?" Mia shook her head, her whiskey-brown eyes widened in dismay. "Another thing, when are these kids gonna learn that you don't keep wearing your new clothes the first few weeks of school? You slowly blend it into your existing wardrobe."

There was the fashion police and there was the one-man Gestapo called Mia Moralez. How she passed dress code with the getups she wore was the magic trick of the century. And today's eye-popping number was no exception. She showed more breast and thigh than an eight-piece combo meal, yet never got called to the office. How did that work? I envied her bravery and her slim physique, but as of late, I envied her ability to ace pre-cal without breaking a sweat. The girl was a walking Pentium chip with expensive taste.

"Ohmigod! What happened to your face?" She spun me around and pinched my cheeks between her fingers. "Sam, who did this?"

Why do people feel the need to poke and prod at a victim's injuries? Ducking her curious fingers, I answered, "Stray dodgeball to the dome." I took a deep breath, knowing I wouldn't get two feet without telling her the whole story.

Female aggression had reached critical mass today

when the girls in third period gym decided to use me for target practice. A simple game of dodgeball had led to a thirty-minute death match, and even the gym teacher had turned a blind eye to the ambush.

Caleb, my main squeeze and fellow Cambion, had experienced his share of rabid females. He'd warned me about our powerful allure and told me to expect hostility from other girls, especially the insecure ones. But oh no, I had to be hardheaded and shrug it off. The daily dose of haterade was bitter and hard to swallow, leaving my thirst for female camaraderie unquenched.

Well, almost.

"Those evil bitches!" Mia shrieked again after hearing my tale of woe. "Of all the days to get a black eye—Picture Day! These are our senior pictures, the ones that are going into the yearbook, for the world to see. Now look at you, a shell of what you once were. Don't worry, I'll take 'em down." She searched around the auditorium as if one of my attackers lurked in the shadows.

And the award for best actress in an over-dramatization goes to . . .

It wasn't that bad, nothing a little concealer couldn't fix, and the swelling had gone down considerably—a little puffiness near my cheekbone. "Forget it. I can take care of myself," I assured.

"I know, but they can't just—"

"Let it go, Mia. I don't want any more trouble. I want to survive the year without further bloodshed."

It took a few minutes, but she finally let the subject drop. Folding her arms, she studied me from head to toe. Her long, dark locks rested over her right shoulder in one enormous curl, accenting her exotic, island features. "You're not gonna wear those contacts for your picture, are you? It would add a little flare to the aesthetics, but it might draw more attention to your shiner."

I froze mid primp. I knew I'd forgotten to do something when I left the house this morning, but I'd been running late and pretending to be normal took a lot of prep work. For the sake of appearances, I'd had to order a lifetime supply of brown contacts to pass as my old color, thanks to the sentient being living inside me. Lilith's occupancy made my eyes extremely sensitive, and she hated weird window dressing obstructing her view. To give her peace, I switched up every few days and I took them out as soon as I got home. As far as anyone knew, my emerald-green eyes were fake, not the other way around.

"Well, I wanted to make my mark," I replied with a bit of sass.

"Suit yourself. I'm out. Catch you later," she said just as I caught Malik Davis entering the auditorium from over her shoulder. I knew as soon as he saw me, he would try to spark a conversation.

I turned to Mia in a rush of panic. "You're done?"

"I was the first in line. Had to get it over and done with. It's hard work to look this good all day." Mia sauntered away before I could grab her and use her as a shield.

Normally, I wouldn't be so clingy, but I so didn't feel like having another run-in with Malik. It was bad enough my black eye would be immortalized in eight-by-ten gloss; I didn't need him rubbing it in.

Malik Davis, a senior and my new shadow, fueled the wet dreams of every girl in school. As if he needed more attention, Malik had become an overnight celebrity when his truck wrapped around a tree last month and he walked away without a scratch, a heroic tale that he never grew sick of telling. Who wouldn't want to hang on the arm of the sexy basketball captain who cheated death? Oh yeah, that would be me.

"How you doin', Shorty?" he drawled in that smooth, magnolia tone that could melt butter. The solid wall of his body brushed my back.

The nickname grated my ears and made my skin crawl. True, the top of my head barely reached to his shoulders, but I wasn't a garden gnome, and pointing out someone's faults was not a good way to spark a conversation.

"Great, thanks. And yourself?" I stepped away as the line moved forward.

"It's a good day, especially after seeing you," Malik whispered in my ear.

"You give me too much credit. You shouldn't need a girl to make you happy. If so, you have plenty to choose from."

"Maybe so, but you've got my undivided attention, girl. I don't know why I never noticed you before; we've got a bunch of classes together and all that. But I like light-skinned girls, and your contacts are hot. They look so real."

Here we go. If I had a quarter for every time someone mentioned my eye color—

"Let me ask you something. What's a fine sistah like you doing with that white boy? You know he's using you, right?"

I stopped. "For what?"

His gaze slid down my body at leisure. "What you think?"

I wasn't even going to dignify that with an answer, but it served to remind me why I couldn't stand him in the first place. Since tenth grade, Malik had made my mixed race a subject of ridicule, judging my choice of friends, my vocabulary, my taste in music, and now my boyfriend. The words *sellout*, *Oreo*, and *zebra* were commonly used in our brief exchanges. "Fine sistah" had never been included, but was a new moniker, courtesy of my roommate's influence, no doubt.

"I don't mean no harm by it," he said. "I just—"

"Just what, Malik? 'Cause I don't like your tone."

"That Caleb guy will never take you seriously, Samara. He's just gonna take what he wants, then leave."

"And let me guess, you're so much better for me, because we all know you would never get with a girl and leave her high and dry," I bit back.

The photographer's perky assistant yelled for the next pair to approach the stage, which was Malik and me.

After handing the assistant his ticket, the cause of my growing headache turned to me. "Look, I'm just watching out for you. How could you even stomach being with somebody like that?"

That did it. Evidently, people didn't get anywhere in life by being polite in this school. Turning on the balls of my feet, I glared up at him. He looked amused, but that didn't last long.

"Look here, there's no nice way to put this, so I won't even try. It's none of your damn business what I do with my boyfriend. I'm sure it eats you up inside that I'm not sniffing behind you like the rest of the herd, or that you will never in life get to sample any of this luscious I got going on, but seriously, you need to get off my ass, or else I'll break my foot off in yours." I strolled to the stage, leaving Malik standing with a stunned look on his face.

The assistant directed me to the stool and ordered me to sit up straight. Malik sat in the station to my left, his stare burning at my profile, but I wouldn't give him the satisfaction of caring.

There was just something about him that didn't sit well with me, even more than usual. An air of danger loomed around him, an unnatural aura that gave me the willies.

Lilith felt it as well, voicing her disquiet with sharp tingles up my spinal cord, and worrying the network of nerves lining my midsection. While the photographer arranged my chin and shoulders in the right position, I snuck a glance at Malik.

He was good-looking, hotter than my boyfriend, though I would never whisper that to a living soul. It shamed me to admit that I'd had a few fantasies of him, most involving a hot tub and a vat of cookie dough ice cream, but that secret will follow me to the grave. Besides, looks meant nothing if you were an asshole, a self-righteous tool who turned into a skeleton in sharp lighting.

Wait, what the—?

I blinked and spun my stool completely in Malik's direction. Did I just see what I thought I did? As soon as the camera flashed, his clothes, skin, and all external material vanished, leaving a framework of bones sitting on the stool. The weird X-ray vision only lasted a second, but that was enough to freak me out.

When the photographer finished, Malik rose to his feet and strolled to the opposite side of the stage. He spared me a fleeting glance and smiled with more humor than the occasion called for. A quick glint of gold flickered in his dark brown eyes, then disappeared.

"Face this way, hon. Shoulders straight." The voice of my own photographer snapped me back to attention.

My heart tapped Morse code against my ribs as I tried in vain to make sense of what I'd just seen. Forcing the worst smile in history, I waited for the camera flash.

Nothing outside of the natural surprised me anymore, but my curiosity would never die. The events of the summer had taught me well never to ignore those feelings, but to embrace them and expect the unexpected. Maybe I wasn't the only freak getting their learn on at James City

High School. Perhaps it was a new power I had acquired that I was just now tapping into, an ability to foresee danger, like in those *Final Destination* movies. More than likely, it was my overactive mind running wild, something that happened a lot lately.

I only knew that this was a warning of some sort, a whisper too faint too make out the words.

2

Despite everything that had changed in my life, things stayed the same at Buncha Books, much like how cartoon characters never aged or changed clothes. I found it refreshing.

Fusion jazz pumped through the speakers. A group of girls giggled and read steamy paperbacks from the erotica section. Young entrepreneurs hovered over their laptops, abusing the free Wi-Fi the store provided. Old men who had mistaken the bookstore for a rest home hogged all the sofas while reading the newspaper. Yep, business as usual at Buncha Books, set under a thick aroma of fresh cookies and hot espresso.

Alicia Holloway was on duty with me at the café, perky and animated as ever, which put a damper on my afternoon. Her elfin face, hopeful brown eyes, and twisty braids always reminded me of a black woodland sprite who couldn't find her way home. She stood by the barista machine, watching a tin of hot milk bubble with foam.

"I'm not judging or anything, but it's just weird," she

began, concerning the unlikely attraction between Caleb and me. "Isn't there, like, a rule somewhere about not dating your coworkers?"

"Isn't there, *like*, a rule about minding your own business?" I mocked while toweling off my wet hands, taking extra care to dry the gold bracelet on my wrist. I rotated the chain so the nameplate stood face up, and Lilith hummed when she recognized her name engraved on it in elegant script.

Alicia let out a shrill meow and set a row of fixed drinks on the coffee bar. "Somebody forgot to bring their charm to work. I'm just saying, you should be more low-key. People talk, you know."

I watched her rush to the register to ring up the next customer. "Yeah, like people are talking in school about your tragic romance with Garrett Davenport."

"What!" she squeaked, dropping the customer's change. She quickly apologized, then turned to me with alarm. "What did you hear?"

Shifting my lips from left to right, I crooned, "Oh, stuff. Like you and him secretly dating before he died and now all three Courtneys want your head on a platter, that's all. You're making enemies in high places. Be careful. Girls in our school are vicious."

Lifting her chin high, she poured coffee mix and ice in the blender. "I'm not scared of them."

My gaze wandered to the book floor and I smiled. "Oh, so if, say, Courtney B. rolled up right now, you wouldn't be scared?"

"Not at all."

"Good to know, because she's heading to the counter right now."

By the time I turned around, Alicia was a ghost with the blender still running. Only the swinging door of the back kitchen told me where she'd disappeared to. After finishing the drink order for her, I took my time going to the register and prayed for patience while in contact with the redheaded diva.

The three Courtneys were renowned in my school for their reign of tyranny, and Courtney B. ruled as the blood-sucking queen of the damned. The recent death of Garrett Davenport had shot the trio to stardom, and they milked the sympathy vote by wearing all black the first week of school. Telling by Courtney B.'s ensemble, the period of mourning was over.

Decked out in designer labels from head to toe, Courtney B. approached the counter with a strut suitable only for the runway. All that was missing were the wind machine and the slow-motion camera. Aside from her being painfully vapid, she owned the unmatched talent of squeezing insults into every conversation. For fear of getting fired, I decided to limit my responses to two words or less.

Her handbag thumped on the counter while she scanned around for the prey that had vanished from sight. Disappointed, she narrowed her icy gray eyes at me. "Hi. You're in my Spanish class. Sam, right?"

"Sí," I said, deadpan. I couldn't believe this chick. We'd shared at least two classes since sixth grade and she still didn't know my name?

"Is that, like, short for Samantha?"

"No." I pointed to my name tag.

"Oh. My bad. Anyway, you know that hot guy that works here, Caleb something?" She looked around the store.

Tapping my finger to my lips, I contemplated. "Six-foot-two, brown hair, purple-blue eyes, always smells like cake? Yeah, that would be my *boyfriend*." I stressed the last word.

"Oh!" She looked surprised for a moment, appalled

even, then swept a cursory glance up my frame. "Well, maybe you can help. I was wondering if you could talk him into deejaying my party on Halloween. He did such a great job at Robbie Ford's birthday party; I'd love to have him, um, spin for me." She twirled a lock of hair around her manicured finger.

I should be used to women drooling all over my man, but that would require more patience than I could afford. "I'll be sure to run it by him, but it would be more businesslike coming from you. You can find him in the music section. That way." I pointed to the other end of the store using my middle finger, a gesture too blatant to over-look.

Applying loud suction, Courtney slid her tongue over her teeth, perhaps to see if her fangs elongated. "Thanks. Doesn't seem to be your kind of thing, but I'll see if I can add you to the guest list too." With a neck-spraining flip of the hair, she flounced away.

Resting my weight against the counter, I exhaled slowly, absorbing the sting of her verbal attack. This was an interesting turn of events. Courtney's Halloween bashes were the talk of school, but unlike Robbie Ford's parties, hers were for the A-list only. Mia would be so jealous if I got an invite before she did. The only down-side was subjecting Caleb to that harpy's whims.

This was a good opportunity for him. Soon he would leave his position here to "scratch" with full force, but his budding deejay career already left us juggling sched-ules to see each other. Music was the mistress in our union, the only love I didn't mind sharing with him.

"Is she gone?" A timid voice came from the kitchen.

When I confirmed that she was, Alicia crept out, a wash of relief ran across her face. I shook my head, knowing this doe-eyed sophomore needed more life expe-rience and pessimism to survive high school. The mother hen in me wanted to keep her innocence intact, so my watchful eyes were never far from her.

Seeing her trepidation, I said, "If it gets too bad, you have my number, okay?"

"Thanks." She gave me a weak smile and went back to the register.

Though I only worked a few five-hour shifts during the weekdays, time seemed to run at a snail's pace. Alicia tried her best to entertain me with the latest gossip, but it didn't seem the same with Nadine gone. Nothing was the same with her gone.

I found myself comparing Alicia to Nadine, noting how she took forever to wrap the food when we closed, where it would only take Nadine ten minutes. Alicia chatted and laughed with the customers, whereas they had been considered lucky if they got service, let alone a smile, from Nadine. Alicia was an old friend and I would flip out if something happened to her, but the injustice prevailed.

That fact prevented me from finding closure, and I kept picking that scab until it bled. Time might patch it up, but the open wounds remained untreated and at risk of infection. Even if I'd known all that would happen, would it have made a difference? If Nadine hadn't died in my arms, Lilith wouldn't have needed to abandon ship and move into my crib. Maybe Lilith was her farewell gift, a secret she entrusted me to keep.

After shutdown, I clocked out at customer service, then ambled to the break room in an almost dreamlike state. Our monthly book club meeting was tonight, which was reason enough to wallow in sorrow, but seeing where Nadine had once sat deepened my depression another notch.

A part of me expected to see Nadine pass through the door, her blond hair bobbing behind her head in a haphazard bun. The staff's seating arrangement was an unspoken rule, so I wasn't the only one who paused at the empty folding chair by the soda machine. Even Linda, the store manager, shifted her eyes to the chair, as if an unholy curse awaited anyone who sat there.

I felt the gentle grip of a hand around my wrist, and that one touch caused my body to relax. Instantly, the doom-and-gloom atmosphere melted away, and in its place laid an intimate cocoon. I knew by heart that hand, and the senses that came with it: the warm sweetness of baked goods and a ton of nerve. Never mind butterflies: a colony of bats flapped inside my stomach, a rush of elation tightened my sternum.

Caleb smiled down at me as he guided me to the seats. He used his free hand to push back his hair only to have it tumble down and cover his face again. I watched the light brown strands fall in a slight curl by his jaw. A blazing amethyst hue filtered through the curtain of locks, a color that projected his mood and his spirit's needs.

"It's just a chair, Sam. It's not haunted," Caleb said and sat next to me.

"Not the chair, just us," I mumbled as my mind drifted again to my belated friend.

Nadine's life energy—the energy that came with Lilith—eventually dissolved, but the memories were kept on file for safekeeping—every birthday party, every bedtime story, every wild adventure, save one. It was strange how every facet of her life opened at the ready to me, all but that tiny blank spot of her history, a scene spliced during post-production.

To say Nadine had been a jaded woman would be a blatant understatement, but even she had loved deeply at some point, and the memory of it was hard to penetrate. This feeling I detected was far more dangerous than the ones she had for her family, a love that those with good sense shouldn't have for a faceless man. So it shocked me that someone with a fairly decent, albeit morbid, head on her shoulders would entertain such mush. And not tell me about it! We used to tell each other everything.

The mystery distracted me through the meeting to the point where Caleb shook me to attention when it was over. I had completely lost track of time, not to mention I hadn't gotten to share my book. While the crew filed out of the door, Alicia tossed me a parting glance, grinning in triumph.

Caleb extended his hand, then helped me to my feet. His smile produced broad dimples, two parentheses buried deep in his cheeks.

"What did I miss?" I asked.

"Alicia got her wish. *Specter: Part III* got voted book of the month. She went through a ten-minute dissertation of the intricacies of having a 'totally hot' ghost boyfriend." Caleb mimicked Alicia's squeaky voice perfectly. "You know there's a movie coming out about it?"

"I heard." I collected my bag, then followed him out.

After wishing everyone good night, I stepped into the cool night with Caleb practically stuck to my back. His arm wrapped around my waist and squeezed, lifting me off the ground. I squealed, which caused the crew to roll their eyes at us from the parking lot as he carried me to his Jeep.

A honking horn came from a blue SUV driving by. "Get a room!" Alicia yelled from the passenger-side window as her dad drove her away.

"That's not such a bad idea," Caleb whispered in my ear before kissing the back of my neck.

I wiggled against his hold. "That's it. You are unfit to be in my company, sir."

"Aw, come on! Don't be that way."

"Unhand me, contemptible cur! 'Else purge such lechery from thine purpose, you knave!"

Snorting a laugh, he set me down. "All right, Lady Macbeth, have it your way."

I pressed against his car door and frowned.

"What's wrong?"

I rubbed my eyes with the back of my hand. "Nothing. I've got a lot on my mind."

"Oh, yeah? Does it have to do with your eye?" He grazed the fading bruise with his thumb.

On contact, the day's events resurfaced as did the slight throb from my injury. "Okay, this is gonna sound weird, but I think I saw something today." I told him about Malik, the Picture Day light show, and the ominous feeling that had come with it. Caleb stayed quiet until I finished, wearing an incredulous look on his face.

"Sam, Cambions don't turn transparent in harsh light, and as far as I know there are no others like us in town. We're kinda spread out for a reason. And you said you've known this guy for years and no warning bells have ever gone off, no strange-color eyes, no girls being rushed to the hospital, so I think you're good on that front. But if it happens again, let me know, okay?" When I nodded, he asked, "Did you feed at all today? That might've been the cause of you seeing weird stuff."

"I did afterward during lunch, but I hate feeding off of guys I know. I have to see them every day, and it's awkward enough as it is. When I take in their energy, their memories come with it and they're hard to get over. Most of them I block out, but others are too juicy to ignore. Don't get me wrong, it has its privileges, but it gets real crowded up here, you know." I tapped my temple, then rubbed my face. "Sorry. I wasn't trying to vent. My brain is all over the place. And I didn't get to share my book."

He leaned into me, getting good and comfortable, not in the slightest rush to leave. "Share it with me. What's it called?"

I put a finger to my lips. "*Shh.*"

He looked around the parking lot. "What?"

"No, that's the title, *Shh*," I explained. "It's about angels and the battle between Heaven and Hell. According to Hebrew myth, an angel enters the womb of every pregnant woman and places a finger over the lips of the unborn child. They silence the baby from revealing the secrets of Heaven, including God's true name. The proof of that secret is that small dent in your top lip." My finger danced over the outline of his mouth, making him shiver. I could tell he felt the attraction, a pull rooting from the chest, joining our two magnets together.

Dropping my hand, I continued, "Anyway, this autistic boy doesn't have that dimple. He's a mute, but he's been leaking secrets all through his writing and artwork. A group of angels come to Earth to kill the kid, because once heard out loud, humanity will remember the secrets told to them and all of Hell will break loose, literally. It's a race against time because the kid starts mumbling in class out of nowhere."

"Sounds good! Let me borrow that when you're done." His lids grew heavy as he inched closer.

I tried to push off his Jeep, but his nearness made it impossible. He was stalling, squeezing a few more minutes alone with me, but our time was running out.

"Did you want to come over to my place for a bit? I made a new playlist that you haven't heard—" He stopped midsentence when I flashed my bracelet in his face.

The gold chain shimmered under the parking lot lights, creating a sufficient force field against his libido.

Caleb's shoulders slumped under the weight of defeat. "I thought that was only activated for emergencies."

"So did I, but Mom's got it synched to her laptop to track where I am. Cambion or not, my curfew still applies until I'm eighteen and out the house. It's just a safety measure. Can't be too careful these days." I offered him a gentle smile.

"Fine. I'll see you tomorrow." He pulled back and allowed me to pass.

Parked in the next row was a metallic gray Nissan Juke, my new ride—*new* being a relative term. It was new to me, and love allowed me to overlook the high mileage and stench of fried bologna that an entire bottle of Febreze couldn't remove. It was mine and I had earned it, and that was enough for me.

I didn't make it two feet before his hand caught my wrist and pulled me back into his arms.

"Caleb," I whined, though I felt just as needy. "I have to go."

"Well, am I at least allowed to kiss you? I've waited all day to do so. Indulge me." He lowered his head for a kiss that never came.

The sound only had a second to register in my ears: soft at first, then louder as it drew closer—ending in an explosion not even a foot from where we stood. Natural instinct took effect and I ducked from the whoosh of air and sailing fragments of glass.

I hit the ground hard—scraping my knee on the pavement—and covered my face and eyes from the blast. Tiny shards rained on my head, over my shoulder, and tinkled against the concrete. Caleb's body fell over mine; his weight crushed me as he withstood the brunt of the attack. It's funny how situations can change. One minute, I held my boyfriend, the next I was on the ground, curled into a ball.

Once silence enclosed the parking lot again, Caleb stood up and assessed the damage. "Stay here," he ordered.

Of course, I didn't listen and I joined his side before he could open his door.

Not one, not two, but every window in Caleb's Jeep was missing. What remained sat in the driver's seat and formed a glittery ring around the vehicle. The weather-proof hardtop didn't fare too well from the impact, seeing that it now laid upside down in the next row.

"What did that?" I asked. "I thought it was a bomb."

Caleb circled the Jeep and peeked underneath its carriage. "Nothing else seems to be damaged, just the windows."

I searched around the parking lot. All of the employees were gone, and only our cars remained. "Maybe some kid shot at the windows," I suggested.

He whipped out his cell phone. As he dialed, his anger mounted with every punch and click. "It wasn't a gunshot and it couldn't have broken all the windows at once." He used his free hand to push me away from the debris. While relaying the situation to the operator, he examined my hands and face for injuries.

If anyone needed medical attention, it was him. Tiny scratches tracked his left cheek and temple. Blood ran in a thin stream down his neck, seeping into the collar of his white polo shirt. He didn't notice any of it; he seemed too distracted with plotting bloody vengeance.

Caleb was slow to anger, but he reached full hotness when he showed aggression and his eyes glowed bright lavender. Though the color was pretty, the carnage that followed that wondrous view was not. That was how Caleb's "roommate" made his presence known and it was clear that Capone wasn't happy with the situation, either.

I pulled away from him, not liking the storm brewing in those eyes. "I'm fine, but you need a doctor. I'll take you to the hospital."

Ending the call, he regarded me with a furrowed brow, his lips tightened. "No. I need you to go home."

Was he serious? "I'm not leaving you!"

"The hell you're not. This is dangerous, and I want you away from it. The police should be here any minute. I'll wait with the mall cop." He tipped his chin to the security vehicle cruising its way toward us. "Now I want you to go straight home. No stops, no detours. Understand?"

"But I—"

"The longer you stay here and argue, the more you'll have to explain to your mom. Now do you really want that? 'Cause *we all* know how laid-back and trusting she is. She wouldn't mind her only daughter getting grilled by police at ten-thirty on a school night. Oh no, it wouldn't freak her out at all." He hid his smile behind pursed lips, because not even in sarcasm could he describe my mom as lax and keep a straight face.

I would've pointed that out, but that wouldn't make him any less right. Mom didn't play these days, constantly checking my comings and goings to the point where I couldn't tell if I was grounded.

I was being pushed in the direction of my car, and I didn't complain. In all honesty, I really wanted to get out of there. The night had a sharp sting to it, very dry, and my breath seemed to freeze before I could even push it out. The frigidness had little to do with temperature.

"Call me when this is over," I said.

"No. I'll call you tomorrow. Don't worry about me."

He took my keys to open my door, then lifted me in his arms for the kiss he had been denied. I knew he needed a distraction, so I obliged his brilliant attempt at redirection. Hell, I forgot my own name.

It wasn't the softness of his lips that put me into full swoon mode, nor was it how he stole my breath and gave me his own. It was the way he held me like I would soon disappear, as if at any minute someone would rip me away from him. I understood the feeling. It had taken us months to achieve what so many took for granted, to share a simple kiss. Maybe we were making up for lost time, because every kiss felt like the first and the last we would ever have. We were Cambions, not cannibals, but I was willing to make an exception for Caleb. I wanted to eat this dude alive, starting with that plump bottom lip as my new chew toy.

Just when it was getting good, he ended the kiss and set me down. My body dragged down the length of his with agonizing slowness. I nipped his lip, his stern chin, his bobbing Adam's apple, every spot I could reach before my feet settled back to earth.

"I'll be fine, I promise. You'll feel it if I'm not." His lips rounded the curve of my cheekbone, planting a petal-soft kiss by my bruised eye.

Knowing exactly what he meant, I nodded at that small assurance. He waited for me to climb in my car and left no room for argument.

I revved the engine, then pulled out of the parking space. Peeling out of the lot, I watched his body grow small from the rearview mirror, and I fought the temptation to turn around. Only when I was two blocks from the shopping center did the pressure dissipate, though my heavy foot on the accelerator wasn't taking any chances.

I rolled down the car window and breathed in the

yeasty musk of Williamsburg. The heavy cloak of dread fell from my shoulders, and I could now ease my foot off the gas. But the discomfort lingered, its ghostly fingers creeping up my neck. There was no camera flash this time, but I heard the whisper in my ear to keep driving. The warning was louder, more insistent than the one before, yet it held a harsh undertone that seemed an awful lot like a threat.

3

I pulled into my driveway; the pop and grind of gravel against rubber filled the car's interior.

Turning off the engine, I sat behind the wheel for a moment. I tried not to think about what happened tonight, but the scene was stuck on instant replay. There was something strange going on, again, and I knew this was only the beginning, the quiet before the shit storm. I liked to be ahead of the curve when something was about to blow up in my face; however, sometimes knowing was worse than being caught off guard.

I closed my eyes and focused on Caleb, searching for his face in my mind's eye. It didn't take long to find him, or rather feel him. Confusion, annoyance, and high levels of pissed-off rushed to my senses, giving me a sudden urge to break something, which was a good thing. He wasn't scared or in danger, so I could at least try to sleep soundly tonight.

I set the dilemma on pause and studied my dingy house with the flaky white paint. The shriveled flower bed lined the front deck, and the putrid yellow porch light made my house visible from space. Pine needles, nutmeg, and my neighbor's chimney smoke sprayed the air with a perfume only worn this time of year. Of all the things that had changed in my life, my birth home stood the test of time. I climbed out and breathed in the cool autumn night, enjoying the crunch of dry leaves under my sneakers.

Once inside, I checked and double-checked the security alarm by the door. My eyes locked on the blinking green activation light, marking the time at which it had been set. It became a habit of mine to test it twice lately, just in case.

Under a floral mist of scented candles, the air still carried that sour hint of paint fumes from Mom's room. Little crumbs of drywall had settled into the crevices between the stairs. The cracks in the ceiling were gone, and the bloodstains had faded under strong bleach and several coats of paint. The repairs had given Mom an excuse to redecorate, but that had only covered the external damage. After a shrewd face-lift, the Marshall residence no longer resembled a house of horrors, but the ghost of that terrifying night still roamed the halls.

Soft light from the kitchen told me where and how Mom had spent her evening. Instead of passing through the hall by the stairs, I entered the kitchen from the dining room to my right. The crimson walls and gold tasseled drapes reminded me of a brothel, but this eyesore hurt less than the one from the living room.

The side route allowed me to sneak up on Mom, a difficult prank with only the top of her brown bun in sight. The rest of her hid under a mountain of encyclopedias, old news articles, and other source material. This had always been Mom's makeshift office, but it had quickly transformed into a library and demonology classroom.

An astute accountant by day, by night Mom moon-
lighted as a renegade myth buster. She burned the midnight oil trying to understand why a succubus spirit had
jumped bloodlines to occupy my body. This type of possession was supposedly a hereditary trait, so this new living arrangement produced a ton of questions and sleepless
nights.

"Hey, Mom." I dropped my bag on the counter and
headed to the fridge.

"Hey, honey." She returned from somewhere behind
the stack of books.

I grabbed a carton of orange juice and poured a glass.
"How was counseling?"

"Awkward as usual. I'm not a big talker, so I end up
listening to other people's problems more than anything
else. The stories they tell in the meetings would break
your heart, Samara. I feel guilty because I always leave
thinking, 'You know, things aren't that bad.' "

"Group therapy: proof that life could get a whole lot
worse." I saluted her with my glass before taking a sip,
but watched her with caution.

I worried about her recent issues with insomnia and
night terrors, and I secretly wished Nathan Ross could be
just a little bit more dead for her sake. Even in death, the
face of Caleb's father taunted her, like some movie villain
coming back for one last scare. Her doctors chalked it up
to trauma, and Caleb and his brothers assured us there
was no lasting damage. Good luck explaining that to a
woman who almost had the life sucked out of her by a
deranged Cambion. In either case, nothing could be left
to chance, not even dreams.

I leaned against the counter, watching her carefully.
"You know, there's better ways to vent if you're upset.
You can always go back to the gun range."

"True. I just hate that they close at nine. I mean, what's a girl to do in the middle of the night."

"Drive-bys?" I offered.

Mom smiled and returned her attention to her laptop. Text and lights dragged across her glasses.

"What you working on now?"

"Trinkets and sanctified objects. Did you know that priests and missionaries use olive oil for exorcism? There's a sacred ritual that expels demons."

"For real?" I rummaged through the overhead cabinet and retrieved the bottle of olive oil Mom used for cooking. As soon as my hand gripped the bottle, Lilith flinched, causing a quick jolt in the middle of my back. It ended as quickly as it had begun, so I figured she was probably hungry.

I let a few drops fall on my finger and hissed at the contact. "Ah! It burns! It burns!"

That got Mom's attention. Immediately, she stood to her feet and raced to my side. "Baby, are you okay? What happened?"

I gave a wide grin and showed her my oily hand. "Nothing. I'm just playing with you."

Mom didn't look amused. She turned away, then did a double take. "What happened to your eye?"

"Dodgeball shows no mercy and takes no prisoners," I said in a dramatic, movie-trailer-guy voice.

After giving me a light whack on the back of the head, she returned to her research.

I licked the oil off my finger, then said, "I don't know why you bother with that stuff. It's hardly accurate."

"Well, it says it has to be sanctified and untainted. That's the cheap stuff; I think I got it on sale."

I rested my elbows against the counter. "You mean like anointing oil?"

"Something like that."

"Doesn't work, either. I tried it on Caleb when he first came to the house." In fact, I thought I still had that little vial somewhere in my bag, among other things I should've trashed months ago. I had a hard time throwing stuff away, resulting in me carrying extra baggage.

"Do I even want to know why you used oil on him?" Mom asked, sounding a bit disturbed.

"The same reason you're looking up folklore in the middle of the night. You're scared of the unknown."

Mom's eyes lifted from the computer screen. "I'm not afraid of you. You're my child. I'm just trying to keep it all in perspective. Evangeline has been trying to answer some of my questions, but I keep coming up with more."

I smiled at the mention of Nadine's mother, making a mental note to call her tomorrow. Evangeline Petrovsky, or Angie for short, was an unstoppable force in her own right. Since Lilith came from her lineage, Angie had pretty much adopted me, teaching me the ways of the Cambion. No matter where she traveled in the world, she was always a phone call away.

"Oh, look at this!" Mom motioned me to her side. "According to myth, Merlin the wizard was a Cambion. That's why he had those magical powers."

I peeked over her shoulder. "Like King Arthur and Camelot?"

She nodded. "Also, they say a true incubus has the physical ability to appear as what a woman most desires, plaguing women while asleep, and seducing them to his will."

The concept swirled around my head for a moment. "So an incubus is going to creep into my room looking like Usher?"

"Not sure. It's what your heart desires, so he might look like Caleb." Crystal-blue eyes slowly met mine.

All sound and good humor fled the room. My mind swam to the night when Caleb's father had used the same trick for personal gain, a deception that nearly killed me. It was a very powerful, confusing ability that few people lived to tell about.

Mom continued, "The folklore varies with each culture. Some say they're gremlin-looking imps that perch on a person's chest to drain energy, like that superstition about cats. This might contribute to their animalistic nature. All in all, these incubi creatures are a randy bunch, enslaving and impregnating women."

"Myth."

Her head popped up. "What?"

"Myth," I repeated. "Incubi first possess a human male, then use him to impregnate a female. A part of its soul passes to the female during conception."

Mom just stared, her mouth agape. After a few blinks, her hand slid to the wireless mouse, ready to scroll down the web page for confirmation.

My hands rested over hers, halting her movement. "You won't find it there. Ask Angie."

"I'm avoiding her calls. She keeps insisting that I'm tired and need a spa makeover. Honestly, how can I look tired over the phone? You see what she made me do to my hair?" Mom nervously patted her newly highlighted curls.

I stroked the top of her head. "I told you before, it looks nice. She just wants you to stop stressing all the time."

"I don't know how she talks me into these things. I can't say no. It's odd, Angie and me, it's like—"

"Love at first sight," I finished.

"Yeah, but in a strictly hetero way," she was quick to add. "How did you know?"

"That's what it was like with Nadine and me. It took

Mia and me years to get to that point, but with Nadine, it was an instant connection. Cambions are attracted to wary women, I guess." For reasons beyond my control, my bottom lip quivered and tears burned around my sockets. Lilith jittered up my spine, letting me know she grieved as well.

Mom removed her glasses and gave me a hard stare, probing my every move. "Samara, maybe you should come to a few of my counseling sessions—"

"No, thanks." I turned away and moved back to the counter.

"Just a few meetings. They're really helpful, and you don't even have to say anything, just listen."

"I'm fine, Mom."

"Baby, you need to handle your grief properly. I can only imagine what you're going through. You won't even enter the living room by yourself. You barely talk about Nadine and you've become detached."

I paused. "Have not."

"Samara, your father and I are worried about you, and you can only hide so much from that man." She quirked a brow.

Mom had a point. Though ignorant of Lilith's existence, Dad wasn't stupid, and it was damn near impossible to lie to a lawyer. Mr. Watkins called more often now, laying guilt trips on me for not coming around. My visits were a test of endurance since listing Caleb's many flaws became his favorite topic at dinner. In Dad's book, no one was good enough for his baby girl, especially the son of a killer. So no, baring my soul to certain members of my family was not a good idea right now.

"Have you talked to Caleb about this? It's not healthy to have all this bottled up inside."

"It's pretty hard to find 'quality time' with the LoJack

I got strapped to my arm." I looked down at my wrist and snarled.

Like Lilith, this trinket had also belonged to Nadine, and it was one of the most stylish and unassuming tracking devices on the planet. Only after it had been placed in my care had I learned that it could never unlock once it was fastened. Waterproof and flame retardant, the tiny chip embedded inside the nameplate monitored the wearer's location and sent updates to the software on Mom's hard drive. This heirloom had been passed down to me as a form of protection, but now held the weight of iron shackles. The bracelet's outrageous retail value kept it from meeting the fate of a bolt cutter.

I tried to reason, though I knew it was a lost cause. "Angie told me that you two were discussing my relationship with Caleb. Why is it such a big deal? We have to see each other; we feed from one another for energy. I'm not going to skank out or anything."

"She said that your body chemistry will change more than usual during the adolescent phase. I've seen how you get when you don't feed. I can only imagine what might happen with *other* cravings, and I'm not trying to be a thirty-four-year-old grandmother."

I lifted my head to the ceiling. "Where is the trust in this house?"

"It's not you I don't trust, baby. It's your roommate— as you call it—that needs to be chaperoned. Which means that outside of work, you're not allowed to see Caleb without supervision. I'm not budging on this, so you can save your breath." Mom replaced her specs and returned to the solace of her laptop.

At that point, this meeting of the minds was over. I snatched my bag and left the kitchen. This broken record kept playing over and over, and I had grown sick of the song. First Dad, and now Mom sung backup to the tired tune. At least it had gotten her off the subject of therapy, a topic that slipped into our conversations a lot these days.

On my way to the stairs, I tried not to look at the living room, but its presence seemed to burn at my peripheral, soliciting one peek, one moment of my time. I snuck a glance at the small area and cursed at my own weakness.

The layout was different, a cheery arrangement of floral prints, cushions, throw rugs, and fake plants tucked in corners. The sofa had been moved a foot or two closer to the center of the room, grouped by the love seat, glass coffee table, and high-back chair. The walls were painted in a pale, cake-batter yellow trimmed with white molding. Carefully selected photographs crowded the wall unit and marble fireplace that we never used. But no amount of remodeling could erase the image of Nadine's body sprawled on the floor.

As Angie had once said, "once seen it can't be unseen," and that truth breathed life into this phantom, giving it substance. My back stiffened and the muscles tightened painfully, causing a bubbling in my stomach. My throat closed up as I tried in vain to keep my dinner down.

The greasy sludge rotting my gut shot me upstairs, down the hallway, and to the welcoming embrace of the commode. Between vomit sessions, the cool tiled floor became my new best friend, my confessional. I wished I could blame it on food or some physical illness, but it had to be psychological. Mom wasn't the only one with issues—I was just better at hiding them.

Gripping the edge of the sink, I pulled myself up and stared at the stranger in the mirror—perhaps a close cousin or a long-lost twin. The features looked familiar, same chubby cheeks, stubborn chin, caramel-brown skin, and the Sideshow Bob mop top that reached my shoulders. The only thing that didn't belong to me were those green eyes—another souvenir from Nadine.

Three antacid tablets didn't ease my stomach, four glasses of water couldn't quench my thirst, stripping down to my underwear didn't cool my fevered skin. The air tasted thick, rusty, and too humid for my lungs to absorb. Too much activity crowded inside my skull, too many voices between my ears spoke out of turn. I needed oxygen and an open space where the walls didn't move.

I went to my room, opened the window, and welcomed the crisp night air, not caring that I stood in my skivvies, giving the neighbors a free show. I had never experienced anxiety attacks before, and considering what had brought it on in the first place, I doubted it would be a one-hit wonder.

As if an answer to my unspoken prayer, my cell phone rang. I didn't need to see the name on the caller ID, or hear the sappy ring tone I'd picked out for him; I just knew.

"Sam, you okay? What's wrong?" Caleb asked as soon as I placed the phone to my ear.

"I'm glad you called. I just . . ." I paused, unsure how to verbalize hysteria.

"You just what?" His voice hitched and his anxiety shot through the line to reach me. Police radios and chatter mingled in the background, so I knew he was still with his car.

"Nothing. I just—I've got a lot on my mind," I dismissed. It was best to keep quiet. Caleb had his own problems. "I'm not feeling good."

"I can tell. Why don't you lie down? I'll stay on the line until you feel better."

"I thought you weren't gonna call me until morning," I nagged.

"That was before I started getting nauseous and scared out of nowhere. Go to bed. I'm right here." His soothing tone melted the knots in my shoulders and liquefied the bones in my legs. Underneath his hard outer layer came a wash of peace that purified me.

I crawled into bed and let his voice cradle me to rest. "Thank you, but you don't have to do this."

"It's not just for you, Sam. I need you nearby for a while. Don't think I can sleep otherwise. Is that okay?"

"Always," I whispered and tucked a pillow under my head. I couldn't blame him, for I felt the exact same way. It came with the package of having a Cambion boyfriend, to share emotions. All. The. Time. Some would consider it intrusive, or even a curse to experience this kind of connection, this empathic intimacy, but it had its perks, especially tonight.

His sigh dragged through the phone, a weary gesture that mirrored mine completely. "Talk to me. Anything you want."

I brooded for a moment before asking, "How would you feel about mixing at a party on Halloween?" I told him about Courtney B.'s proposal and the free press that would come with it.

He sucked in a sharp breath. "Yeah, I heard. Some redhead approached me earlier today about doing a gig. The pay is good and all, but . . . *high school girls?* I can't deal with all that whiny—"

"Hey, grandpa, in case you forgot to take your meds today, *I'm* one of those high school girls. Plus, it's supposed to be the biggest event of the season, with free candy," I added, knowing that anything involving sugar would seal the deal.

A long pause passed between us until he asked, "Will you be there?"

"I gotta check with my parole officer, but I think I can swing it," I said while toiling with my love-hate battle with my phone. Despite all its buttons and high-tech features, it had no arms, no lips, no breath. This tiny device served as both a gateway and wall between us. "I wish you were here."

"I feel you," he whispered. The double meaning made me laugh out loud, as did the next topic of discussion.

"So . . ." Caleb drawled, trying to sound sultry, but coming off extremely sleazy instead. "What are you wearing?"

4

Lunchtime: where social lines were clearly marked in the sand and where group status hung in the balance of the faintest whisper.

Legends were born, hearts were broken, and the weak were herded to the slaughter in front of a live studio audience. Here lay the watering hole for all members of the food chain and hunting ground for predators. And I was the deadliest of them all.

Just a taste. That was the Cambion policy, our credo. *Just take enough to appease the spirit, then move on.* It sounded simple enough, but sometimes taking a little was worse than taking none at all.

I inhaled the boundless life that hummed in the air and consumed the electricity just under their skin. I could see their energy if I squinted my eyes—a turbulent haze or sweltering heat on the horizon line. This was my daily vitamin and Lilith's food supply.

Energy in assorted temperaments mingled in large gatherings like these, serving up a convenient buffet platter of human life force. Each sip of energy, no matter how small, gave me joy and replenished my starving psyche, a free-for-all without guilt. Though strictly for dietary purposes, I still felt weird about feeding from anyone who wasn't Caleb. I didn't want a stockpile of memories of another guy in my head. It was too intimate, too personal, so direct contact was for emergencies only.

I sat at the far end of the cafeteria with the leftovers their peers chewed up and spat back out. These discarded table scraps assembled into a patchwork of loners, from bookworms to goths, to that one weird kid who never bathed and talked to himself. My allure didn't work on the willful and chaste, which revealed more about my lunchmates than I'd really wanted to know.

What no one realized was that they were the nicest people in the entire school. Unfortunately, this was a dead zone for anyone who was part of a preexisting clique, but it was an excellent place for those like myself who wanted to stay under the radar. Not even Malik had the nerve to come over, but he watched me from the east wing of the cafeteria, licking his chops.

Trying my best to ignore him, I dove into my writing assignment headfirst. Papers and folders spread across the rectangular table, sorted by priority, subject, and difficulty. Between Caleb and work, I had to squeeze every moment to keep up with classes. I had to write a poem for English, which now seemed to be an effortless task. No doubt Nadine's lingering influence had something to do with it, because much like her prose, mine was now leaning toward the dark and dismal.

While I was trying to find a word that rhymed with "fester," a voice whispered my name. "Hey, Sam."

I lifted my head in time to see Mia sitting next to me, wearing a hoodie and shades over her eyes. "What are you doing here?" I asked.

"I should ask you the same question." She nudged her chin toward my lunchmates.

"Unlike you, this is *my* lunch period and I want to keep a low profile. How did you get out of class?"

She waved her hall pass in front of my face. "I needed to go to the nurse—woman problems and all that."

"That's like the fifth excuse this month. People will think you're pregnant."

"Whatever. Actually, I'm here on business. I was supposed to meet Jason at twelve-forty-five on the dot." Mia examined her watch.

I leaned away from her, just in case crazy was contagious. "Am I about to witness some shady drug deal?"

She crouched lower in her seat. "No, but I gotta keep it on the DL. Dougie's in this lunch and I don't want him to see me."

I glanced sideways at her. "Uh-huh."

Even though I'd seen it a mile away, it had still come as a shock when it arrived. Mia and Dougie's breakup had hit our trio hard, leaving me in a messy custody battle for friendship. I refused to take a side. I only had a small handful of true friends, and I was surgically attached to all of them, including Dougie.

Scanning the cafeteria again, Mia leaned in and whispered, "Don't look, but Malik Davis is checking you out."

"Good for him." I sniggered, not bothering to lift my head from my notebook.

I didn't need to. His heated glare was burning a hole in my neck. I did wonder how his pictures would turn out, but I would have to wait another month until they came back from the studio.

What happened on Picture Day stayed close to my mind, but not enough to exchange words or follow him around. He did plenty of that for the both of us; it was kind of his thing. Okay, I may or may not have taken pictures of him with my camera phone when he wasn't looking, but all the images turned out fine. Until further evidence came to light, the case of the skeletor mug shot remained unsolved, and Malik still held the title of douche bag of the year.

"Man, he is straight up *on your six*," she exclaimed, indicating his position clockwise. "The guy looks hungry, and not for what's on his tray. I don't know, Sam. He's pretty hot and has a shiny new truck," Mia teased.

"I'm quite content with the guy I have, thank you very much."

"Oh yeah, I forgot you like your men older. Nineteen is the new thirty." Continuing her stakeout, Mia spotted her inside man.

Rail thin and covered with acne, Jason Lao was anything but discreet. The head editor of our school newspaper was the fast-talking, Korean equivalent to Perez Hilton, with a not-so-secret gossip blog that the superintendent had tried in vain to shut down. This tenacious news hound could find dirt on dirt, but he always gave us the week's scoop before it hit the web.

Spying the area for any witnesses, he scurried to the table. "Wow. When you said you wanted to meet in private, I didn't think you meant no-man's-land." He swung his legs over the table's bench and plopped down across from us.

Mia drew closer and whispered, "I'm on the clock here. What you got?"

Getting right to business, Jason pulled out his notepad and flipped through several pages. After clearing his throat, he reported, "Courtney B. is sending out invitations this week. I managed to sneak a peek at the guest list first period. Sorry, kid, you didn't make the cut."

Mia sobbed and rested her forehead on the table.

"Don't feel bad. You can tag along with Sam."

"What?" Mia looked to me with surprise. "You got an invite to the Halloween party?"

"Not really. She wants Caleb to deejay, so I'm invited by association."

Mia closed in on me. "Why didn't you tell me? Sam, you have got to get me into that party."

"I'm not sure if I have power like that."

She grabbed my shoulders and shook me. "Of course you do. Caleb's the deejay. Just tell her that we're a package deal; one can't go without the other."

I groaned, knowing that my classwork would have to wait yet again. My theory became fact when a shadow darkened my notes.

"Hey?" called a voice behind us, snatching all humor from the building.

Mia turned around, removed her shades, and stared her past in the face.

Dougie was a sight for sore eyes, and what a sight he was. He'd put on some extra weight since he joined the wrestling team, with muscles popping out the yin-yang. His sudden interest in school activities didn't harm his position as the most thugged-out white boy I'd ever met.

My recent purchase of a demonic man-magnet kept my visits with Dougie brief, but the allure had diminished over time, thanks to the recognition exercises Angie had taught me. As practiced, I corralled all the memories of Dougie and pushed them to the forefront before Lilith had a chance to pounce. Since my draw didn't work on virgins, Jason Lao wouldn't be a threat until he was thirty.

Dougie tipped his chin in greeting. "Yo, SNM, what's good?"

"Same old," I replied.

His smile faded as he locked eyes on Mia again. "What are you doing here? I thought you had second lunch."

"I'm just talking to Sam." Mia wrapped her arm around me possessively.

He nodded. "So, how you been? You a'ight?"

After undressing him with her eyes, Mia stammered, "Good. I mean, I-I'm good."

Dougie did some visible disrobing himself, his hazel eyes twinkled with longing. My head panned to our growing audience. Everyone at the table stopped eating to watch the action like it was the Thursday night lineup. This table had seen more action within the past five minutes than it had in all four years of school.

Suffering a long and thoroughly awkward silence, Dougie spoke up. "Listen, what are ya'll doing for Halloween? We should try to do something. It's our last year and I miss hanging out." He stared at Mia with a look that almost broke my heart. "We used to have fun."

I turned to Mia, my invisible pom-poms waving in the air, encouraging her to make a move. She worried her bottom lip as she searched the cafeteria for a reply. "Well, I just—"

"There you are. I was looking all over for you." A short girl clung to Dougie's arm, and slaughtered any trace of hope. At first glance, I could tell she was one of those high-maintenance girls who usually had small dogs hiding somewhere in their purses. She used her X-ray vision to size up Mia, then rose to her tiptoes and planted a kiss on Dougie's cheek. "Dougie, I wanna go eat now."

Say what? I was ten seconds away from snatching those extensions off that chick's head. Nobody, and I mean nobody called Douglas Emerson III "Dougie" but us. It was official law, and no one dared transgress and expect to survive.

Mia had the same reaction, but she hid it well under a guise of cool. I knew that look of deadly calm, a look that usually preceded bloodshed and a police report. Mia may not have known karate or kung fu, but she had mastered the ancient art of *kut-a-bitch* at an early age.

Dougie squirmed away from his arm candy. "I told you not to call me that."

The girl pouted. "Why? It's so cute."

" 'Cause only special people call him that," I answered through gritted teeth.

Little Buffy narrowed her eyes at me. "Well, I'm special. Aren't I, Dougie?"

The bell chimed on Mia's side of the ring. Rising to her feet, she rounded on her target. "Obviously not if he told you to stop, and obviously not if you continue to ignore him. You don't know him like that to use the title."

Resting her head on his shoulder, the girl caressed Dougie's chest. "Oh, I know him *real* well. Don't I, *Dougie?*"

The suggestion did not go overlooked by Mia or anyone else in the cafeteria. Heads whipped in our direction, mouths dropped, and Jason's pen rapidly scribbled away at his notepad. And Dougie just stood there sporting a mask of dumb, neither confirming nor denying the claim.

Mia's gaze iced over as she stared at the couple in front of her. "Nice seeing you, Douglas. But let's not do it again." Like the Hollywood starlets of old, Mia lifted her chin in the air and brushed past them, preceding her graceful exit—stage left.

Dougie turned to me, almost pleading. "Sam, I—"

"I'm staying out of this. You had your chance to say something and you didn't. Besides, you have your hands full. Good luck with that." I patted him on the shoulder, gathered my stuff, then met up with Mia at the double doors.

Though both parties had agreed to see other people, Mia hadn't expected Dougie to adhere to that contract. Mia had never told me what happened that caused the big break, but I had a feeling that that "something" had to do with little Miss Clingy. I figured Mia would tell me in her own time. Telling by her robotic walk and stiff shoulders, today wasn't it.

"So, Dougie's trying to date my body double? He should know that nothing can replace the original," Mia grumbled with a taught jaw.

"Didn't *you* break it off with him?"

"That's not the point. You don't date one girl and then go try to find her designer knockoff. He could at least own the decency to upgrade." She put on a brave front, but the heavy bags under her eyes revealed worry and fatigue.

"Mia, you sure you're okay? You've been acting strange lately."

"I'm fine. Just haven't been sleeping, that's all."

"You would tell me if there was something wrong, wouldn't you?"

"As much as you would tell me." Her gaze met mine for a moment, drilling her point home.

The events of the summer had put a veil of awkwardness between us that we couldn't remove. I had to choose my words carefully; every action, every excuse ran through a censoring filter, so I thought it better to say nothing.

We stopped in front of her physics class when Mr. McNamara snatched open the door. "Good of you to rejoin us for the last five minutes of class, Miss Moralez," he barked, his sunken brown eyes narrowed in accusation.

Lowering her head, Mia fumbled with the pass in her hand. "I'm sorry. I just felt a little faint."

Stepping in front of Mia, I held his unblinking gaze. "She's not feeling well, sir. I wanted to walk her to class in case she fainted again. She's a bit under the weather. I'm sure you understand." I spoke the words in a low, even tone, allowing my influence to reach his hardened heart.

After several blinks, Mr. McNamara gave a lazy smile. "Of course, I understand. Mia, if you're not feeling well, you can go home. I don't want you hurting yourself." His offer was as smooth and sweet as molasses.

The sudden change of attitude took Mia aback. She shot me a puzzled glance, then said, "No, I'll be fine. It'll pass."

I was sure that baffled expression stayed long after she entered the classroom. And for as long as Mia remained in the dark about Lilith, that look would be permanent.

For the sake of all involved, only my mother and the other Cambions in my life could know what I was. That was our policy, our credo. The secret slowly ate at me, but it was something I would have to live with. For now.

5

The slow drag of the following week didn't affect the weather's natural timetable.

Autumn leaves set fire to the landscape, determined to die in a blazing glory of red and gold hues. People donned leather and fleece and sipped hot drinks to keep warm. Pumpkins, scarecrows, and ghosts sat on porches and lawns. Orange and black streamers garnished the cafeteria and classrooms. Cackles and squeals echoed the halls; plastic fangs and fake blood dripped from painted lips.

And where was I? Locked in the girls' bathroom, blowing up Caleb's phone for the fifth time today. Caleb and I were quickly turning into the couple we'd sworn to never become: strung out and wondering what the other was doing, and calling at random just to hear them breathe. How disgusting is that? But there I was, in the handicap stall, sending cutesy text messages with numeric hearts and smiley faces. Satisfied, if only for the moment, I tucked my phone in my bag and went to my last class.

School, work, Mia's ongoing drama, and the suspicion of supernatural doom had me running around like a headless chicken. Caleb was the only thing that kept me going, my life support.

During our wireless romance, he bitched about his Jeep, from repairs to the crooked insurance company, and wondered whether he should pimp his ride with new rims. The police reported the incident with Caleb's car as vandalism, though all the evidence pointed to a failed Mob-style hit. This didn't surprise me. Last summer had Williamsburg's finest running scared, and they stuck to the "Don't ask, don't tell" policy when it came to Caleb and my family.

However, what did surprise me was Caleb's flippant attitude. Whether it was denial or stubbornness, he was ignoring the signs that bad times were a-comin'. He had always been protective and fought hard to keep me out of danger, but there was a fine line between protection and omitting vital information. His secrecy had caused a rocky start to our relationship, but I'd believed our link would've put an end to that. When I went home to change for work, I realized we had more ground to cover in the trust department. This latest bombshell came in a FedEx box that waited at my front door.

Carrying the package to the stairs inside, I noticed it was addressed to Mom and me with a European zip code and stamp. I ripped at the cardboard and burrowed into the crumpled Styrofoam until my fingers retrieved from the bottom what appeared to be two old spell books. Bound in aged leather with a buckle fastening, each volume carried the thickness and weight of a dictionary.

My fingers played with the buckle when a cream-colored envelope caught my eye. I recognized the handwriting immediately, and the smile on my face started to hurt. I had become accustomed to her long-winded emails, so this one-page note left me intrigued.

> *Dearest Samara,*
>
> *How are you, little one? I hope you are doing well and that you're excelling in your studies. Are you practicing the memory exercises I showed you? They're tedious, I know, but you must stay vigilant to accelerate the recognition process. The spirit will not draw from those it knows. This may not work with new people you meet now, but it will help you with the male friends you already knew from school, so please practice at least three times a day.*
>
> *Forgive this brief letter, but I'm away on business and my time is limited. I regret to say that my schedule will not allow me to visit you as I wish. By now, you are probably wondering about the books I enclosed with this letter. They are a collection of letters and journal entries from my ancestors that your mother requested. I have also bookmarked several passages that might be of interest to you, mostly involving Cambion bonding.*
>
> *This is a very serious matter that you and Caleb need to discuss before you consummate your relationship. I have already discussed this with your mother, and though your bonding is inevitable, she agrees that this is not a matter to take lightly. So please read the marked passages so you don't enter a situation blindly, because this decision will affect the rest of your life and it cannot be undone.*
>
> *I wish I could share these things in person, but these books will have to suffice until we meet again. Until then, give Caleb my love.*
>
> *Take care and celebrate life.*
>
> > *Angie*

After reading the letter three times, the data still wouldn't process—perhaps there was a clog in my mental frequency. The confusion had nothing to do with the Polish dialect, but the ready-made assumption behind the request. Had Angie just given me the green light to bump uglies with my boyfriend? And what business was it of hers if I did or not? And what the hell was Cambion bonding?

Sitting on the bottom step, I plopped the first book on my lap and unfastened the buckle. As promised, pink and yellow tabs marked several entries. Since this book had no index or table of contents, I skimmed through the marked pages.

And that's when I lost my mind.

"Caleb!" I yelled, loud enough to hear from the Buncha Books parking lot. Heads turned as I charged the metal detectors of the music department, intent on murder. I peered over the CD shelves, DVD kiosks, and trendy kids littering the aisles. Children hid behind their parents, women clutched their purses, and shoppers gave way for the fiery wrath of hell that was Samara Marshall.

Caleb stood behind the counter and, as usual, chatted up a group of girls, including Courtney B., much to my disgust. Batting lashes and lip biting, the groupies clung to every word out of his lying, conniving mouth.

Shoving his entourage to the side, I slammed my hands on the counter and met him nose to nose. "We need to talk. Break room. Now!" I stomped away without another word, while the shocked audience watched my swift retreat.

Thank goodness no one was in the break room, and the manager's office was locked. No one should witness the lashing that was headed Caleb's way—the less collateral damage the better. The room always reeked of burnt popcorn and fried rice, and the combination made my stomach turn. I paced the floor, breathing hellfire, my fingers itching to lock around his neck. I didn't have long to wait, and I spun around when the door opened.

Caleb pressed his back and left foot against the wall with hands shoved in his tan khakis. Wearing his trademark grin of conceit, he stood as if waiting for the photo shoot to begin. "What's wrong with you?" he asked.

"What's wrong with me? With *me*? You're the one keeping secrets again. I thought I could trust you."

"You can, so tell me what's wrong." Wincing, he asked, "You're not PMS-ing, are you? Because I can't go through that again."

"Trust me, if I was, you'd be dead right now," I snipped, though I inwardly smiled at his apprehension.

One small penalty to our link was that Caleb suffered the hormonal roller coaster that came with my monthly visitor. Oh yeah, payback was a bitch. Too bad he didn't endure the cramping part, though time would tell on that score, if what I had discovered proved true.

I handed him Angie's letter and a scanned excerpt of her journal. "You care to explain this?"

He glanced at the page, then handed the letter back. "Sam, you know I can't understand Polish. Read it to me."

I'd forgotten that with Lilith came the ability to understand Nadine's native tongue.

"I'll give you the punch line: You were planning to sleep with me without telling me about this bonding thing. If two Cambions mate, they are intertwined for life, and one cannot survive without the other." His puzzled look annoyed me, so I decided to dumb it down. "Our emotional connection will take a physical extreme. If I get cut, you bleed; if I itch, you scratch."

Once awareness hit, he sighed in relief, as if this wasn't the end-all, be-all of bad news. "I figured you knew. I mean, Nadine knew."

I balled up the printout and threw it at him. "I'm not Nadine!"

He watched the crumpled paper bounce off his chest and tumble to his feet. "But you have her memories, her knowledge."

"Not all of it. And this surely wasn't part of it." I paced the break room, looking for something else to throw at him. "No wonder Mom's all freaked out about us being alone together. I thought she was just being paranoid as usual."

"Wait, so you're mad because of the bonding or mad because I didn't tell you?"

"Both!" I snapped. "Is there anything else, *anything else*, that I should know about what we are? Any key factors hidden in the fine print? Stuff keeps popping up out of nowhere and I don't know how many more surprises I can take. I'm so ready to walk out of that door and not look back."

Pushing off the wall, he stalked closer with a smooth, predatory quality. He kept his distance, ambling around the long folding table in the center of the room. I followed his lead in this odd waltz, drifting in a circle with only the table dividing us.

The dance ended when he pulled out a dollar and slinked to the snack machine for his sugar fix. He took his time choosing the one he wanted, which only pissed me off more.

Finally, he said, "We're not a normal couple, Sam. You know we can't just quit each other and walk away. Our kind mates for life, and no man, no religion, and no court can go against that."

Scooping up the chocolate bar and his change, he continued, "You ever see an old couple who's been married for eighty years, then they die within months of each other? They were bonded, a process that takes normal people decades to achieve where it would only take us one night."

I crossed my arms. "Can you break that down for me?"

He pulled out a chair and sat, not even thinking about sharing his treat. Cake Boy would give me the moon if I asked, but it would require the Jaws of Life to pry sweets away from his greedy clutches.

"Take my father, for example. When his spirit began to recognize my mom's presence, a link developed, like the one we share. Dad could sense her mood, her pain, even knew when she was near, like you can with me.

"Since Mom was normal, the link was one-sided and they could never form a solid bond like we can. That partial link was enough to destroy him when she died; he went insane from withdrawal. So, can you imagine if two Cambions got together? I can't even wrap my mind around it." He pinched his eyes shut, cutting off the negativity before it could sink in. Telling by his burdened expression, these thoughts occurred regularly.

Riveted, I crossed the room to stand between his parted legs. My fingers danced around his jaw and I enjoyed the color contrast, his creamy beige skin against my golden brown. Despite the temptation to strangle him right now, I couldn't let a moment go by without touching him, to remind him that his pleasure, as well as his discomfort, was mine also.

I tipped his chin to look at me. "You do realize this is a serious problem in our relationship? I can barely go a day without seeing you, but we're talking long-term commitment here. What if you become a jerk in ten years?"

He scowled. "You're one to talk."

"And if I get really nasty and super fat?"

"Hey, more cushion for the pushin'." He took a huge bite of his candy.

I rolled my eyes. "Or what if I get hit by a car—"

"Then I would die with you, simple as that."

I gasped at the thought. "At the same time?"

"I don't think so. Maybe a couple of weeks, less than a month for sure. It's unavoidable, Sam. Our link is just a precursor to a lifelong bond that the beings inside us will demand. And they will demand. It's what most Cambions dream about: being with someone without fear of killing them, having a permanent outlet for all that tension building inside." The worry lines melted away as he reveled in the concept.

Mindlessly, I played with his hair. Cool strands glided through my fingers as smooth as water. "You dream about me?"

"Only when I sleep." He shrugged, then tossed the candy wrapper over his shoulder, missing the waste basket by three feet. "And as far as the sex issue, well, I'm not gonna lie and say I don't want you. Badly. I'm not too quick to sign my life away either, but if it had to be to someone, it would be you. Just know that I'm ready when you are, and not a moment sooner."

I closed my eyes and pushed the air from my lungs. I could sense his disappointment, that balloon deflating and losing shape, but it was too soon in our relationship to go that extra step. This bonding thing was no joke, a decision we shouldn't make in the heat of passion. It didn't help matters that Caleb kept gawking at me like I was hot dinner.

I dragged a thumb across his bottom lip. "Are you really okay with us waiting?"

"The question is whether you can wait."

I drew back my hand. "Why?"

"You have a succubi spirit in your body. Its appetite is legendary, in more ways than one. Some of the folklore may be exaggerated, but not about that. You saw what happened to me when I denied Capone simple nourishment. It's only a matter of time until it will desire *other* things, and having a similar being around you will only make the need stronger. So yeah, there's cause for concern."

"We could always see other people," I suggested. "You slept with hordes of girls before you met me."

His face hardened with a mixture of disgust and rage, both expressions shooting fire to my torso. "You make me sound like a whore. Sex is pleasure. Pleasure is energy. Energy is food, nothing more. Yeah, I had women, but I never stayed long enough for Capone to recognize their presence, nor did I want to until I met you. What we have is something completely different and you know it, so take that righteous look off your face."

The words slammed into me, stunning me for a moment. I was mad and hurt, but I had no right to judge a past that didn't include me. We were carnal creatures, a call that we both had to answer to at some point, and adding more conflict was unnecessary.

After a moment, Caleb's eyes cooled to a darker, less hostile shade. He rose to his feet and closed the space between us. "Bonded or not, we will still need to feed from others to survive. That will never change. But being with anyone else in an intimate way would be as pointless as drinking sea water. It would never quench my thirst, no matter how much I drink. So I'll take whatever you can give me, even if it's just one sip at a time." He took my mouth in a searing kiss, stealing my breath and all argument with it.

Greedy fingers crept under my shirt and caressed my back. I stood on my tiptoes so we could be at eye level. My arms circled his neck, digging my nails into his scalp. No light could pass between our bodies, yet we shook with the need to get closer.

A current passed from my lips to his, its high voltage crackling and sizzling against my tongue as his life crossed my vision in a jumbled montage: his twelfth birthday party in Rome, his first day in India, his school in Germany. I sat with him during his final conversation with his mother before she died. I relived the moment he first saw me in the café, and hundreds of other moments fluttered around like fireflies. I tried to catch as many as I could and add them to the thousands I already had in my collection.

While feeding from each other's energy, our inner beings tingled with delight as they were let loose to play. Capone and Lilith tangled and rolled together, frolicking within their spiritual plane. They whined and begged for a deeper connection, a throb rooting to my core and forcing me to press harder into Caleb's body.

Suddenly we noticed Alicia, paused in the doorway with her mouth open. I buried my head in Caleb's chest, my cheeks burning.

Clearing her throat, she moved to her work locker and dumped her backpack inside.

"Well, I was gonna heat up my Hot Pocket, but I seemed to have lost my appetite." Fighting a smile, she left the room, leaving us locked in the same position we'd been in when she'd entered.

6

Though the Cambion motto dictated that we celebrate life, death deserved a holiday as well.

Once a year, at this hour, that dark stranger crosses our path and offers us candy. Despite our fear of the unknown and the warnings of elders, what child could truly refuse?

This occasion inspired me to dream, at a time when the clouds bruised the sky and the air turned purple. The sun retreated behind the trees, resigning its post while the moon began a new shift. I lived in that impasse, being neither shadow nor light, but the median amid two rivals.

Sighing, I turned away from the bedroom window and finished dressing. I'd wasted too much time staring into space and channeling Nadine's inner poet. Call it a coping mechanism, call it a crutch, but slivers of insight crept into my subconscious to numb the pain. It was aspirin for my clotted bloodstream, a treatment for my lifelong disorder. I couldn't dwell in that deadened state for too long or else I would develop a habit. The night was young and alive, and I owed it to Nadine to enjoy it sober.

Halloween with the gang was no casual affair and we took our sugar raid to almost militant proportions. Back in the day, Mia, Dougie, and I had been the original A-Team, laying waste to the entire junk food industry one block at a time, leaving devastation and candy wrappers in our wake. We outgrew plastic masks and pumpkin buckets, but those three kids laughing in the night stayed trapped in time. Which was why I resorted to blackmail to reunite the trio for one last stand.

Caleb managed to squeeze an extra invitation to Courtney's party for Mia, and I dangled that carrot over her head until she called a truce with Dougie. The holiday just wouldn't be the same without him, leaving Mia no choice but to put up or shut up.

It took me over an hour to get dressed, but seeing the results in the mirror was well worth the trouble. Covered from head to toe in my favorite color and five pounds of glitter, my costume revealed plenty of leg for Caleb to drool over. They were my best asset, Caleb's Kryptonite, and a foolproof weapon against Courtney B.'s advances during the party.

Just after seven, Mia picked me up, wearing a short-cropped wig and a spandex suit with neon lining that had to be painted on. She had spared no expense on authenticity, and I wouldn't have been surprised if she'd bought the costume from a studio back lot.

"Why, if it isn't Quorra, the rebel without a Clu," I called from the top of the stairs.

She whirled a glowing Frisbee with her finger and watched my awkward descent to the foyer. It took true agility to walk through narrow passages while rocking a four-foot wingspan.

Crossing her arms, she conducted an MRI on my attire, her eyes missing nothing. "What are you supposed to be, again?"

"The green fairy." I twirled around, and my frayed ballerina skirt and sheer wings danced around me.

Mia's nose crinkled, her mouth shifted from side to side. "Like the one from *Pinocchio?*"

"That's the blue fairy. Mine is more provocative." I rolled my shoulders and swayed my hips.

"No, you're definitely not a Disney character. More like Tim Burton." She smirked.

I stopped mid-spin and frowned. "You ready to go?"

"Yep. I've got a score to settle and I wanna make Dougie squirm. Always let your ex see what he's missing," Mia replied and pushed up her cleavage.

I swooped up my bag waiting by the door when Mom entered the foyer.

"Oh, don't you two look . . . nice." She grimaced. "Won't you be cold?"

"We'll be fine, Ms. M. I got an extra coat in the car," Mia said.

"All right then, you two be careful. Don't touch any candy that looks tampered with and don't eat anything people baked. I just saw on the news where this man slipped rat poison in his cookies and—"

"Thanks, Mom. We'll keep that in mind. Later." I opened the door and shoved Mia out before Mom gave us nightmares.

"Have fun, baby. And remember what I told you." Mom tapped her wrist, indicating the bracelet on mine.

With a groan, I nodded, then closed the door behind me.

A ten-minute drive across town led us to the back entrance of Kingsmill, an upper-class neighborhood with a guard gate, a dozen golf courses, duck ponds, and a plethora of wild parties. On top of the hill, overlooking the James River, was the clubhouse where the big shindig took place. Just pulling into the car show posing as a parking lot, I knew we were in for a night of pretension.

Mia was halfway to the door when she noticed I didn't follow. "Sam, where you going?"

I didn't answer and let her chase me around the building to the service parking lot in three-inch heels. I broke into a run, following the sound of heavy bass growing louder. When she finally caught up to me, she didn't look happy at the change in plans.

Dougie's Range Rover parked in the fire zone with the engine roaring. The tinted windows and metal framework shuddered under the sonic boom of gangster rap. On sight of us, he climbed out, unleashing lyrical turmoil and Auto-Tunes on the neighborhood. As if to enhance his street cred, Dougie wore the exact white suit that had made Al Pacino infamous in the hip-hop world.

I shook my head. "Douglas, Douglas, Douglas, why do you do this to yourself?"

His lips twisted to the side of his face as he shrugged. "I gotta do me, naw mean, man?" he said in an impressive Tony Montana parody. "What you 'spose to be?"

I threw my hands in the air in frustration. "What is wrong with you people? I'm the green freaking fairy! You know, the one that appears when you get high after drinking—"

"Absinth," Caleb said behind me. Flashing a grin, he dropped his box of equipment and reached our side.

I bowed my head in gratitude and pulled him to me. "Thank you. Finally."

With a look of indifference, Dougie said, "Okay, whatever. You look like Tinker Bell with a drug problem."

"Shut up, Dougie!" I hissed, then wrapped my arms around the lost inhabitant of Middle Earth.

Wearing a long blond wig, pointy ears, and gray leggings, Caleb was a dead ringer for the arrow-slinging elf. He approved of my choice of costume, judging by the subtle glow to his eyes. The luminous effect spoke volumes and brought this ethereal character to life. Strapped to his back was a custom-made bow and arrow that I had seen numerous times on his living room wall.

"Nice costume. You'll use any excuse to show off your longbow, won't you?" I joked.

His lips touched my ear as he whispered, "I don't need an excuse, and you are more than welcome to see my *longbow* at any time. It's quite impressive, if I do say so myself."

Shaking off the delicious tingle, I backed away before I took him up on his offer.

"Caleb, hey," Mia cut in and flung herself in his arms.

Holding her tight, Caleb took her for a spin before setting her down. He spread her arms wide to take in the full package. "Wow, great *Tron* outfit. You trying to get back on the grid?"

A nice shade of pink rushed to Mia's cheeks, but drained away at Caleb's next statement.

"Well, it's closer than you think. Doug's helping me set up, so you have plenty of time to talk to him." Caleb tucked in his lips to hide his smile.

Mia cut her eyes at the group, now coming to the realization that this had been a trap.

Dougie walked backward toward the main door, still wearing that hard look of thug life. "Y'all rollin' or what?"

I could see Dougie was getting to her, but that chip on her shoulder put up a fight. I bumped Mia in the arm when she didn't move. "Come on, Mia. One night won't kill you."

The next hour went by in a string of activity. While Caleb went to work, Mia and Dougie scattered to opposite sides of the hall to avoid killing each other. Stranded, I dove into the throng of the repetitive, half-naked clichés. Peppered throughout the skin parade stood the Dark Knight, six variations of Lady Gaga, Freddy, Jason, Shrek, Optimus Prime, and EVERY Anime character known to man.

Lost on the dance floor, I ate my fill on life, consuming the electricity in the air, licking the pulse that kept in sync with the throbbing bass. Bodies brushed against me, hot and clammy with their exertion, and rolled with the current of the music. Shafts of light dragged over this living sea, capturing split-second flashes of movement within the surf.

After my meal, I went to the bar and ordered a hot drink. Instead of coffee, a mug of hot cocoa rested in front of me with pumpkin marshmallows floating at the top.

"Best I can do, kid. Sorry. Don't wanna get you guys hopped up on caffeine," the bartender in a Frankenstein costume said remorsefully.

After one sip, I realized he'd done me a favor. This was gourmet hot cocoa with melted chocolate bricks and cream—no powdered mix crap. Its yummy warmth coated my insides, hitting all the right spots. I wasn't that surprised at the high-budget fare. The party screamed of rich-girl decadence, including a punch fountain and a witch and broom ice sculpture. Black and orange balloons floated to the ceiling, blotting out the row of chandeliers. Platters of mouth-watering sweets sat on each cloth table, a dieter's nightmare, but a Cambion's utopia.

Lifting my head, I winked at Caleb, who bobbed under his headphones in the deejay booth. Our eyes locked, and as always, the world disappeared only to return when he looked away. I could tell I was getting to him as he drained his bottled water. He was almost due for a break, so I called Mia to kill time. Yes, I was one of those people who call friends just to look busy, even when that friend is in the same building. I didn't feel too bad about it because Mia did the same thing.

"Can you believe him? He's rubbing it in my face!" Mia wailed. The hollow echo through the line told me she was hiding in the bathroom.

"What did Dougie do now?"

"First, he's all over me on the dance floor, right? And he's talking about 'girl, I sure do miss how you move,' and of course you know what he means, because you know I can't dance, but I keep flirting and laughing. Then I turn my back for a second and he's pushing up on some blue chick at the bar."

I looked to my far left, and sure enough, Dougie was yuckin' it up with one of the aliens from *Avatar*. Dougie was a fan of the movie and he seemed to have found a kindred spirit to geek out with. Even from this distance, the body language appeared friendly, but Mia had always had selective vision. This couple-counseling thing was going to be harder than I'd thought.

"Two can play that game, you know," Mia fumed in my ear. "You just wait; he's not the only single one around here. . . ."

Mia wasn't the only one with jealousy issues, either. I looked to the booth and spotted Caleb and Courtney B. talking and standing a little too close together for my taste. Decked out in an ironic she-devil costume, she did everything but shove Caleb's face in her chest. While her Wonderbra did most of the talking, Courtney handed him a bottle of water, which he eagerly took. When he finished the bottle in a single chug, she readily supplied another.

No one was that damn thirsty.

I'd hung up on Mia and leapt from my stool, ready to throw my hot drink in Courtney's face, when I spotted a man in a cape and mask watching me. That stare alone created its own gravitational pull, with those rich brown eyes that gleamed like brass. My hands shook so bad that I had to set down my mug before I dropped it. It amazed me how one look could suggest so many things—and all of them indecent. The look alone sent nerve endings on high alert; the slight brush of air shot a cold rush over my entire body. Lilith hummed between my ears, begging to come out and play.

He moved quickly through the multitude, as if he knew I would drop everything just to follow him. Heads and shoulders drifted past us, only giving me the floating hem of his cloak to go by. His eyes followed mine as the crowd entangled us; his stare glazed over with undiluted hunger.

From what little I could see, he was tall with deeply tan skin and full lips that curled seductively. This stranger had me running in circles around the party solely to confuse me, yet the urge to just touch this man reached past the bone to the marrow. I wanted—no, needed—to see his face, to know him. But something in the back of my brain told me that I already did.

After a few minutes, I'd found no trace of the man in the cape, which slathered an extra coat of disappointment to my evening. I returned to the bar to drown my sorrows in hot chocolate and stress eating.

"Good thing you're not driving." A low voice traveled close to my ear.

I turned to my right and saw Caleb sitting next to me at the bar, sipping from my mug. That was a pretty sneaky move—I should've seen him leave the deejay booth. How had he gotten here so fast? He leaned his elbow against the bar, staring as though waiting for an answer to a question I hadn't heard. "You feeling okay?"

"Yeah, sure," I said warily, shaking away a sudden

head rush and the lapse in time. "So, it looks like you were having fun with Courtney over there. Not that I care or anything. I mean, you're free to talk to people— it's a party after all, so . . . yeah. Did you feed from her?"

"Jealous?" He bumped my side with his elbow.

"No," I answered quickly.

He laughed. "Really, there's no need. And no, I didn't feed from her. It hurts just to hear her talk, so can you imagine having pieces of her swirling in my subconscious? I've been taking pulls off the crowd here and there, but I'm holding out for later when I can have you all to myself. Alone."

Why did he have to look at me like that? I wanted to melt down my chair and puddle to the floor. I'd been checking the clock too, counting the seconds before we could sneak off to feed and grope each other like a normal couple. It was a rare treat to be together outside of work and I was ruining it by being petty.

"I'm sorry," I said. "It seems no matter what, I keep dragging you back to high school drama."

"It's fine," he replied, rubbing his face with both hands. "I needed a change of scenery to take my mind off stuff anyway."

I studied his burdened expression. "What's wrong?"

He didn't answer immediately, but consulted his drink for the answer. After taking a few timid sips, he said, "There's a private detective in town out of New York. He's taken up an interesting hobby—shadowing me. That's why I didn't want you sticking around when my car got smashed, in case he showed up. I wouldn't be surprised if he followed me here. Oh look! Candy apples!" He reached over the bar and grabbed two pieces of fruit wrapped in cellophane. He unwrapped one and offered me the other.

As tempting as it was, I declined, trying to stay on the subject. "You think he knows anything?"

"No, and that bothers him. I told you, investigators were following my dad while he was alive, and now this detective, David Ruiz, has joined the crusade," he explained with his mouth full. "My guess is one of the victims' family members hired him, but Ruiz is having a hard time connecting the murders. He has a whole file on my dad tracing all the way back to his time in the military. He's thorough, so he might even interview you to find out what I'm hiding."

No matter if Caleb changed towns or his last name, there were some things he could not escape. One of those involved the shame of having a psychotic father and the string of deaths that remained unsolved. Nathan Ross was a cautionary tale for any Cambion who loved too deeply and OD'd on human energy. That old ghost had risen from the grave to settle a vendetta, and its main target was Caleb's peace of mind.

My fingers combed through the long blond strands of his wig. He looked way better with dark hair. In fact, there was nothing I would change about him. "I'm sorry. I know you want to put all that behind you."

Caleb shoved my untouched apple in his pocket for later snacking. "It comes with the territory, I guess. I did some checking and from what I hear, Ruiz is an ex badge with a hell of a mean streak. Cops at his old precinct call him 'the Cuban Necktie.' Fitting description if you think about it."

"I don't get it. Cuban Necktie?"

"I'll tell you when you're older." His thumb caressed my cheek, and that simple touch turned my limbs to jelly. "I don't want to worry about it now. Let's just enjoy the night and let tomorrow work itself out." Seeing me nod, he took another sip of chocolate heaven. His eyes rolled in the back of his head in rapture. Our spirits had an affinity for sugar, but Caleb made consuming sweets a religious experience.

"So are we doing this or what?" Courtney B. approached us, holding Caleb's bow and arrow case in her hand.

"Yes, and please don't touch that. It's not a toy." Caleb reached for the weapon, but she tucked it behind her back.

"I wanna see how it works. You said you'd show me. Oh, come on, please, please?" she pouted. Her antics were drawing a crowd. Not getting the desired reaction, she took the longbow and raced through the party. In a moving streak of red, she disappeared through the patio doors leading to the golf course.

I lunged forward, but Caleb pinned me still. "No fighting here. Too many people," he whispered, yet he was the one who needed to cool down. He finished my cocoa in one gulp as if it were a shot of courage and slammed it on the table. Before I knew what was happening, I was being led outside by the wrist.

"Caleb, you don't have to do this. This is dumb," I pleaded, trying to keep up with his long-legged stride.

He wasn't listening. Caleb was really sensitive about his weapons, and Courtney had gone and messed with his ego. We stepped out to the back deck of the club out onto the grass facing the golf course. The moon shimmered over the river in veins of silver. More guests rushed out of the clubhouse, murmuring in curiosity. Even Dougie and Mia came out of hiding, looking just as confused as I felt.

"Come on, Caleb, show us how you work your weapon." Courtney and her mob waited on the green, looking smug at the new entertainment. "Can you shoot it, or is it just for show?"

Fellow guests joined the argument, taking her side. "Come on, man. Let's see what you got." Hoots and cheers followed, egging Caleb on.

Caleb crossed the grass until he towered over the petulant redhead. Courtney's chest heaved under her corset; her eyes drooped, no doubt feeling the effects of Caleb's draw.

"All right, Britney, but I'll need assistance for this trick," he said and reclaimed his property.

"It's Courtney!" she huffed.

"I don't care." He whisked past her and crooked his finger at me to come forward.

Oh, the pitter-patter. Even Lilith felt a little woozy at the invitation. As I pushed through the group, the world progressed in cinematic slow motion. Licking my lips, I took my time crossing the distance, adding more hip swing in my strut. Cool wind passed around me, taking my glittery wings into flight.

Long blond strands whipped at Caleb's face as he dove into his pocket. With a roll of the wrist, he presented the candy apple and the same smile that probably tempted Eve.

"You see that big tree over there? Stand there and place this on your head."

My love-induced daze died a quick death. "Say what?"

"You ever heard of William Tell?"

"You ever heard of involuntary manslaughter?"

Singling out an arrow from his case, he dragged its feathered end over my cheek, beginning a languorous journey down the front of my dress. "Come on, Sam. Don't you trust me? Relationships are built on trust."

I plucked the arrow away with my fingers. "And stupidity."

Courtney leaned in. "If you're too scared, I'll do it!"

"No!" was our unanimous reply.

"I know what I'm doing. Trust me. Just keep still and I'll do the rest." Caleb planted a soft kiss on my forehead.

I don't know what made me agree with the idea—curiosity, peer pressure, or temporary insanity. But this was definitely a test of trust and courage. Caleb's weapons were the real deal and sharp as hell, which had inspired countless slaps on the wrists and scoldings whenever I tried to touch one on his wall. I had heard tales of his impeccable aim, but I'd never expected to one day become a target.

I reached the aged pine, a good twenty yards from where the gang stood, and flushed my back against the trunk. Balancing the apple to my crown, I yelled, "Do you need more light?"

"I can see you!" Nervousness made Caleb's voice uneven. "Just keep still. Don't move, don't even breathe!"

He didn't have to worry about that. Statues could never attain this level of stillness. A painful jolt zapped my chest as Caleb squared his shoulders and pulled back the string of the bow. A hush swept over the night, even the air froze around my skin. Some jerk in the crowd yelled "Miss!" and I almost wet myself. As the group grew quiet again, I closed my eyes and awaited my fate. The seconds slithered by, my hesitation grew, but I couldn't move. Caleb's face appeared behind my eyelids when a loud, wet crunch cut through the air.

Racing feet brought me back to current events. Hearing my name, and relieved that I was still alive, I opened my eyes to look up at what was left of the apple. The impact had broken the fruit into three pieces, speared in a gooey kebab of ribbon and clear wrapping.

"Sam! Are you okay?" Mia asked, pushing onlookers aside to gain a better view.

"Yeah, I guess."

"Wow, that was some crazy Robin Hood shit!" Mia tried to pull the arrow from the bark, but it wouldn't move. "Man, it's really in there." She tried using both hands, but not even Dougie's added strength could budge the lodged arrow.

I stared in a blank daze. Two inches lower and that would have been my head.

I looked over to my curious audience, scanning each painted face, but not seeing the one I wanted. "Where's Caleb?"

The crowd gave me room to walk, seeming to wonder the same question. It took only a moment to learn the answer. Moonlight silhouetted his body but made every spastic movement clear as day. Low grunts of pain filled the night as Caleb shrunk into himself like a dying spider.

"Caleb!" I screamed and reached his side at record speed.

Something sharp and tight took me to my knees. I no longer felt the cold or the ground beneath me, but the acidic burn that ate at my gut. It resembled the worst stomach flu in the world with a splash of malaria, and a freaky acid trip as garnish.

Fitful heaves emptied the contents of my stomach even when there was nothing left. I crawled to Caleb and held his head in my hands, and he clung to me like a life raft. His jaws flapped as he clutched at his throat, fighting for one breath of air. He was drowning in some private sea of torment, quickly dragging me with him.

I wasn't the only one having a reaction. Lilith went into a full wild-out, itching from the inside out as if covered with ants, scrambling for an exit, an answer, something.

Somewhere in a galaxy light years beyond the Earth's sun, I heard a stampede of footsteps. "You okay, Sam? What's wrong with Caleb?" a panicky voice asked. Shoes crunched the chilled grass, followed by speculative chatter. "Oh my God, look at her eyes! What the hell is she on?" someone yelled.

Before I could reply, bolts of fire struck my midsection with such force I fell flat on the ground next to Caleb. My muscles locked, causing joints to snap violently. The stretching of tissue, along with overwhelming sorrow, had me curled into a ball and crying for my mother.

Time held no true measure for these heart-stopping moments of fear and agony. Hands tucked underneath me and lifted me off the ground. I had no idea who spoke to me or where the flashing lights came from. More hands grabbed at my wrists and ankles, cruel in their assault and unmoved by my pleas to get to Caleb.

Where was he? Was he okay?

Through blurred sight, I saw Mia crying and squeezing my hand. A long, cold tube scraped my already raw throat, burrowing its way downward. Words floated in and out of range, loud, garbled noises that pertained to me in some manner. Everything after that was anyone's guess because the fight soon left my body. Death's cold finger rested against my lips and whispered, "Shh," bidding me to sleep. Despite my will to hold on, what child could truly refuse?

7

The next thing I remembered was waking up in a hospital bed with a tiny construction worker jackhammering my skull.

Turning over, I saw Mom dozing in a chair by the window. Something bad had happened, bad enough for Mom to wear holey pajamas in public. Judging from the dried tears and dark circles under her eyes, it had to be serious.

"Mom?" I called with a swollen, scratchy throat.

Slowly, her eyes fluttered open. "Samara?"

"Hi, Mom. What's going on?"

She sat up straight and rubbed her eyes. "Oh, thank goodness, baby. Are you all right? How are you feeling?"

"Groggy. Why am I in a hospital, again?"

"You were brought in two nights ago. You had a seizure and fell into a coma. Do you remember what happened?"

"Not really." I dragged my hand through my hair and

leaned back against the pillow. "We were at Courtney's party. Caleb had a bow and arrow and—Caleb!" I sprang upright, but Mom pushed me back down.

"Easy now, just relax. He's down the hall. His brother is with him. Tell me what happened."

My mind reeled, straining to recount the event in its proper sequence. "He was having a fit, some sort of reaction."

Mom's expression was indiscernible. Several emotions flashed in those blue, bloodshot eyes, and hitting the top of the list was fear. "Samara, I'm so sorry. I'm so sorry." She buried her face in her hands.

"What happened, Mom?"

"He's in a coma. The doctors believe he suffered an allergic attack, but they're having trouble diagnosing his symptoms. The paramedics arrived to the scene pretty quick and were able to pump his stomach and give him insulin, but he's still in bad shape. We'll have to wait and see."

"Like a food allergy? What did he eat?"

"I was hoping you could answer that question," she said with a hint of reproach.

"You think he took drugs or something? Come on, Mom, Caleb does not do drugs. I would know if he did. I was with him the whole night, and I didn't see him OD on anything but candy," I said in his defense.

"No, no, I believe you. They're pretty sure it's an allergy to something he ate." Mom took her time getting to the root of the matter, bracing herself for my response. "I thought maybe it was just a coincidence, but then he wasn't the only one affected. You had the same reaction."

"To what?" I yelled. "Were we poisoned?"

"I didn't want to rouse any suspicion, no more than

there already is, but . . ." Mom glanced at the door before saying in a low, sneaky tone, "Remember what I was telling you about last week, my research about olive oil?"

"Olive oil?" I repeated, not sure if I heard her correctly. "Why would Caleb drink olive oil and what does that have to do with him being sick? That's all myth, Mom."

"Is it? Cambions are myths as well. Incubi and succubi aren't supposed to exist. Why wouldn't this rule apply?"

"Because it doesn't work—just crazy superstition. I even proved it that night, and I was fine. . . ." I paused, my mouth forming the word yet to be spoken, when a recollection struck. Its truth seemed to have caught in my throat and gone down the wrong pipe.

While talking to Mom in the kitchen, I'd licked the oil on my finger and soon after, I'd gotten nauseous and spent half the night puking. My stomach muscles had curled into knots and Lilith had writhed in her own sphere of agony, a feeling very similar to the one on Halloween night. But only a few drops had coated my finger, not even a teaspoon.

Staring off to the far end of the room, I shook my head. "Are you sure about this, Mom?"

"There's no other explanation. You don't have any past medical conditions, and you rarely got sick as a kid. And these aren't exactly textbook symptoms of a food allergy. In fact, it's more of an 'internal' issue." She stressed the word with air quotes before continuing. "The staff around here have a lot of unanswered questions. No one has seen anything like this." Mom tucked in her lips, holding back the sob that was ready to break loose.

I sat there in an unblinking trance. My thoughts ran in opposite directions, and each path led to a dead end. Aside from pizza, I'd never liked Italian food. Salads of any kind were against my religion, let alone fancy dressing. Which posed the question: How did olive oil get into my body?

Closing a shaky hand over her mouth, Mom broke into another fit of tears, but this time I joined her. "My God, you could've . . ."

I reached over and fingered her curls. "Mom, please don't cry, please. I'm fine."

"Come here." Mom pulled me in her arms. "Now do you see why I keep hounding you about your bracelet? I'm not trying to run your life, I tell you these things for your own good. You're the only child I have, and I'll do whatever it takes to keep you safe." Mom smoothed back my curls and rained kisses on my cheeks and temple. "The doctor says you'll be fine in a few days, but you need to rest and stay hydrated. Your father came to see you this morning. He should be back tomorrow. He'll be glad to know you're awake."

"Is he mad at me?"

There was something very creepy about her laugh. It seemed to mock me as if I should know better. And I did. I could almost see Dad barging through the door demanding answers that I didn't even know how to give.

Pulling away, I wiped the tears from my eyes and focused on one crisis at a time. "I need to see Caleb, just for a few minutes."

"I know, but not tonight. Get some rest. I'll take you to him as soon as the doctors check on you." Mom stroked my tube-covered hand.

Lying back on the bed, I shut my eyes. I didn't have the strength to analyze this tonight, so I closed all programs and saved the data as a WTF file. Besides, whatever was tunneling inside my IV drip was making me drowsy.

"Will you stay until I fall asleep?" I mumbled against the pillow.

She kissed my nose. "I'm not leaving you, baby."

In moments, sleep took over and I dreamt of Caleb, my knight in shining armor. He stood proud on a mountain summit, surveying his newly conquered terrain with a sword in one hand and a powdered doughnut in the other.

I could have been asleep for maybe an hour when a nagging throb attacked my stomach. It caused a pull, an unrelenting need to act. This distress call seemed to come from miles away, a desperate plea for help. I tried my best to ignore it, but that only aggravated the ache more. Like a baby wailing in the night for its mother, this alarm pulled me out of a sound sleep to see to its need.

"I'm coming," I croaked and threw the covers off of me.

I ripped off the medical tape, and my eyes watered as the top layer of skin peeled with it. Eyebrow waxes were never this brutal. Thankfully, removing the needle in my hands was far less painful. I eased out of the bed and rummaged the supply cabinets for bandages while keeping a watchful eye on my dozing mother. Once I'd dressed the wounds, I tiptoed to the door.

Mom would have a fit, but I had to see Caleb, just a peek, just a moment of consolation. The vacant hall left me free to walk undetected. If I hadn't been awake before, the icy tiled floor and cool draft creeping up my hospital gown did the trick. The strange pulling sensation grew stronger with each step, creating a navigational system that allowed me to reach room 278 without conscious effort.

I opened the door and peered inside. The hall light leaked into the dark space, drawing around the sleeping body in the middle of the bed. I slipped inside and leaned against the closed door, listening to the monitors chirp like nocturnal wildlife. It took my eyes a moment to adjust to the darkness, but my patience was well rewarded.

I admired his peaceful demeanor, even with the tubes

and wires wrapped around him. However, his position made him too inert for sleep, and looked more like preparation for burial. The thought left me drained of strength, and the continuous draw seemed to suck the life from my body. At least now I knew where the compulsion was coming from.

"You shouldn't be here, Sam." The voice carried a faint Irish brogue.

I spun around to a pair of purple lights flickering in the dark. It followed my every move as I pushed off the door, but I wasn't afraid. If anything, his presence offered comfort. Last time I'd heard he was doing volunteer work overseas, forever the philanthropist who opened his hands rather than his checkbook.

The keen glow in his eyes told me that my visit was an unexpected one. His spirit was livid, and he didn't care who saw it.

"You'll make yourself sick. Go back to bed," Haden advised.

"I will. I had to see him." I turned back to Caleb. "How is he?"

"Unresponsive. They managed to get his heart rate under control and he's breathing on his own."

Footsteps drew closer. That soft, lavender glow bumbled in the dark.

"How could this happen, Haden?" I whispered.

"The lives inside us aren't human, but we are. Our bodies are just as susceptible to the elements as everyone else." Rough, callused hands rounded my shoulders and squeezed. "But this is an internal injury. His spirit is the one that's afflicted, not him."

"Did you know about the olive oil?" I asked, my eyes stinging with tears.

He let out a long, heavy breath. "We all knew about it as lads. Basic household oil is not as harmful; it'll make you sick. The deadly kind has to be organic and blessed by the church. Michael got a hold of some when he was seven, but Brodie and I were there to give him enough energy to fight it off."

Seeing my look of confusion, he added, "Feeding as soon as it happens works as a vitamin C shot; it strengthens the spirit's defense system in a way. Every second counts if you want to catch it before it settles into your system. After that, it's a coin toss."

I couldn't believe this! All this fuss over a cooking ingredient, a toxin known to everyone in the Cambion community but me. Hell, if Mom could discover our weakness, then this little fun fact was available to anyone with a decent search engine. If only a certain kind could do harm, that meant someone else knew about us, and they had gone through a lot of effort to single us out. But who? In light of this, I couldn't help thinking that somehow this was my fault.

I let my weight rest against Haden's chest. "When did you get here?"

"This morning. Brodie's here in the States, but he's stuck in New York on business. And Michael . . . well, he's a little upset."

I stared up at him. "He blames me, doesn't he?"

"He's a bit more rational than that. There's a method to his apparent madness, but no, he's not angry with you. He was more concerned for you than Caleb."

"Why?"

"As I said, the oil lingered too long and Caleb didn't feed to build his strength, and if he did, it wasn't enough. There is no logical reason why he isn't dead yet. His spirit hasn't abandoned his body, which means there's life left to salvage. Yours."

"I don't understand. We're not bonded yet."

"But you're linked. You feed from each other constantly, strengthening the connection," Haden explained. "Capone is borrowing energy from Lilith, a type of life support until Caleb can recover. That's why you had your seizure. They only found a small trace of the oil in your body, not enough to do serious damage. You're taking in Caleb's illness, you're keeping him alive, and the fact that you're walking about is a good sign."

My next question was difficult to get out. "Since we're not bound to each other, what will happen to me if he dies?"

Haden leaned closer to my ear. "You want the truth?"

"It's always nice."

"You'll survive, but you'll wish you hadn't. Your spirit will grieve and suffer extreme withdrawal and you'll go mad. For starters."

I flinched. I had asked for honesty, but damn. "Starters?"

"Best case scenario, you'll become suicidal and succeed. Worst case." He swallowed hard. "You'll become like my father."

The reply sent a chill through the entire room.

Whirling machinery cut through the silence as our predicament lay out before us, unmoving, wrapped in tubes and adhesive. Bonded or not, I was stuck with Caleb for life. Though I hadn't signed up for this when we began dating, I couldn't imagine life without him. Not now. Not after all that had happened.

"Does he need to feed now?" I asked.

I felt Haden nod. "Badly."

That was all I needed to know. I rushed to Caleb's side and touched his face. "How will that work if he can't draw it in?"

"I have no idea, but if his spirit can feed off you from across the hall, it should sense you up close. Try it, but don't let him take too much."

Opening Caleb's mouth, I lowered my head. His lips

were cold and lacked the sweetness that served as the norm. After long moments of stillness, a pulling sensation dragged at my insides. Lilith twitched and prickled in both pain and frenzy. I only had my imagination to help me understand the internal battle taking place. One injured animal nursed the other, licking the wounds and offering food. Meanwhile, no trace of Caleb was present, no warm coat of joy, no scent of sweets, no memories.

"Caleb," I whispered against his lips as hot tears burned my cheeks. My body shook as I drew deeper into the kiss, giving all of myself to him, praying that my strength was enough. But all I got was dead air and further anguish.

"That's enough, Sam. You're still weak. You don't want to overdo it," Haden whispered from some great distance. His hands latched on to my arms when I didn't respond. Opening my eyes, I strained to remember where I was. I stared at Caleb, motionless and lifeless as when I'd last seen him.

"He needs more," I insisted.

"Not right now. You need to feed, rebuild your strength, then try again. He'll kill you if he takes too much now." Haden pulled me to his chest and squeezed me tight until I stopped struggling. "Go on back to bed. You can try again in the morning."

His chest rose and fell in angry tremors in an effort to keep it together. More times than necessary, Caleb's brothers had seen death, that uninvited guest who had taken permanent residence in their lives.

"You know I can't leave him," I mumbled against his shirt.

"I know. I figured I'd toss the idea out there anyway." He kissed the top of my head as an orderly walked into the room and clicked on the light.

"Miss, you can't be in here. Your mother is looking for you. Come back to your room," he ordered.

Pulling away, Haden lifted my chin to meet his gaze. Dingy black hair fell around his face in tangled locks. Fading white scars creased his leathery face. His nose hung slightly bent and set off center, evidence of rough living and a short temper. But seeing those violet peepers made my stomach jerk. I had almost forgotten how all the Ross boys looked alike. Caleb and his brothers shared that vagabond appearance, as if they had simply rolled out of bed, looked in the mirror, and given up. Then again, they all had an incubi spirits living in their bodies, and having women dogging their every step left no real reason to try.

Six and a half feet of bulk made Haden the most intimidating of the four. He looked like he should be in Special Ops combing the jungle, but his cinnamon roll cologne killed all element of badass.

After a few blinks, the glow in his eyes faded away, retreating behind the cornea. "Are you hungry?"

Knowing what he meant, I said, "Starving."

Wearing a wicked grin, Haden turned to the male nurse. "Sir, she's a bit weak. Could you be so kind as to take her back to her room?" His voice was as low and persuasive as any villain.

"Sure." The orderly stepped closer, then froze as our eyes met. He was a husky guy with loose-fitting scrubs. His athletic build and baby face screamed med student, but I had to be careful. My allure affected men of all ages, and it would be a shame if he was arrested tonight for improper conduct.

Meeting him halfway, I brushed my hand over his face. Almost instantly, he gave in to the draw, leaning closer to capture my mouth. I stopped and lightly danced my lips against his, grazing his cheek, his neck, then returned to the source, drinking in my fill on much-needed nourishment. My finger stopped at his pulse, waiting for that indicative skip in his heartbeat. As soon as I felt it, I pulled away.

He stared back at me with hooded eyes, silently begging for more, offering anything for another turn.

"Leave me here and tell my mother I'm fine," I said. "Insist that I stay. My presence calms Caleb. I'll return in the morning."

He nodded keenly, then set off to do my bidding.

Haden stood by the door with an appreciative smile, looking like Caleb's alter ego. "A true Cambion at work. Nadine would be proud."

"Thanks." I crawled on the bed and curled next to Caleb, mindful of the wires and cords.

Haden left the room for a moment, no doubt to keep Mom from dragging me back to my room. I needed this time with Caleb, a period of regeneration and peace. At some point, I fell asleep whispering words of encouragement and love, words that I'd never had the nerve to say aloud, words for his ears only.

8

I remained hospitalized for the next few days, still unable to imbibe solid food.

The doctors ran more tests and gave me the royal treatment, perhaps in fear from the last time the Marshall women darkened their halls. Maybe the extra attention had something to do with me snacking on every man on staff, including the custodians. Whatever the deal was, I didn't complain.

Mom stood guard as usual, fending off police and the obstinate private detective, David Ruiz. He seemed adamant about interviewing me, and not even Mom's threat of disembowelment could deter him.

Despite his relaxed, Brooklyn-bred tone, Ruiz sported an air of authority that had me tripping over my own words. His shiny black curls, Colgate smile, and designer suit couldn't diminish the "don't eff with me" vibe that clung to his skin like cologne. For that reason, Lilith decided to sit this one out. He seemed immune to my draw anyway, which was a phenomenon within itself. He didn't seem like a forty-year-old virgin, not the way he was eye-balling Mom all through his visit.

Having knowledge of our connection, he asked about Caleb's father. My answers remained vague, but he kept drilling that rig until he struck oil. The detective and I shared one belief: There was a cause and effect to everything, and there was no such thing as coincidences. Maybe it was part of his strategy, but he seemed to know more than what he let on. Since neither one of us were going to show our cards, we wasted a good part of an hour calling each other's bluff.

"You really got the staff around here spooked. Even the police in this town freeze up at the mention of your name. Any particular reason?" Ruiz asked.

"My grandpa is a very influential man and he enjoys scaring people, including us. Not a good idea to step on his toes."

He gave a shrewd nod. "So I hear. Must be comforting having so many powerful people backing you. You can get away with just about anything."

"Mr. Ruiz, just out of curiosity, why are you called the Cuban Necktie?" I asked, remembering what Caleb had told me at the party.

With a wry grin, he answered, "Because I'm Cuban and I have the reputation of being cutthroat when I need to be." He left it at that, some clever anecdote everyone in the room got but me.

I caught Mom giving him the eye during the interview, adding an extra flip of her hair whenever she interrupted him. Her efforts brought a smile to his stern features, and his line of questioning took a detour into her marital status.

I guessed stubborn people attract each other. If I hadn't been strapped to the bed by IVs, I would've given them some privacy. After twenty minutes of the sickest flirting contest I'd ever witnessed, the detective left defeated with promises of a rematch.

And the Awkward Train just kept on rolling.

Dad swung by to check on me, which led to another Caleb-bashing session. He figured Caleb's vegetable state was a fitting punishment for endangering his baby girl yet again.

To make matters worse, he'd brought his shrew of a wife, Rhonda, who looked as though she'd been dragged there by knifepoint. She made a show of concern, but the disdain wafting off her body was enough to choke a horse. The woman couldn't stand me, but her contempt was exacerbated by her belief that I harbored bad juju, which made her visit blissfully brief.

Dad brought the twins with him as well, dishing out a mouth-watering treat for Lilith. She loved the pure, concentrated energy children produced, which my siblings owned in abundance. I watched the six-year-olds nap in one of their brief breaks from anarchy. Kyle curled up in the chair in the corner, snoring with his mouth open. Kenya leaned on her brother, wearing a Princess Tiana costume that she refused to take off, a stubbornness I would've never gotten away with growing up. Dad was getting soft with his old age.

I didn't get to see my brother and sister as often as I should. Much like this meeting, they mysteriously fell asleep after the first hug. This strange occurrence only Lilith and I could explain, and our silence added another brick to the growing wall between Dad and me. Though Lilith recognized Dad's presence, with the right amount of concentration I could use her "powers of persuasion" to cool his temper. It had gotten me out of binds before; why fix what isn't broken?

"I think it's a bit strange that so many 'accidents' are happening in Williamsburg." Dad strolled in front of my bed and continued his cross-examination. "First one of your classmates, then your mother, your coworker, and now this. A lot of odd events this past summer, and they all occurred right around the same time you started seeing that boy."

Here we go. Dad had some serious Angus beef with my boyfriend, and he needed to get over it. Gathering what little strength I had, I sat up straight. "Daddy, don't blame Caleb. We're all victims in this."

He swept a meaty hand across his bald head. "All I know is that something happened to you, something strange. Not just your eye color—which the doctors still can't explain, by the way—but your whole demeanor. You're like a different person." He reached inside his suit jacket and pulled out a folded pamphlet. "Samara, there's a psychologist in Alexandria who specializes in abnormal cases of post-traumatic stress," he began, waiting for my reaction.

I didn't say a word, but stared at the worn brochure in his hand and wondered how long he'd been holding on to it.

"I know you think you're fine, but it's clear that you're not. When I met your friend Nadine, the first thing I noticed about her were her eyes. And you have the exact same pair. The mind is a powerful thing, baby girl, and I believe that your change is a physical sign of your grief. Now this specialist handles all sorts of anomalies: women who miscarry but still have all the effects of pregnancy, twins who share physical symptoms of their siblings, people who claim to have stigmata, and so on. Now these sessions are completely confidential and . . . just think about it, okay?"

"What if I can't be fixed, Dad? Are you gonna have me committed like Grandpa tried to do? I don't want any more tests, blood work, or pills thrown at me. I just want to be normal. So please, just let me."

Fear and disappointment gripped his face for a moment. I wasn't sure what had caused that look, my secrecy or my quantum leap into adulthood, but he seemed to think I was a stranger.

He glanced back and forth between me and his other two children as if comparing our differences, not in complexion, but age. The twins had just started first grade and I was about to graduate, a lengthy gap that Dad had trouble measuring. He'd never looked as resigned as he did in that instant, demoted from his proud station as protector and provider.

I reached out and pulled him closer. His big body covered what little room was available on the bed. His hands dwarfed mine as dark brown fingers enclosed them. He had a way of making me feel small and delicate by proximity alone.

"I'm the same ol' Sam, Daddy. It's just a newer version of me—Samara 2.0. I'm seeing the big world out there, and I like what I see for the most part. I'm still your baby girl. No matter what, that fact won't change."

"I know." He leaned in, planted a warm kiss on my forehead, and in a slick move that almost made me proud, slipped the brochure under my blanket.

An hour later, Mia dropped off my classwork with an extra helping of tension that was bigger than her handbag.

"So you gonna tell me what the hell is going on, or do I log this in the 'things Sam won't talk about' shelf?" she began. "I've seen some weird things in my life, but Halloween night was off the chain."

"There's nothing to talk about. Had some bad reaction to some food," I explained with a mouth full of lime Jell-O.

She didn't buy it for a second. "I've taken three years of biology and not once have I ever read about foreign bacteria that make your face start glowing like a radioactive mutant. If so, why was no one else at the party affected but you and Caleb? Come on, Sam. It's *me*. Talk to me," she pleaded.

Though each syllable cut at my insides, the lies rolled off my tongue like Polish. This skill would come in handy once I started law school, so it was good to start early. Her parting glare as she left the room told me I needed more practice.

For the rest of the day, I replayed Halloween night over and over in my head, wondering what Caleb had eaten that could have been tampered with. I remembered the bottles of water Courtney had been chucking at Caleb, but could oil mix with water without him noticing? At my request, Mom rechecked my clothes and found nothing. We were about to give up when I recalled the hot cocoa I'd drank that night. I'd set down my mug at the bar while chasing after some stranger around the party. Anyone could have gotten a hold of it.

I cupped my head in my hands and cried. For years, Mom had warned me of situations like that, to never leave my drink unattended. The one time my guard dropped, I became the newest cautionary tale. But Caleb had gotten caught in the cross fire, more collateral damage, another life in danger because of me.

Guilt and damnation rode me hard that night, granting only minutes of sleep before another round of abuse. But I swore I would find out who'd done this, even if it killed me.

The middle child of the Ross dynasty signed the visitors' guestbook the next morning. Michael Ross was the emaciated version of Caleb with a long, brown braid that reached his waist. I would never get used to these body doubles running around. It conflicted with the "Holding It Together" campaign I had going. But each had their distinct style and endearing quirks.

Though I was unsure of his preferred poison, Michael carried a perpetually drunken sway and could never sit in one spot for very long. He also had his paranoid moments, looking over his shoulder and answering questions only he could hear. Oh yeah, there were some screws loose, but he was always aware of the things around him.

Of the three times I'd been in Michael's company, I'd never seen him stone sober, just in fluctuating degrees of blitzed. Today was no different.

"It keeps the voices quiet," he'd told me once after his dad's funeral. "I can hear the lives I take, and not all of them are pleasant. It becomes harder to sort out which memories are mine."

Everyone coped differently with the Cambion lifestyle, I guess. None of the brothers confronted him about his self-medication and I thought I'd better do the same.

On sight, this walking skeleton drew me in for a hug that almost hurt. I could feel his ribs under his baggy trench coat, and his red-rimmed eyes avoided mine. He never looked a female in the eye unless he fed, so I didn't take offense.

Once the pleasantries were over, he told me that Brodie was still missing in action, and I wasn't sure if I was happy or sad about that fact.

"Do the police have any leads on a suspect?" Michael asked.

Haden looked puzzled. "Nothing so far, but I don't expect the police to come up with anything useful. This wasn't an accident. Someone was trying to get to Sam and Caleb, and if it was a Cambion, then he won't stop until he finishes the job."

Michael staggered around the room, pulling out drawers and opening cabinets. "We'll have to stay here in shifts. I'll take the morning and you take evenings."

My head volleyed between the brothers. "You think he might come back?"

"We're not leaving anything to chance." Michael smiled, stuffing alcohol wipes and rubber gloves in his coat pocket. He was so weird. "Let us worry about this. You gather your strength. Caleb needs you more than ever."

With Michael and Haden's help, I snuck into Caleb's room for the next couple of nights and tried to nurse him back to health. I had to up my food intake threefold in order to sustain us both. Holding Caleb's head in my arms, I would offer all life force as a sacrifice. I entered the room full as a bloated tick only to be carried back to my room depleted. These night visits turned me into a lifeless zombie, too weak to stand on my own, which lengthened my stay at the hospital. On the upside, I lost ten pounds within a span of three days.

No matter how often I fed, how much energy I donated, it wasn't enough. Capone was getting stronger, but he needed more than what I could give. I would offer every last drop I had to keep Caleb alive. Haden and Michael voiced their concerns, but no other alternative presented itself. I was no good to Caleb weak, but that utility went both ways.

Hour by hour, Caleb resembled a soulless, capsized vessel, and I was slowly going down with the ship. Though still new to the world of dating, the thought of being without my Cake Boy dropped me into a void with no bottom. All I had was hope. And time.

On the fifth day, the doctors sent me home with a clean bill of health. They might as well have left me there because I camped out in Caleb's room. Mom's absurd de-

mand that I return to school at some point kept me from
building a fort out of blankets.

My first night home was one of melancholy and isolation. Mom kept her distance, but her shadow passed
under my door every few hours. She told me that Dougie
had dropped off a card. Thank goodness Mom was there
to intercept my messages; I wasn't up for company. Questions abounded, and I could barely eat, let alone wrap
my lips around a decent explanation. Things would only
get worse in the morning when I returned to school.

I couldn't stay in one place for too long, and my skin
prickled at the slightest touch. Lilith whined and clawed
at my insides, pining for Capone as I did for my own
companion. Conversations whispered in my ear; laughter
and arguments tickled the hairs on my arms with their
ghostly presence. Phantoms emerged, transforming my
room into a crowded house party of memories, multiply-
ing and taking more than their share of space.

I was a nervous wreck, crying at random over the
dumbest stuff: running out of shampoo, burning my
tongue on the soup Mom had brought me, and staring at
the jar of quarters sitting on my dresser. For months, I
had collected those coins as tokens of Caleb's affection, a
code only we could understand and truly cherish. Two
hundred and fifteen "I Love Yous" safely deposited in an
old mason jar, gaining interest by the hour.

I sat on the floor and poured out the jar and counted
the quarters, carefully tending to each one of my children. When the numbers didn't add up, I tore my room
apart trying to find the missing quarter. Screaming my
anger to the heavens, I checked under tables, chairs, and
piles of clothes with no success. My hands shook, report-
ing my crisis to every known part of my body. Breathing
and all other functions stopped in response to this state
of emergency.

Mom burst into the room with a baseball bat, ready to do battle. "Samara! What's wrong? What happened?"

"One is missing! It's gone. It was right here." I crawled on my knees and swiped my hands across the carpet, my eyes scanning for anything small and shiny. Tears blurred my sight, so I had to rely on touch to continue my search. "I remember fifty-three-seventy-five. There's only fifty-three-fifty."

Mom dropped her bat and joined me on the floor. "Samara, calm down. We'll find it. You probably miscounted."

"No! It was here. I lost him. I can't find him. Mom, help me, please!" I burrowed under my bed, tossing out items I hadn't seen in years. A solid grip captured my waist and pulled me out. "No! I have to find it. I can't lose it. It's mine!"

"Baby, stop. Please, just stop." Mom trapped me in her arms and rocked me back and forth. "Hush now. Just breathe. We'll find it, even if it takes all night. I'll count with you. Accountants are good with numbers, remember? Baby, please, just be still." Her voice broke as she crooned and shushed me quiet. I didn't know who trembled more, me or her.

I now had a taste of what Mom had gone through when she finally split with Dad—the loss, the vulnerability. I wondered which hurt worse: watching someone you love marry and start a new family without you, or helplessly watching a loved one die before your eyes like Caleb's father had. Both paths ended in grief, the slowest kind of death.

I wiped my eyes on Mom's sweatshirt. I'd never told her the significance of the coins, but I was sure she knew it had to do with Caleb. Cradling me in her arms, she dragged the jar to us and began counting one by one. After twenty minutes of searching, we found the missing coin in my sock. Too drained to do anything else, I climbed into bed in a full-body collapse, tucking the coin jar next to me.

Mom sat at the foot of the bed, having watched her daughter lose her mind over pocket change and been powerless to do anything about it.

"I knew this was going to happen. Evangeline warned me about this, but . . ." Mom swallowed noisily. With a broken voice, she said, "This is only the beginning."

9

Finding something to wear for my first day back to school was a true act of futility.

The person staring through the mirror wasn't me, but an addict fresh out of detox. A hooded sweatshirt and jeans draped over my body in shapeless layers of fabric. My skin looked waxy and almost green from the lack of sun. Unfocused eyes hid behind dark shadows with their emerald luster gone. No need to sugarcoat it, I looked busted. It mirrored my enthusiasm for school, so I was good to go. Just the thought of solid food made me nauseous, so I downed some orange juice, pecked Mom on the cheek, and set out.

James City High's welcoming party came with a powder keg and a hard dose of reality. Word of the Halloween freak show had gone viral, reaching both students and faculty. The good news: my instructors fell into a more diplomatic approach to teaching, even offered a sympathetic ear if I needed counseling. Their compassion helped ease the burden of makeup exams and overdue projects.

The bad news: I got more hostile glares and dubious whispers, along with the most outlandish yarns I'd ever heard. The ringleader to this circus was Courtney B., who recommended drug rehab and gave unwanted dating advice. As if I would take any advice from someone who couldn't remember my name.

"You know, Samantha, you have your whole life ahead of you," she said, walking beside me on my way to gym. "Hanging around bad elements is bound to ruin your future in fast food, but it's good that you know now. Poor Caleb, what a tragic end, but in time you'll move on." She looked down at me in feigned sympathy, then strolled ahead with the other two Courtneys flanked at her sides.

Not even ten seconds later, Alicia leapt into my arms, frantic and out of breath. "Ohmigod, Sam! I heard you were in the hospital and the police are after Caleb because he tried to kill you with an arrow. Are you okay? Did you get stitches?"

"What? No, Alicia, I'm fine. He had a food allergy and now he's in a coma."

She sprang back in shock. "Oh no! I hope he's okay." She covered her mouth, then frowned when a question struck her. "Wait, if Caleb was the one that got sick, then why were you—"

"Wow, look at the time!" I announced a little too loud and checked the clock by the bulletin board. "I'm gonna be late for gym. I'll let Caleb know you asked about him—'kay, bye!" I quickened my steps before she could follow me.

It only got worse from there. The rumor mill kept churning out hit after hit, more exaggerated with each telling: epic explosions, bloodshed, and supernatural fervor that would make Stan Lee slap his forehead. Only my lunchmates dared to ask about that white elephant in the room, so I gave them the director's cut of what happened. For the obvious reasons, specific scenes were removed and would forever remain on the cutting room floor.

Girls became more vicious toward me, which resulted in a scuffle in the girls' bathroom. I could hold my own in a fistfight, but I was outnumbered by four irate girls with sharp nails and a false sense of entitlement. During this ambush, my enemies accused me of stealing boyfriends, ruining prom and future marriage plans, and jeopardizing the survival of mankind.

"You think you all that, don't you?" a very butch junior asked while shoving me against the sink. It was a rhetorical question that I had no time to answer.

"Yeah, she does, with her phony contacts, trying to look white. You're so fake!" A toad-face-looking girl with no neck joined in, yanking my head back by the roots of my hair.

I now understood why Caleb abhorred violence. Our spirits needed no reason to go on a murderous rampage, and I couldn't risk the exposure. Lilith was pissed, eager to wring these heifers dry on my behalf, but to unhook her leash was straight suicide.

With a busted lip and a chunk of my hair missing, I survived the catfight and wound up in detention for my selfless act. At least there I would get a chance to do homework.

Or so I'd thought.

After the final bell, I made my way to the in-school suspension class. My smart mouth had led me to this room more times than I'd like to remember, so I knew the drill. Occupying the desks in the front was a set of clones, wearing black high-laced boots, heavy eyeliner, and a practiced look of boredom.

The usual suspects loomed in the back, the potheads,

the brawlers, and to my surprise, Mia. She couldn't have stood out more if she lit up in bold neon, and it threw me off guard to see such an elitist kickin' it with derelicts. I gave my detention slip to the dozing teacher and scooted my way up the row toward the back.

I took a seat next to her and smiled. " 'Sup."

Mia's head whipped around, her dark curls slapping her cheeks. " 'Sup, Sam. Figured I'd see you here today. Heard about the bathroom throw-down. Any survivors?"

"Barely," I grumbled, knowing this was yet another rumor I had to recover from. "What brings you to this neck of the woods?"

"Fell asleep in sociology three days in a row and I wound up here."

"Why were you sleeping in class? Something keeping you up at night?" I asked, though I had a sneaking suspicion about what.

In this week's episode of *The Bold and the Reckless*, Mia decided to play hardball. Using her status to her advantage, Mia had started spreading rumors about Dougie's new love interest. In retaliation, Dougie had gone to Jason Lao with a tell-all exposé about their relationship, revealing to those unaware that Mia was a jealous psycho. This not-at-all-groundbreaking news solidified their position as the Mr. and Mrs. Smith of our school, and served as fodder for the tabloids.

Before fifth period, Dougie had stopped by my locker in order to uncover Mia's next move. He had every right to be concerned. The loud, aggressive Mia he could handle, but her silence proved lethal for all involved. If she kept me in the dark about her counterattack, her intended target didn't have a prayer.

"Why are there so many girls in here? And why do they look like they attend the goth girl academy?" Mia asked, derailing my train of thought. "That's like the eighth shirt like that I've seen today. What is *Specter* anyway?"

I looked to the short girl sitting by the window, wearing three layers of shirts, including a T-shirt that cut across her stomach in an unflattering way. In the center of the shirt was a translucent blue boy embracing a girl with black lipstick. The phrase LOVE BEYOND THE GRAVE stretched across the top.

I rolled my eyes. "It's a book series that all the girls are obsessed with. Hot ghost boys are *en vogue* this year. The main characters met in detention," I explained, recalling what Alicia had blathered on about in the book meetings. "You visit me at work all the time; you've never seen it on the shelves?"

Mia cut her eyes at me and pulled out a spiral notebook from her backpack. "Sam, you know I don't book. I go straight to the magazines."

This was true. Mia worked better with pictures, including pie diagrams and charts. High-strung as she might be, she had brains, which I steadily probed to complete my take-home quiz for biology. The next twenty minutes consisted of me asking random vocab questions.

"Psst, Mia, what's a polyploid?"

"An organism with more than two sets of matching chromosomes," she answered, not lifting her eyes from her papers.

After jotting that answer down, I moved to the next question. "Oh, okay. What's a zygote?"

"A fertilized egg. Sam, are you even trying?"

"Yes," I said indignantly, then went to the next problem. "Hey, what's a—"

"Just give me the damn quiz!" She snatched the paper off my desk. In exchange, she slapped her folder on my desk. Mia breezed through my homework, her pencil flying across the paper.

Quite familiar with the routine, I opened the folder, whipped out a red pen, and began proofreading her English essay. She was seriously the yin to my yang, one of those left-brained people who couldn't write a compound sentence, but could formulate the time-space continuum in their sleep. I'd miss her so much when she went to Columbia next year; it gave me heartburn just thinking about it.

Handing back my quiz, Mia whispered, "So, is it true that you and Malik Davis are hooking up?"

I almost jumped out of my chair. "Who-with-the-what-now?"

"Quiet down!" Mrs. Braxton ordered from the front of the class.

While pretending to work, Mia whispered, "That's what Malik's been saying. I gotta tell ya, I was a little shocked. I know I teased you about it and all, but wow, I didn't think you would creep like that. Did you know he almost died in a car accident?"

"So I hear," I dismissed with a flip of the hand. "You said Malik's been saying we're dating?"

"More than that," Mia mumbled with a hint of suggestion. She pulled out her phone and fiddled with the touch screen while hiding her actions within the shelter of her lap. Finding what she was looking for, she passed me the device.

Jason's blog appeared with a picture of him giving a cheesy thumbs-up. An entire page was devoted to me and the grocery list of rumors. Most of them were ridiculous, but the others cut me to the quick. I couldn't believe how many people in school saw me as conceited, mean, and butt ugly.

"Do I really look like a brown Cabbage Patch doll?" I asked Mia.

Her whole body turned as she gave me a good once-over. "No. Well, a little bit—right around the face. Why you ask?"

"Never mind." I continued scrolling, my dignity shriveling with each comment. The false reports by the guys bothered me the most. These accounts had been relayed in such graphic detail, they should've been deleted by the webmaster. The most outrageous entry came from MalikD757, who claimed that he and I had partaken in acts that only someone freakishly double-jointed could accomplish.

I was ready to toss the phone out the window when Mia caught my wrist.

"Hey, hey, calm down. Don't break it." She wrenched her defenseless phone out of my clutches.

"One more outburst, ladies, and I'll see you back here tomorrow," Mrs. Braxton threatened with a slam to her desk. Apparently her nap time was over.

I returned to my editing task, seething and crossing out errors with angry red stripes. My entire week came to a head, the sickness, the uncertainty of Caleb's recovery, not eating a decent meal in days, and having my ass handed to me by four of Malik's biggest groupies. The attack in the girls' bathroom began to make a bit more sense. Malik had gone too far, and his pissing contest placed me at risk of getting shanked by every girl who claimed him.

I was quickly learning that playing by the rules didn't work in this school. I wished it hadn't come to this, but now, I had to take care of business, Samara Nicole style. I had another thirty minutes until detention ended, so I needed to act fast.

*   *   *

Once my sentence ended, I stormed into the gymnasium, absorbing the echoic blare of bouncing balls and squeaking sneakers. The smell of hot funk and industrial cleaner almost knocked me out. This was the guys' turf, and I made it a point to never invade this domain, unless absolutely necessary.

Malik raced along the court, doing off-season relay drills with the rest of his team when I called for him. Sporting a fiendish grin, he called a time-out, then met me halfway. He didn't get a chance to speak before an upper cut to the jaw knocked the taste out of his mouth.

"You lying son of a bitch!" I yelled. "Why are you spreading rumors about me, you evil—"

"Whoa! What the hell is your problem?" He tumbled back, struggling to gain his footing as his partners rushed in on the scene.

"What's my problem? You're telling everyone we're having sex, and you know good and well it's not true!"

His hand shot out and caught my wrist before I delivered another blow.

"Says who?" he challenged. Dude didn't even own the decency to deny it.

I shoved his chest. "Says me!"

"Uh-oh, your girl is getting mad!" a teammate mocked. "You gonna let her carry you like that, Malik? You better handle that."

He tossed his fellow teammates a sneaky grin before all eight members crowded around me. Only then did I realize the error of my ways. Emotions impaired judgment, and I'd managed to walk into the middle of a trap. No coach or teacher stood in sight, and class had been dismissed hours ago. It was just me among eight hormonal athletes and a thick cloud of BO. Not wanting to be the next Lifetime movie of the week, I backed away toward the double doors.

A boy pivoted to my left, blocking my escape. "Where you going?"

"Don't try to run now. Say what you gotta say," another guy added as the circle closed in on me.

"Let go of her," Malik ordered. It was a calm, low-spoken command that the team immediately obeyed. "No one—and I mean no one—touches her but me. You feel me?"

The team nodded as one of the boys shoved me into Malik's arms. My sense of rescue lasted a blink as he gripped my arms and smiled.

"I hear your boy is still in the hospital. He got messed up pretty bad. Looks like you need a new one," he teased.

I tried to get my anger under control, tried to remember Mom's teachings about the virtue of patience and to be a lady at all times. But this lady was in the middle of a nervous breakdown with a sentient that would Hulk out at any second.

"You guys go ahead. I'll catch up with you in a minute." He pulled me toward the bleachers.

This was not a good sign. I tugged and jerked my arm free, but my efforts only made it worse. Before a scream could escape, he covered my mouth. His strong arm wrapped around my waist from behind, lifting me off the ground. My legs wiggled and kicked in a fruitless attempt at his shin or kneecap.

A lanky guy tried to step in, but the others pulled him back. "Hey, just let her go, man. We've still got practice. You don't need to—"

"I'll be out in a second. Samara and I need to talk," Malik interrupted.

"Let go of me!" I yelled under his hand.

"Now get out and watch the door. Don't let anyone come in." Malik waited for his crew to file out of the gym one by one.

He carried me behind the bleachers against the wall. In seconds, his big body trapped me in.

"I shouldn't have to work this hard to get a girl's attention. I see how you look at me, trying to get under my skin. Nobody likes a tease, and you're the biggest one in the school." He finally removed the hand from my mouth.

"Look, Malik, you're obviously seeing something that isn't there. I never gave you any impression that I was interested in you."

"You did when you kissed me."

Whoa! I must have missed that episode. "What are you talking about? I never kiss—" was all I could say before his lips crushed against mine, shoving all arguments back down my throat.

Oh, the slimy feeling that curled my body! Hands, lips, and tongue went everywhere, a feeling that could only be boiled away.

Yet somehow, this all seemed oddly familiar.

Purely by instinct, I inhaled the trail of energy radiating from his skin. I knew he was under the draw, but I hadn't realized to what extent. This guy took an all-expenses-paid trip to La-La Land. Scenarios flashed in my head, events that he could swear on a Bible were real.

Perhaps it was the dizziness or the indignant sense of disbelief, but once realization rolled up, so did my stomach. Caleb had warned me about the lengths people would go while under the draw; their desperation to be with us could turn violent at the flip of a switch. But Malik had picked the wrong time and the wrong chick to mess with.

All my torment, all my grief took center stage. The thought of losing my mate and enduring this perv's unwanted touches shot my anger to Defcon one. I snatched away from Malik and pushed him against the wall with strength I'd never known I had. His body slammed against the brick surface, stunned at the sudden change of plans.

"You can't just lead me on and leave me hanging." Malik grabbed the back of my sweater before I could run. A rough jerk spun me around as his hand latched on to my face. Long, callused fingers dug into my cheeks, making my eyes water. Though I'd watched a basketball shrink to the size of a grapefruit in his grasp, I'd never realized how big Malik's hands were until now. All that strength gathered in one hand, and something as delicate as bone could easily break under its power.

"You gonna play nice, and no one has to get hurt." Seeing me nod, he backed me against the wall again. "Good girl."

After licking his lips, his head leaned in for another kiss, but this time I didn't fight him. His dark eyes, runny and crazed, made it clear that no one was leaving until he got what he wanted.

There was only so much one could take before the barricade broke. The floodgates of rage burst free as I opened my mouth wide and unhooked my roommate's collar. I wished I could feel bad about what was about to happen, but human rules and sensibility no longer applied.

And the timing couldn't have been any better. Lilith was hungry.

10

Mom flung open the door before I could slip in my key. Her fingers curled into the wood, ready to rip the door off its hinges. Her chest heaved and swelled under a red silk shirt. "Where in the world have you been? You should've been back hours ago!"

My eyes lowered to the floor. "I figured you'd check my status from my bracelet."

"Answer the question," she demanded. "What happened to you? How did you get that cut on your lip?"

"Shaving," I grumbled.

Blue pools of fury told me that she wasn't in a mood for jokes, nor was she about to let me cross the threshold without an explanation.

"I got into a fight," I said in resignation.

"I figured that much. The principal called my office saying you had an incident in the bathroom. What I don't know is why."

"Girls at school think I'm stealing their men-folk."

After several blinks, her heated gaze cooled to a low

simmer. "They have no right to lay a hand on you. I should press charges."

"Mom, I'm fine." I pushed my way inside. "The girls got suspended and that's that. Don't want any more drama than necessary."

Mom followed me to the dining room. "You should have called me."

"It wasn't an emergency. I had a really rough day, all right? I don't need you hounding me." I moved to the kitchen, but Mom foiled my escape.

"Too damn bad. How long has this been going on? If someone's harassing you at school, you need to tell me."

"What good would that do? I'm a freak, Mom. Every-one in school knows it. I have a succubus in my body. Girls are naturally hostile to me; nothing's gonna change that. It will continue well after school, and bugging out over every little scrape is pointless. I'm gonna go to bed. I'm tired." I raced to my bedroom, then locked the door before she could catch me.

The shadow of her feet paced in front of the door. "Samara, talk to me, please? Something happened, and you're scared. Come out and talk."

The worry in her voice tightened my gut. Instinct begged me to open the door, grief ordered me to wrap myself around her and cry, but fear kept me stationary. "Mom, please, I just wanna be alone right now. I'll talk to you later. Please, just let me sleep it off."

After several long minutes, the shadow disappeared as she left me to my angst.

I changed into an oversized T-shirt, then fell on the bed and buried my head in a pillow. I knew Mom meant well, but her pep talk would just go to waste. My methods were cruel, but she couldn't know the real reason I was upset. I couldn't understand it myself, and I'd never been so scared and thoroughly freaked out in all my seventeen years. Death had a way of doing that to a person.

Tears didn't come, but a lump emerged and clogged my windpipe. Eventually, sleep took over, surrounding me in darkness, pulling me back to the events of the afternoon as if I needed a reminder. . . .

I leaned over Malik's body, lapping the traces of life from his lips. The thin string of energy, translucent and delicate as smoke, danced around my tongue and filled my inner being to capacity. Not just a taste, but a feast of life, a five-course meal generating power to my spirit.

I sat back on my haunches and lifted my head to the ceiling, withstanding the euphoric seizure of the intake. I now understood why so many people got drunk. The eye viewed the world through a soft focus lens, and every crisis lessened in gravity. However, my sense of direction shattered to pieces.

And then I saw him, a limp, waxy mannequin stretched across the filthy gymnasium floor, his limbs akimbo. Unblinking eyes stared skyward, engaged in a wordless discussion with Heaven. His mouth gaped open, as if shocked at the reply. His pulse didn't exist, which shriveled my buzz to dust.

I backed away slowly, but returned to the body and wiped his mouth. I checked for stray hairs and other evidence that could lead to me. Though the police would attribute his death to a heart attack, I'd watched enough forensic shows not to leave anything to chance.

Slow, elementary facts drilled in my head, as if rephrasing would somehow soften the blow or facilitate knowledge. A boy was dead. He was no more, no longer among the living. But, no matter the wording, no matter how I sliced it, I was still the one holding the knife.

"Hey, Malik, hurry up, man! The coach is coming!" The voice of one of his teammates echoed against the gym walls.

I didn't know what to think at the moment, but I knew getting the hell out of there was a good start. I stood up and straightened my clothes, trying my best not to look at Malik's body. I stumbled through the labyrinth of support beams and metal framework under the bleachers. Coach Reynolds corralled the basketball team through the side door of the locker room.

I had to stay cool, keep it together, and by no means let them wander behind the bleachers. I inched toward the door, staying close to the walls, hoping to sneak out before anyone saw me. The screech of a whistle ruined that plan.

"What are you doing here, young lady?" With a clipboard in one hand and his eighty-proof energy drink in the other, Coach Reynolds stood in a reprimanding stance. Though he wore a maroon track suit that had probably fit twenty years ago, this ex-Marine was not one to tangle with, unless you wanted to risk triggering his famous war flashbacks. His disapproval was palpable as he zeroed in on my location.

Fellow teammates leered at me in humor. The ones who had left me with Malik offered knowing smirks and shared private comments. If they'd known what had happened to their boy, they wouldn't look so smug.

"I asked you a question. What are you doing here? This is a closed practice," the coach demanded.

Giving my best impersonation of a deer in headlights, I said, "I-I-I was looking for Malik. I wanted to give him something."

"I'm sure you did." A tall kid with cornrows snickered. Others joined in with laughter and high-fives.

"Quiet down!" Reynolds barked before darting his

beady eyes at me. "You socialize on your own time. Now see yourself out." He nudged his head to the exit.

He didn't have to tell me twice. I nearly tripped over my feet crossing the gym, when the coach asked, "Where is Davis anyway?"

Murmurs spilled from the group. "I dunno."

"Haven't seen him," another said.

"Oh, for crying out loud!" Reynolds threw his head back and groaned. "Somebody had to have seen him. He was here ten minutes ago."

I kept moving, not waiting for the fallout, the screams of horror, and the impending police visit to my house. Those boys would know I had been the last one to see Malik alive. Of course they would point me out in a lineup. How was I going to explain this to my mom? I'd cross that bridge when I got there. All I knew was I had to get home.

I pushed the handle of the double doors when the last voice I ever expected to hear called out.

"I'm right here, Coach!"

Slowly, I turned and saw an image that shouldn't have been there, a knowledge I wasn't equipped to comprehend. I blinked several times, but the vision remained, gaining focus with each step.

"Davis! Front and center! Now!" Reynolds yelled with the conviction of a drill sergeant.

Malik emerged from behind the bleachers and trotted toward his teammates. Reaching the group, he said, "Sorry I'm late. Something came up."

"I'll bet." Coach Reynolds grunted, eyeing Malik's wrinkled shirt and shorts. "Twenty laps around the gym. Now. The rest of you, pair up and grab a ball." The quick chirp of the whistle shot everyone into action, including me.

Malik jogged the outer perimeter of the gym, his long,

toned body working in a uniform pace, lithe and very agile for a person who had no business being alive.

Glancing in my direction, a slow smile crept to the corner of his mouth as he flashed me a wink.

What had happened behind the bleachers had been real. Malik was dead, an ex-person who ceased to be. I hadn't been seeing things, but the dozen witnesses littering the gym could attest to the contrary. I felt Malik's energy inside me. His life and all it entailed churned and digested within, and Lilith practically belched after her devoured meal.

Given the situation, I should consider myself lucky. If there was no body, there was no crime. I was off the hook. My newfound freedom died quickly as a question crept to the surface.

If I hadn't taken Malik's life, then what the hell did I just eat?

I sprung upright, the dream dissolving into mist, bringing the murky design of my room into focus. My skin itched from where the bedsheets stuck to my sweaty back even through my T-shirt. I rocked on the bed, my pulse racing to keep in time with my rapid thoughts. It was just a dream, but not really; more of a recap of the day's weirdness, the brain counting its earnings once business hours were over.

The thing I really hated about nightmares was waking up alone. No one hid under the bed or lurked in the closet, but the imagination ran wild and every shadow posed a threat. Everything was still, quiet, and set to rest but me.

Needing a drink, I tiptoed downstairs to the kitchen, successfully avoiding a glimpse into the living room. But turmoil persisted, oozing through the woodwork and cracking static in the air.

After clicking on the kitchen light, I headed to the fridge to down the half gallon of orange juice straight from the carton. I thought of Mom's olive oil and the questions it provoked. It piqued my curiosity several times before, but now that interest leaned more toward scientific research. Units of measure, quality, quantity, and religious dogma swirled around my head, thick and greasy as the oil itself.

I checked the top and bottom cabinets, even the pantry off the side of the kitchen, and found no oil. Opening the fridge again, I noticed that the jar of green olives Mom liked was missing from the shelf on the door. She'd probably thrown it away and likely child-proofed the house. She'd even cleaned out my purse while I was in the hospital, which explained how the old dried-up bottle of anointing oil mysteriously disappeared. Tossing the empty O.J. carton in the trash, I made a mental note to hit the grocery store tomorrow.

No sooner did I come to that decision than an eerie vibe locked me in place, a brush of a presence in close range. Something alive and moving occupied the first floor; its energy fluttered around my skin, creating goose bumps. That familiar signal always alerted me of Caleb's nearness, and I reveled at the welcome vibration. I starved for my Cake Boy, and I quietly begged for him to end my famine, to hold me again. I could almost feel his breath on my skin, that warm kiss on the back of the neck.

Lost in emotion, I didn't bother with the plot holes of the scenario, like the impossibility of someone entering my house without tripping the security system or Mom's keen sense of hearing even in deep sleep, or that Caleb, by all logical extremes, should still be hospitalized.

Eventually, reality set in once a whining noise poured from the living room, a low, raspy yelp of an injured animal, or a crying dog. Mom's allergies prevented me from having a pet, yet that failed to explain how a dog had wandered into my house.

I spied the security box by the door, noting the flashing green light indicating its activation. Slowly, I turned to the living room and almost screamed at the tall figure standing by the couch. His back faced me; the light from the window outlined his form, but gave no real detail to identify. What I knew was a man stood still with hands in his pockets and his head low.

Memories of the last home invader had me paralyzed in terror. My heart pounded in my chest and I fought to keep everything in my body in working order. I was going to need all my faculties to go into battle mode, and it would be a fight to the death before another man tried to hurt me. He stood a good foot taller than me, so I had to find a weapon.

I backpedaled into the kitchen, pulled a knife from the rack on the counter, and crept back to the living room entry, all achieved with the deadly silence of an assassin.

My bare feet crossed the threshold, that distinct line where hardwood floor met soft carpet. I lifted the knife in the air when his head turned toward the window, casting his profile in gentle moonlight.

"Lilith, be still." Though barely a whisper, his voice ricocheted against the walls, summoning unseen forces to his bidding.

Those three words sobered me up quickly, bringing disturbing facts into play. This man standing in front of me operated on a first-name basis with Lilith. What's more, Lilith jittered down my vertebrae at the acknowledgment. If she'd had a tail, it would've been wagging.

The knife wobbled in my hand. "What did you say?"

Instead of a response, he returned his focus to the floor, concentrating on a singular spot near the couch. As a cop would a crime scene, he circled the area. A shadowy hand traced the outline of a shape that only he could see. His whole body engaged in this exploration, crouching lower as he studied what lay there, or rather what once laid there.

"This was where it happened?" he asked with his back still facing me. "This was where she died?"

I didn't try to deny it or pretend not to know what he was talking about. "Yes. She broke her neck, and stopped breathing soon after. I tried to revive her, but it was too late."

"You were with her?" He sounded surprised but then sniggered at some private joke. "Of course you were."

"I didn't want to leave her alone. She was very close to me, a good friend," I rambled on while I inched toward the stairs.

I'd barely made it two paces when he said, "Don't bother. She won't hear you."

Not taking his word for it, I dashed up the staircase, my screams going unheard by my mother. Was she hurt? Had he gone after her first? A vision of Nadine flashed before my eyes, her broken body discarded without a second thought, an obstacle that had to be eliminated. The risk of Mom sharing a similar fate fueled me with rage.

I opened the bedroom door and found Mom stretched across the bed in a graceless sprawl. Her night mask covered her eyes at a slant. Tangled within the covers, she rolled onto her side and rooted into a deep sleep that had eluded her for too long.

Her peaceful state left no doubt that some mad paranormal activity was taking place. If the intruder could enter the house undetected, he could leave just as easily, making a quick call to the police a moot point. I quietly closed the door and trotted back downstairs to find the stranger standing where I left him.

"What did you do to my mom?" I demanded, pointing the kitchen knife at his back.

"Nothing. She's only asleep. She won't hear us unless I let her."

I couldn't have been any more spooked out if I'd tried, and I really did try. Gathering all my courage, I bit the bullet and asked the question of the hour. "Who the hell are you?"

"Whoever you want me to be."

"Can you be more specific?"

In response, he turned around. The glow from the window trapped his body. A light ripple rolled from his torso to the roots of his hair, darkening his skin, and distorting his features to a different shape altogether. In seconds, Malik Davis stood before me with hands on his hips, looking pleased with my astonishment. He hiked his chin in greeting. "What's up, Shorty?"

"Malik!" I leapt back and whacked my head against the wall.

"No. Malik is dead. He's been that way for several weeks now."

I was going for the gold for the number of freaky events that can occur in one day. "Malik isn't dead. I saw him a few hours ago at practice."

"No. You, the coach, and his teammates saw *me* walk from under the bleachers. If anyone cared to look, they would find Malik at the bottom of the James River . . . where I left him." He bit out the last part. The energy you took today was mine, and with it, some of the memories I'd taken from him."

"Wait. Malik was already dead? But how?"

"Friends don't let friends drive drunk," he intoned.

A cold streak followed that answer and it froze the blood in my veins. "He had a car accident last month. He didn't survive, did he?"

"No."

I glared up at him. "Was there really an accident?"

"Yes. He was dying when I found him. I took the pain away, and while doing so, I saw a few memories of you at school, and I jumped at the opportunity. What better way to get closer to you, much easier than hovering in shadows."

"And you've been walking around looking like him all this time?"

"Not the whole time, but a while. I've been waiting for a time where I could get you alone, a chance to reveal myself without frightening you."

"Right, because showing up in my house unannounced isn't frightening at all."

"Are you frightened right now?"

I opened my mouth to respond, but shut it again. I was a lot of things: surprised, angry, annoyed, confused, but fear didn't factor into it at all. A false sense of security seemed to trap my body in a warm, protective coating. I would have been stupid to trust that feeling for a second, but it was there.

"You're a cold, slippery one, Miss Marshall." He stepped closer, his eyes hooded in recollection. "I saw you on Halloween. I thought I would have my chance then."

"Hold up, so you were the man in the mask?" His affirmative recharged my anger. "Why are you following me? If you wanted to talk to me, then why not just come up to me and say hi?"

"I tried that, and as I said, you're a cold, slippery one—emphasis on 'cold.' You really don't like this Malik fellow, do you?"

"Not really. He was always mean to me, but that's not the point," I dismissed irritably. "So, that epic death scene behind the bleachers, it was all fake?"

"One of my best performances. Lilith left me winded, but as you realize, the spirit won't truly harm what it knows, and she knows me quite well." He smiled. "But I wanted to see what you would do, how far you would go should a real danger cross your path. I must say, I'm quite proud of you. A true killer instinct."

His words made me shiver. "You tried to take advantage of me, you crazy rapist!"

He moved closer, not in the least bit threatened by the knife aimed at his chest. "Sweetheart, I don't have to rape any woman. I am every woman's fantasy. They come to me without a fight. Well, except you, of course."

I took a minute to ponder his reply. That was something a Cambion would say. Cambions inspired lust and for that reason, were usually victims, not aggressors. Then I remembered what Mom told me about demons and how they could appear as any person they chose. Oh yeah, I knew these glamour tricks well, but something wasn't right.

"What kind of Cambion are you?" I asked.

He looked at me like I'd insulted his mother. "Cambion? I'm not some demon mutt, Samara, and you wound me deeply for even insinuating it."

"Well, this *demon mutt* is offended by you busting in her house and trying to . . . whatever you were trying to do." I fell back against the wall, resigning to the absurdity of the argument. Taking a deep breath, I added, "Just answer three questions for me: Who are you, what do you want, and what did you plan to do with Malik's body?"

"You have nothing to worry about. As far as anyone knows, Malik went home after practice like he does every night. I made sure plenty of people saw me as him, including his mother. Business as usual."

"Ohmigod!" I had completely forgotten about his family. Before I could regard it any further, he continued.

"As for your second question, I'm here because I've come to claim what is rightfully mine. But I can't take it by force, nor should I have to. It already belongs to me. But there are some people who are trying to trespass on my territory, and I can't have that." To show an example of said trespassers, the ripples returned. His skin lightened, his hair grew, resembling an image that drained the fight from my body. The knife slipped from my hands and hit the carpet with a dull thud.

To the smile, to his height, to the way his hair fell around his face, the man in front of me was Caleb's carbon copy. Déjà vu hit me with such strength it made me dizzy and I lost my balance. Once again, I stood before a predator that used my one weakness as camouflage. Was this some sadistic wheel that kept reverting back to this same moment in time, history repeating until I learned from it? Or maybe Mom was right: I needed professional help.

A pair of arms caught me before I hit the floor. Through barely parted lids, I stared up at the man, frozen beyond any normal range of shock.

I knew he wasn't Caleb, and the inner connection hadn't come from Capone. Lilith agreed, but no complaint came from her end. She flipped and yipped with excitement, the only one amused by this new circumstance. She didn't fight back, but beckoned him into her inner sanctum as one would an old friend. Or something else. Then I saw it, the secret that I could never uncover, the puzzle that had gone unsolved until now.

"You have an interesting taste in books, Samara," he said in Caleb's voice. Then he placed a finger to his lips. "Shh."

The gesture brought a distinct memory and a new series of righteous anger. "You're the one who broke Caleb's windows!" I shoved his chest, which only pushed me back toward the wall. "Did you put olive oil in my drink? You could have killed him and me!"

"I may or may not have taken my anger out on his car, but you were never at risk. You're no good to me dead. Him on the other hand—most beneficial."

His admission made me sick to my stomach. Anger tainted my system to the point where I couldn't move. "Why are you after me? What did I do to you?"

"What makes you think it was something you did? And that's not one of the questions." He turned his back to me and faced the window. "As for who I am, I'm pretty sure you figured it out by now."

He was right. We stood in silence as if some solution would appear without our input. I remained motionless for several minutes until the stall tactic grew tiresome, even for my own reasoning.

"You're a . . ." I strained to get out the word. "You're an incubus. A full-blown incubus."

He turned and held me with a look just shy of antagonism. "That takes care of *what* I am. The question is *who* am I?"

That answer was more terrifying than the first. It was a truth that had haunted me since I'd entered the room, but it couldn't be denied. I fingered the bracelet on my wrist, thinking of Nadine, and understanding her reason for keeping this secret locked away. Memories within her hidden archives now made themselves available for my private viewing. Past and present mingled in a swirl of gibberish within the posterior lobe. Errors of another life, the regret of others weighed down my heart with unwarranted guilt.

If I was honest with myself, it was the real reason I couldn't seal the bond with Caleb and why I could not in good conscience ask this guy to leave.

"You didn't have a name, but Nadine called you Tobias," I said with a crippling sense of defeat. "She gave you that name the night you gave Lilith hers. The same night she became your mate."

11

This latest development was still too fresh to analyze, so I pushed my nervous breakdown to a later time slot.

Suffering a numb, almost out-of-body detachment, I watched Caleb's imposter wear down the carpet with aimless pacing. I quickly grew distracted by that noise grating my ears, that odd shrill of some tortured thing in need of a mercy kill. It then dawned on me that those whimpers came from my uninvited guest. His chest rose and fell in rapid speed with every shallow breath.

"Why are you panting like that?" I asked finally.

His body stilled. "This is how we cry, Samara."

"Like an injured dog?" I joked, but I was the only one amused. "Do you shed tears?"

"Rarely. We grieve differently from humans. I don't expect you to understand."

"I think I understand, despite everything else I don't know. I've noticed Lilith has animal-like characteristics, the way she communicates with me."

"That barely scratches the surface. We're primal creatures. We rely solely on instinct. Our senses are heightened beyond what any human mind could grasp, and we feel *everything*." His voice broke. His entire body tightened on the brink of combustion. "Was he here, that demon mutt that killed her, the one who broke her and threw her away like trash?"

Again, I didn't need to ask who he was referring to, but his body language told me to tread lightly. "Tobias . . ."

"Was he?" he bellowed.

"Yes. He killed her to get to me and my mother."

"Two offenses on his head." His eyes rolled in my direction, heated with accusation and disgust. "And you let his spawn touch you after that, kiss you? How can you even look at him after what his father has done?"

"It's more the other way around. I killed Caleb's father that night. How do you think he feels?" I had never confessed this aloud and the words sounded alien to me, almost vulgar. I had killed Caleb's father, the first life I'd ever taken and consumed in its entirety. Caleb had forgiven me, understood that it had to be done, but it wasn't his forgiveness I needed.

Tobias scoffed, unimpressed. "They know the rules. They know to never kill a Cambion, and a mated one at that. This is punishable by death among your kind."

"On what grounds?" I argued. "Nathan Ross was insane, taken over by grief. You of all people should know what it's like to lose someone you love, someone connected to you."

"I'm only aware of that feeling *now*, thanks to him." He proceeded pacing, more agitated than before.

I sympathized with his anger, really, but he didn't know the whole story. It wasn't black and white—a villain preying on helpless damsels, kicking puppies, and pushing old people down stairwells. The evil in Mr. Ross came from a good seed planted in tainted soil, the same earth used to bury his wife. Tobias didn't know the private moments that man had shared with the woman he loved, the hours he'd cried and prayed when the doctors had diagnosed her with cancer, the deterioration of her health and his sanity. I would never excuse his actions, but I understood more than anyone else. After all, once seen, it can't be unseen.

"What about the other women he murdered, huh?" I asked. "You gonna shed a tear, or whimper for them?"

He stopped midstride to look at me.

"Yeah, I thought so. It's one thing when it's humans, but killing one of your own is another story, isn't it? It's all wrong, no matter who it is or why. Everyone is at fault. So if you're gonna convict someone, convict me too." When he didn't reply, I continued, "Nadine died months ago and you're just now showing up to pay your respects?"

"You think this is my first visit here? I come here and watch the house every night. It's a comfort to know you're just feet away, so close and yet so far." He saw me freeze up, then said, "I told you, I can't force you. Lilith will protect her host no matter what, so I need your consent. Won't be too long though. I sense her stirring in you, getting used to me, demanding her mate—"

"See, I have to cut you off right there. I'm not your mate. In fact, I'm no one's mate."

"Yet. But I plan to fix that," he assured with unwavering confidence.

"So do I—just as soon as Caleb wakes up."

His hard stare glued me to the spot. "It won't do any good. In the end, he and his brothers will die. You buy them valuable time by keeping away."

I pushed off the wall and closed the distance between us, unconcerned by my state of dress. "You can't do this! They didn't do anything wrong!"

"They knew what their father was capable of. They knew the insanity a broken link could cause. As far as I'm concerned, they had a hand in Nadine's murder."

"They couldn't do it. They couldn't harm their father and their spirits' source."

"You defend them, yet claim to care for Nadine. Why?" Hurt and betrayal flashed in his eyes before he concealed his emotions. "I have unfinished business, Samara. I strongly suggest that you don't interfere and accept the inevitable."

I knew a threat when I heard one. My finger jabbed into his chest and rebounded against the solid surface. Using both hands, I tried to push him, but he didn't move an inch. That didn't stop me from getting my point across. "You lay one hand on Caleb, and I'll kill you."

He smiled as one would at an adorable child. "Caleb's already dead. You just need to let go."

It took me a minute to regroup after that acidic reply. It didn't help that Tobias still held Caleb's likeness, the same man he marked for death. I called on the four corners of my resolve and fought the tremor grating my voice. "He wouldn't still be a threat to you if he were really dead, nor would I be standing here. You're lying."

His eyebrows rose in a gesture of defiance. "Am I?"

"That's what you do. You manipulate everything around you to get what you want." I swept a glance over his appearance. "Look at you. You can't even get a woman on your own. You have to pretend to be someone else."

His lips curled as hooded eyes ran up and down my body. "I don't need silly parlor tricks to get what I want."

He could have fooled me. I took a few steps back. "Then show yourself. Come as your true form. No disguises."

He flinched for a split second, then quickly recovered. "And you call me manipulative."

He closed his eyes and inhaled deeply. The surface of his skin began to swell and ripple until the image of Caleb dissolved and a new form appeared. His deep tan reinforced a distinct Mediterranean ancestry, with high cheekbones and sleek black hair tied in a ponytail. Thick muscles and a whole lot of "hot damn" tucked underneath a black shirt and slacks. The more I stared, the more difficult it was to stay on topic. I was mesmerized by his face, yet totally aware that I stood in the presence of something unearthly.

Amused by my ogling, he said, "I told you, I don't need to trick a woman into wanting me. They just do."

I ignored his unbuttoned shirt and the muscles peeking underneath, I really did. "Look, I don't care what kind of heated affair you had with Nadine, but it's over. Please leave me out of it. You have to let this go."

Tobias crossed his arms and shook his head. "I disagree, but that is beside the point. I'm connected to Lilith, and there's no getting around that. The only thing that's standing in my way is you." He stepped closer, controlled and soundless across the carpet.

His slow advance made me painfully aware of his six and a half feet and the powerful body that could throw me across the room, or worse should the feeling move him. That knowledge forced me to retreat to the safety of the loveseat.

He stopped in front of me, so close his legs brushed against mine. The heat of his skin filtered through his slacks to warm where our bodies touched. He lurched forward, invading my breathing room, and I offered not one token of protest.

Glowing amber eyes held me captive when he said, "You were not part of the deal. When Nadine died, I was supposed to ascend with Lilith. So, imagine my surprise when I discovered that not only was I still alive, but that my mate was hiding in someone else's body."

"And this is my fault because . . ." I guided.

"It's no one's fault but Nadine's." The hand on my knee almost scorched my flesh, and I pushed it away before it traveled any higher.

"I'm sure this is a lot to take in, but after what happened today, I had to see you, to let you know who I was. Next time, we'll have a chance to talk and answer your questions."

I leaned back and sized him up. "Next time?"

Humor touched his eyes, which shimmered like polished brass. "You thought that I would give up that easily? Lilith and I may not be bonded anymore, but we're still linked. I've come to get my mate back, and I finish what I start."

"But you're a free agent now. You don't have to be tied down by one person."

"Who said anything about being free? I'm more obligated now than I ever was while bonded with Nadine. I sacrificed a lot to be with her, and I intend to get back what I lost. In order to do that, I need a mate, *my* mate. I'm sorry, Flower, but it looks like you're it." He stood up to move to the window again with a balled-up piece of cloth trapped in his fist.

Shaking the fog from my brain, I called after him. "Where are you going?"

With his back facing me, he shoved the fabric in his pocket. "I'm hungry. I'm going to feed and probably get laid." He paused and looked at me over his shoulder. "Why? Do you care to join me?"

"Uh, n-no," I stammered. "If you wanted me so bad, then why are you so quick to sleep with someone else?"

"Are you judging me now? I'm an incubus, or did you

miss that part? Sex is not a primary source of energy for you Cambions, but we heathens need it to survive. You're linked to more than one male, yet I'm not condemning you," he replied in a tone dripping with disdain. "I'm not going to force your hand. I'm not a monster."

"And you seemed like such a nice guy," I returned with a snarl.

"As far as my kind goes, I am a very nice guy. But I'm selfish, and according to you, manipulative. Don't mistake patience for concession. In the end, I always get what I want, damn the consequences." And with that, he disappeared from sight in a plume of vapor, leaving no trace of his presence.

When he left, everything went with him: the air, the warmth, and my last thread of reason. A chill swept up my leg, causing a peculiar draft under my T-shirt. Lifting the hem, I learned never to underestimate his power. If Tobias managed to steal underwear off a girl without her knowing, what else could he do right under her nose?

Then, and only then, did the panic attack take effect, bringing everything to a head with astronomical force. The long-awaited meltdown began at its newly scheduled time, without further interruptions, even as my scream echoed the walls of the house.

12

"Angie, I need to talk to you. Please call me as soon as you get this—no matter the time. It's an emergency."

I ended the call, climbed out of my car, and steered through the student parking lot.

For some reason, Angie had gone AWOL and I was beginning to worry, especially with everything going on. She needed to know what was happening and maybe shed some insight about Tobias.

His little visit last night wrecked my world up, making sleep a comedic impossibility. After crying, screaming, pacing the floor, and slipping a sleep aid in a mug of warm milk, I caught three hours of rest before school.

I dragged my feet to class, dreading first period. Malik, Tobias, or whatever he was calling himself today, would be there, and I had half the mind to ditch. How was I expected to carry on with life knowing what I knew? How long did he plan to walk around impersonating a dead guy? Someone was bound to suspect.

Shouldering through the crowded hall, I did a quick

recap of the past month, listing all my encounters with Malik, his sudden interest in me, and the female hostility that had followed. The obsessive vibe made perfect sense now, and yet, it confused me even more.

Of all the people in the world, why did I get stuck with an incubus, a demon intent on making me his boo? How was I going to explain this to Caleb? What would his brothers think? And I wasn't going to whisper a word of this to my mother, not until I'd collected all the facts.

I entered my government class barely a second before the bell. Keeping my head down, I scurried to my desk, not sparing a glance to anyone, including Mia sitting in the row ahead of me. Not one to be ignored, she threw a ball of paper at me and mouthed the words, "You okay?"

Nodding, I dove into my backpack and pulled out my binder. Halfway through class, I worked up the courage to lift my head and look around.

No sign of Malik.

I couldn't believe my luck. I'd been spared forty minutes of tension and sideways glances. I sat back in my chair and eased into the lesson, which was marginally interesting. Anything was better than my own problems right now, even the untold corruption within the legislative branch.

I made it all the way through fourth period without incident, and saw no sign of Tobias or his alias. Maybe he'd decided to end the charade? Maybe he wanted to give me space? No. It wouldn't be that simple. Though out of sight, he remained a clear and ever-present danger, his aura weighing down my back worse than my book bag. I could feel his hot breath graze my neck as suggestive phrases infected my ears.

When I didn't see him at lunch, I enjoyed the peace among my table of outcasts. I'd barely taken a bite of my ham sandwich when I felt it, that telltale humming vibration. That zip across my spine quickly turned ominous, and I waited for the evil theme music to kick in. Not even a moment later, the vampire kid sitting across from me was shoved aside and Malik sat in his place. Spitting a catlike hiss, the boy scooted to the far end of the table.

I gawked at the scene with my mouth open, the sandwich slipping from my hand. My mind stalled for a moment, then sputtered as the image before me stared me down. He didn't carry a tray or a bagged lunch, just two hundred pounds of muscle and evident frustration.

"Thought it would be that easy, huh?" A cocky grin tugged at his lips.

"No. I know better than that." I dropped my sandwich on my tray. "I take it your evening went well, Tobias."

If there was any doubt of the live-action Malik costume, the quick flash of gold in his eyes removed all suspicion.

"Not as well as I hoped, but it was a decent substitute. Want to hear the details?"

"Not really. How long have you been following me?"

"Since you left your house this morning. I got bored and wanted to talk to you."

"You know that's called stalking, which is illegal in all fifty states and all U.S. territories, right?"

Grinning, he asked, "I'm aware, but who would convict me?"

"Me and my mom's loaded Beretta," I replied. "So could you please leave me alone, and could you give me back my underwear?" I whispered the last part, wary of the ears around us.

"Oh no. I have them framed and mounted on my wall. A motivational tool, if you will."

"You're disgusting." I slid my tray away, my appetite gone with the wind. "And you need to apologize to Midnight."

"Who's Midnight?"

I nudged my head toward my disgruntled lunchmate. "The guy whose seat you took. That was rude and I don't appreciate it and neither does he. Apologize."

Tobias looked over to the pale kid in all black who glared behind his raised collar. "Sorry, man."

Displaying a row of prosthetic fangs, Midnight hissed again, then continued his meal.

Tobias cringed away from him and returned his attention to me. "Nice circle of friends you got here."

"They're good people. If you don't like it, you can take your sorry butt back over to your end of the cafeteria," I replied, doing everything to avoid making eye contact. His power source lay there, and I needed to keep my sanity. The large, dark hand that slid over mine shot that plan to hell.

His gaze met mine with a blend of remorse and longing. "I'm sorry. I promise to behave myself."

"Too late." Snatching my hand away, I peered around the cafeteria, noting over fifty pairs of eyes trying not to look our way. "You're causing a scene, and you coming over here is making your stock plummet."

"Do you really think I care what any of these kids think about me? The only reason I'm in this school, this town, this hemisphere is because of you."

"Waste of time," I sang.

"Correction, it was a waste of time, but not anymore. I've hesitated for too long and now I'm taking the initiative. I need you, and if that means I have to walk around like this to achieve that, so be it."

I took a moment to observe his appearance, the even brown complexion, the thin layer of waves on top of his head, the broad, slightly flat nose, and the full, sculpted lips. The resemblance was uncanny, and no one could tell the difference. But I knew, and I silently grieved for such wasted beauty and unmet potential.

"Cambions have a way to trick a person's mind into seeing what they desire most. But you *physically* transform your body." I shook my head in awe. "So, you can turn into any person?"

He bowed his head. "I can be *any* human I see, whether in person, or in photographs."

"Why bother? Can't stand the sight of yourself?"

His smile widened. "On the contrary. It's just easier to cater to a woman's specific desire, like my companion last night. She was a widow, and I appeared to her as her late husband. She thought she was dreaming, and who was I to deny her one last chance at happiness?"

"That's just it," I whispered. "It wasn't her husband. You're playing with people's heads."

Looking offended, he placed a hand on his chest. "I'm providing a service to lonely women, and I even let them live. What more can you ask for?"

I dragged a hand over my face and rubbed my temple. Fighting to keep my voice and temper low, I said, "Answer me this: How long do you plan to walk around like a seventeen-year-old kid? His family is going to notice something is off."

"Surely you know how consumption works. I acquired memories that came with Malik's life energy. I can revert to those to fill in the blanks, the way he talks, his gestures, his attitude, and his family life. It isn't that difficult to play the part. After all, it fooled you."

Not sure if I heard him right, I leaned over the table. "Wait, you're living with his family, under their roof?"

"They have a nice house and his mom's a great cook— best apple pie I ever tasted."

There was gumption, there was audacity, and there

was Tobias's complete lack of shame. How could he just prance around posing as someone else and not feel a hint of guilt? True, I hadn't liked Malik, and that dislike was a two-way street, but he and his family didn't deserve this disrespect. Lowering my voice, I muttered, "Her son is dead, Tobias."

He hovered closer, his face mere inches from mine. "I'm aware of that, Flower. As strange as it sounds, I don't have the heart to let her find out. She's a really sweet woman, and that kid was her pride and joy. Could be why I haven't approached you sooner."

The distant look in his eyes stopped my snappy comeback. He seemed sincere, but that could mean anything. At the end of the day, he was still a demon, and a crafty one at that. Demons didn't feel anything, didn't have compassion. Or did they?

"How old are you anyway?" I asked.

He blinked away his little daydream to join the conversation. "Age is not really a factor for me. You could pretty much say I'm timeless." He pressed the skin around his cheekbones and eyes. "Must be this new night cream I'm using."

I glared at him, ready to give him a piece of my mind when a voice asked, "What language is that?"

I looked to the girl next to me. Melissa Graham's one gray eye watched me behind her face mask of curly brown hair. She was painfully shy and what little she did say seemed to come at the cost of physical comfort.

"Is that Russian?" she asked in a soft, broken voice.

I paused, confused by what she meant, but Tobias was quick on the draw and said, "Polish."

"Oh. Cool," she said, then buried her face in her book.

Stunned beyond words, I whipped my head in Tobias's direction. He could speak Polish? Had we been speaking in Polish the whole time? And why hadn't I noticed? For an answer, Tobias pointed a finger gun at me and winked. At least I didn't have to worry about anyone eavesdropping.

"So yeah, I was thinking, is there any chance of you moving somewhere that's like, *else*," I said.

He examined his nails in boredom. "Nope. You intrigue me and I wanna get to know you." He lifted his eyes to my hair. "I've been dying to ask, why do you have that red and white streak—"

"None of your business," I interrupted. "Why waste time pursuing someone who's already spoken for? You may have known Nadine, may have even loved her, but you don't know me. What if we did bond and you find out you can't stand me? You'll be stuck for life."

"What's not to like about you? You're smart, witty, and cute as a button."

His answer stopped me mid-outburst. "You think I'm cute?"

"Not in the conventional way, but yeah. Every time I see you, I have this unyielding urge to just squeeze you to death. You're so . . ." He searched the ceiling for the right word. "Delectable."

I stood up and collected my tray. "I'm going to class."

He caught up with me in three long strides. "I didn't mean to insult you."

"Your very presence is an insult." I dumped my food and added my empty tray to the growing stack on top of the trash bin. When I turned to pass through the double doors, I almost ran into his chest. I scowled at his grinning face. "Why are you so bent on getting in my pants? I'm sure there's plenty of girls who are far more experienced in that department."

"You're right, but this isn't a discussion to have here. Have dinner with me tonight."

"No." I kept walking.

"No?"

"Not just no, but *hell no*. I know better than to go anywhere with a demonic sociopath. What I do know about you, I don't like, and the things I don't know are probably a whole lot worse. So I'll pass."

"Ah, come on—"

"Dude!" I snapped before lowering my voice. "I don't know how many ways I can tell you to leave me alone. You've succeeded in creeping me out, and this is only our second conversation. During which, you've confessed to committing the following offenses." Going into lawyer mode, I counted the charges against him on my fingers.

"Breaking and entering, personal theft, attempted murder, destruction of property, sexual assault, stalking, improper disposal of a dead body, identity fraud, and working my last good nerve. This suave routine may work on other girls, but as I said before, You. Don't. Know. Me. Have fun with those underwear, 'cause that's as close as you're ever gonna get to me." I strolled to my English class, leaving my new shadow to his day.

Considering the kind of mischief he could cause, I knew it was a bad idea for him to be running around unattended. I just couldn't bring myself to care. Honestly, if he'd been roaming the halls incognito for this long, what was another day, or week? It's not like anyone had died since he got here.

Well, no one except Malik, of course.

13

Visiting hours at Williamsburg Community Hospital ran between the hours of 4 and 8 PM, a schedule I knew now by heart, and seriously wished I didn't.

The facility could probably treat over two thousand people if necessary, a bit presumptuous, not to mention gaudy, for the snooze-worthy tourist trap known as Williamsburg. Illness and death came the natural way around here, but the definition of "natural" seemed to stretch these days.

Wringing my hands in aggravation, I fought the sudden impulse to run laps through the parking lot before going inside. I had a body full of life force, delicious nourishment that fueled the capricious spring in my step. It made me giggle, sigh, touch everything, and note my reaction to each new texture. I'd never felt this peppy before, a power surge that topped caffeinated energy drinks and would take a good week to burn off. My skin glowed with a healthy sheen of gold, my vision clear, picking up the slightest movement from yards away.

It could have been due to the overbearing demon it came from, or the countless lives he'd taken over the years, but this particular strain harbored a rich blend of the best qualities in life. It twined inside like a braid, each delicate fiber distinct in personality and history, leaving a carbon print of its owner.

Michael was right—memories were strange things. It became harder to determine which ones were mine. I'd thought the listlessness, that foggy drift regarding the how, what, and whys, only happened to donors. But it affected the one who fed as well, for these new lives, these new memories had to be accounted for.

How many files could one's hard drive store before the entire system shut down? To feed completely, to consume an entire life, loaded to the hilt with experience and knowledge required valuable space, and pieces of myself would compensate. If enough lives were taken, what room was left for me? Where would my life fit in? And could I recognize it as my own, or would I become the old saying, 'you are what you eat'?

Feeding always put me in a philosophical mood, searching for rhyme and reason that clearly didn't exist. And if it did, knowing would only kill my buzz, so these hard-hitting questions were strictly rhetorical. A part of me wanted to keep this experience for myself, savor the electricity lacing my veins, but someone else had a greater need for it.

Operation: Cambion Recovery hit a snag when the nurse at the sign-in desk gave me the third degree. She must have been new or drinking on the job if she thought not being a blood relative would keep me from Caleb. Hospital regulations and security guards wouldn't save her from my wrath. Just when I moved in for the kill, a voice called behind me.

"Ma'am, she's with us."

I knew that English accent anywhere. Turning around, I shook my head at his clumsy swagger up the hall. Michael chomped on a rope of licorice and wore that old rumpled gray trench coat that he undoubtedly slept in. Though we were indoors, a pair of dark shades hid his eyes, either to conceal his spirit's allure or the fact that he was hung-over.

The nurse found it difficult to look away or utter a complete sentence, a natural response while in a Cambion's presence. "Sir, um—only family members can see patients at this time" was the only coherent phrase from her. She patted her mousy hair and straightened the front of her teddy-bear scrubs.

Michael bent over the desk, lowered his shades, and leveled her with a stare that could dissolve clothing. "She *is* family. She's my brother's fiancée." He snuck a wink at me before I could correct him.

Shaking out of her daze, she slid the clipboard to me, still unable to take her eyes off Michael. "Yes, of course she is. How silly of me."

After signing the clipboard, Michael escorted me to the room with my head tucked under his arm. I liked being considered one of the boys, but his knuckle sandwiches were brutal. I could only shudder at what Caleb had to deal with growing up.

"So what happened to you? Thought you'd pop by."

"Something came up, couldn't be avoided," I answered while fighting out of his chokehold. "But I'm here now. I've gathered some energy for him. Any little bit helps, you know?"

"Yes, it does. We're trying to give what we have, but he seems more accepting of yours. It's sweet, actually.

We're one big happy family." He held my neck tight, locking me into yet another odd contortion.

"Caleb and I aren't married or mated or whatever you want to call it," I choked out.

"But as soon as you marry Caleb, both families will be united," Michael assured, ignoring my struggle.

I planted my heels into the floor, stopping our procession. "Whoa, back the spit up, caveman. I'm not getting married. I've gotta finish high school and seven years of college before I'll even entertain the idea."

"Yes, because no married woman in history ever passed the state bar. You're a modern woman. You can't multitask?" Michael started walking again and dragged me with him.

With a few calculated twists, I broke out of his hold when two giggling nurses entered the hall. They smiled and twirled their hair in a shameless play for his attention.

Here stood the second reason why no woman should ever hook up with a Cambion, at least none who valued a full night's sleep. I'd been told on numerous occasions that only a strong, self-assured woman could tolerate these chick-magnets, but even the most confident woman had her limits.

Michael turned to me, his playful demeanor melting away. "Speaking of the law—you know that P.I., Ruiz?"

"*O, I see that nose of his, but not that dog I shall throw it to,*" I replied. As Michael stared slack jawed at me, I explained, "It's from *Othello*, one of my favorite quotes."

"Right then. Well, I had the pleasure of meeting him a few days ago. Nasty bloke, that one. I don't care to meet him in a dark alley."

"Yeah. He's been around asking a bunch of questions about your dad."

"Like what?"

"About his death and his life in Europe. I don't know. I get this vibe like he knows something, and he's waiting for us to slip up."

"Interesting. Sounds like I'll have to intervene." He gave me a lazy smile and opened the door for me.

We entered the room, where rumpled blankets and pillows were piled in the corner. Haden lay between two chairs, snoring loud enough to rouse Caleb out of his coma.

I reached Caleb's side and traced a hand over his pale fingers, applying the slightest squeeze to let him know I was there.

"How is he?" I asked.

"Not much change. He hasn't stirred," Michael reported.

I kissed Caleb's eyes and cheeks before moving to his lips. Allowing my body to relax, the energy poured out of me in waves, fast at first, then puttering as the seconds inched on. Lilith had a time relinquishing her energy, as I'd already suspected she would. She seemed a bit indifferent to Capone today, not her usual dancing flickers of electricity. This was not a good sign.

"Sam, I think that's enough. Don't want to give too much," a voice warned from across the room.

I looked up at Haden, who was now among the living. "I'm okay. I'm not tired."

"You sure? That's an awful lot. What did you eat?" he asked.

I avoided the question and returned my attention to Caleb. Capone ate greedily, pulling for every ounce of strength. This time, Lilith seemed more eager to give it, but her previous reaction confused me. Normally, she would be jumping at the chance to be with Capone, and now she was barely interested. I closed my eyes, trying to decipher the feelings as best as I could.

I finally pulled away, gasping for air. "I think that should do it for now." I wiped my lips, then stopped at the sight of the brothers looking at me in shock. "What?"

They continued staring. Michael looked to Haden with concern.

"What?" I yelled.

"I'll handle it." Haden patted Michael's arm before crossing the room and steering me out of the door. "We need to talk."

I didn't have much choice in the matter. One moment I stood inside Caleb's room, the next I'd reached the far end of the hall, out of earshot of wandering staff. Haden cornered me against the wall. His big body eclipsed the overhead lights, casting me in shadow. Though he was soft-spoken, one wrong word could set him in a murderous rage, and disturbing his nap made him that much grumpier.

"Samara, I'd appreciate it if you were honest with me," he began in a calm, even tone. "We have a lot to deal with right now and we don't want to have to worry about you, too. There was no way you could've let him feed for that long and not be on the floor. You're practically glowing. So, I'll ask this one time. What on earth did you eat?"

I had given a lot of my energy away, and though I felt the drain, I still had enough to get me through the next few days without feeding again. If he was this upset over energy, I couldn't imagine his reaction if he knew where I got it from.

I wanted to tell him. The words perched on my tongue,

ready to fly, but couldn't. I was feeding his brother energy from the demon who'd put him in this position to begin with. This was truly messed up from all angles, but I couldn't risk Haden doing something stupid, like killing Tobias. Lilith was linked to him, after all, and I needed more time to figure this out.

"Don't worry. I didn't kill anybody," I said.

He didn't look convinced.

"Haden, I may be desperate, but not *that* desperate."

After a moment, he drew back. "You say that now, but I know the extent our kind will go for a mate. We walk a very tight rope, Samara. Taking a life in its entirety is an intoxicating and dangerous thing. The power will seduce you into wanting more. With each life taken, you become more demon than human."

"I know."

"Be sure to remember that. These demons are not cute, they're not friendly; they are not pets. They kill without prejudice and will turn on you the second you show weakness. Our humanity, our strength keeps them re-strained, but they're patient. Your reasons might be noble, but it will destroy you and Caleb in the end. You're new to this world, and this is a hierarchy you've yet to understand. There are laws that we have to follow, rules brought down from centuries that have kept our kind in line. Disobeying rules will result in death, and I won't lose any more family. You understand?"

Swallowing hard, I nodded. "Yes. I'm just trying to help him."

"I'm not just talking about Caleb." Haden gave me room to pass.

We watched Caleb in shifts. Haden brooded in the cor-ner, while Michael kept taking pictures of Caleb on his camera phone and texting updates to Brodie. Unable to will the strength to leave just yet, I sat by Caleb's bedside, doing homework.

After I read aloud my poem for English, Haden reclined in his seat, playing air violins. "You really do have Nadine's spirit in you. Try not to slit your wrist or anything."

"Shut up, Haden. I think it's deep." I stuck my tongue out at him.

"She's taken after her in many ways; her draw is very strong," Michael commented and took a swig of his flask.

Heat blossomed on my cheeks. "Let me ask you guys something. You knew Nadine longer than I did. Did she mention anything about a boyfriend?"

"Not that I know of." Michael looked pensive. "She dated this one bloke a few years back, but he was married and—"

"What happened to him?" I asked eagerly. I remembered Nadine telling me about her shocking affair, but not a whisper of the two-year tryst appeared in her memories.

Glancing around, Haden said in a hushed tone, "Well, I heard she tried to kill him when he wouldn't leave his wife."

"No!" Michael gasped and covered his mouth.

Haden nodded. "Yeah. 'Hell hath no fury,' they say. I swear, Cambion women are vipers. No offense, Sam. She didn't kill the tosser, of course, but she fell into depression after the split and never came out of it."

The brothers crowded together like clucking hens, only regarding me for confirmation. When I told them that that area in Nadine's life was blank, they continued with their beauty shop gossip.

Why didn't I remember any of this? Did Tobias have

something to do with it? And if he was involved, I wondered if her old squeeze was alive. Maybe Tobias had performed his masquerades on all of his victims and seduced Nadine somehow. Hottie or not, she had to be all shades of crazy or desperate to willingly bond with an incubus.

"Do you guys ever think of Nadine?" I asked, lost in the mystery.

The brothers looked at each other, silently debating over who should speak first.

"One of many lives we have to pay for, Sam. It's harder for someone we know," Michael said. "But Evangeline showed us mercy and will speak on our behalf to the proper authorities. A powerful ally to have, and she's extended her umbrella to us."

"What authority? Like the police? The feds?" I asked.

"It's an agency of sorts," Haden intoned. "There are powerful Cambion families all over the world; a few operate in the U.S. In order to keep track of the Cambions in their region, every newcomer must be registered and accounted for, like a census. Foreigners who come into a new country have to notify the family of the region if they plan to stay. By doing so, you relinquish your power to those governing the territory."

"So these families are like a Cambion embassy?"

"Strange way of putting it, but, yeah, I suppose," Michael said. "No worries, love. You're a Petrovsky now, one of the most influential names in the fold. And when you tie the knot with Caleb, he will carry the honor as well, with Evangeline's blessing." Michael rubbed his hands together and laughed—clearly he was already plotting the decorations at the ceremony. "Evangeline is a good woman, and Nadine was a good friend, almost a sister."

"Better than the ones we have." Haden sucked his teeth in distaste.

I'd known Caleb and his sisters were estranged, but I didn't know things were that bad. "Why are your sisters so mad?"

Not meeting my eyes, Michael said, "They're not mad, just afraid. Our sisters cut all ties with us when Mum died. We haven't heard from them in years. They could never understand what we were. They were afraid that one day we would turn on them."

"Bunch of bigots if you ask me," Haden grumbled. "Not once did they phone us to see how we were. They didn't even come to Dad's funeral."

"What did you expect? Dad was the reason they took off. Can't blame them, they're not like us. They have every right to fear us," Michael argued while checking his cell phone for messages again.

The mood shifted as I tried to follow the thread of the conversation. "Why would they be afraid of you guys? You're family. The spirit won't attack what it knows. Didn't you explain the recognition thing?"

"They weren't convinced. Regardless of the years we all lived under one roof, they were suspicious. As soon as they were old enough, they took off. And when Mum died, Ava and Grace blamed Dad and we haven't seen them since. Whenever we tried to find them, they moved away. After a while, we got the hint." Michael's eyes fused to his cell phone, but his brows furrowed in evident hurt.

Haden stared to the door, focusing somewhere beyond the room, beyond the hospital, beyond the planet. His jaw flexed, his full lips drew into a tight line.

I knew what it was like to be ostracized by family for

being different. My own grandfather had disowned my mother for something as petty as race. I could easily sympathize with the prejudice the brothers had to deal with.

"If you guys are siblings, can't you use your link to find them?" My question was followed by scoffs and gagging. "What?"

"To establish a link, you have to feed from them directly, several times. And doing that with our sisters, well, that's just disgusting." Michael took another drink and moved to Caleb's bed.

A new question struck me, one that had been on my mind for a while. "If the Cambion curse only affects the males of your family, then how do you have sisters? Wouldn't your dad's spirit make sure all the offspring were males? Does it have any control over the gender of the baby?" I asked.

"In a way. Our spirit is a conscious being and at its core, male. He must feed from his opposite and can recognize his equal down to a single chromosome. To reproduce, he has to give up a piece of himself during conception. He can never get that piece back, so every try must count and the timing has to be right. It's the game of life. Sometimes you score; sometimes you don't. Our family is just gifted with tactical players." Haden winked.

"Hey, guys, look!" Michael motioned us to join him by the bed. Noting the sudden excitement in Michael's voice, Haden and I circled around Caleb.

I hopped up and down, trying to peek over their wide shoulders. "What's going on? Let me see."

"Come on, come on. Do it again!" Michael coaxed.

"Do what? What happened?" I asked.

"Come on, Caleb, you can do it. Come on."

"Let me see!" I cried when Haden's arm swooped around my waist and pulled me into the fold. I looked down at Caleb, searching for some grand event, but he lay as motionless as before.

"Look right there," Michael said.

We followed where he pointed and gasped. I covered my hands over my mouth as tears leaked down my cheeks. My chest contracted, never so overtaken by joy. Not even feeding could grant this much satisfaction, this small sign of hope.

Swallowing my sob, I bent down to kiss each finger that twitched under my lips.

14

Caleb moved his hand.

To anyone else, this wasn't worth running and screaming to the rooftops about, but that didn't keep me from doing cartwheels in the hallway. Again, I got questioned by the brothers about my strange behavior, but not even their suspicion could kill my good mood. After visiting hours ended, I kept with the plan to buy olive oil. But first, I had to stop for a victory slushy.

The occasion called for the divine trinity: ice cream, flavored syrup, and whipped cream. Despite the cold weather, the line wrapped around the parking lot of the tiny mom-and-pop yogurt shack, but it was worth the wait once my tongue reached sugary nirvana. With that task done, I continued my mission.

I drove to the ritzy grocery store across town instead of the nasty one near my house, and it was a relief not having to smell the meat department from the parking lot. Slurping down my icy treat, I pushed a squeaky cart through the condiment aisles. Haden said it had to be pure and unrefined, which led me to the organic section. I was a stranger around these parts, and all this green-conscious, eco-friendly crap that tasted like air made me itch.

The entire area was set away from the rest of the food, where I met two men in powdered wigs and stockings comparing prices on tofu. No matter how many times I saw the historical actors, it always took a second to get over the initial shock, to allow the flux of surrealism to level out. Their costumes were not the usual farm worker or politician, but more of the sophisticated people of the era, complete with saggy britches, black tri-corner hat, and matching waistcoats with brass button trim.

No colonial speak came into the exchange as the two huddled together, bickering like an old married couple. They must have seen the lost orphan look on my face because they took pity on me. With plenty of "honeys" and "sugars," they pointed me in the right direction, offering info on organic food and alternative living.

"Oh, that one is good, great on garlic bread," the shorter of the two commented while loosening the bind of his neckerchief.

"No, she said she's looking for pure oil—unseasoned. Put that back. Um, let's see. They're all pretty good, but if you're willing to chuck out some cash, I recommend this." The taller one with the ponytail tied in a ribbon reached up and pulled a small, decorative bottle from the top shelf. The bottle was no bigger than a saltshaker, which meant it was way out of my price range.

"It's Dio Bellucci, the Lamborghini of olive oils. All the famous chefs use it." He turned the bottle so the label came into view.

When I saw the price sticker on the shelf, I nearly fainted. "Forty bucks! For this?"

Ponytail Guy placed his hands on his hips. "What do you expect? Dio Bellucci doesn't come cheap."

"Is that name supposed to mean something?"

The shorter man blanched and covered his mouth in a gasp. "It's like one of the most well-known companies in the world. All of their products are handmade in a monastery in Naples. They make perfume, designer fabrics, and beauty cream with finely crushed pearls inside. Expensive! All the celebrities use it and it has to be specially ordered."

"They also make the best wine—three hundred dollars a bottle," Ponytail Guy added.

"Wow. All because some monks crushed the grapes themselves?" I asked.

"That, and the region and the special blend of the soil. It's all very spiritual, and rich people eat all that up," the short one supplied.

"So, do you think it might be, um . . . sanctified?"

Ponytail Guy rolled his eyes. "Honey, it came from a monastery full of Catholic monks. Their toilet paper is probably blessed."

That was all I needed to know. I dropped the oil in my cart along with a few others from varying prices and regions of the world. Waving my thanks to the colonial duo, I grabbed my cart and whimpered all the way to the checkout line. My bank account was gonna bleed from this cut, all in the name of science.

On the way back to my car, a black sedan pulled up next to me in the row. The window rolled down and I groaned when I saw the face behind the tinted glass. The timing was just terrible.

Don't ruin my good mood. Don't come over here. Please, I chanted in my head. But it was too late.

"Evening, Samara. Fancy seeing you here," Ruiz said as if this was a real coincidence.

"Yeah, what are the odds?" I agreed in a flat tone. Did no one have a life in this town? My life wasn't interesting enough for someone to want to follow me around. "I'm celebrating Caleb's recovery. He moved his hand today."

He looked genuinely surprised. "Congratulations. I'd love to hear what he has to say when he wakes up. You shouldn't be walking around by yourself like this."

"My car's right here. I'm heading straight home after this." I went to open my car door.

He nodded. "Be careful out there. Someone's got their eye on you. Have a good night," he said, then drove away.

When he was far enough away, I shuddered from the creepiness of that moment. This guy seriously needed a girlfriend, a hobby, a *real* job—something. After I climbed into my car, I gave Haden a quick call and warned him in case Ruiz made a surprise visit. The dude was straight shady and nothing could be left to chance.

On the drive home, I grew excited with possibilities, but I was alone in the celebration. Lilith trembled and curled within, dreading some impending punishment.

"Lilith, what's wrong? Are you scared?"

I couldn't explain the sheer absurdity of talking empathically with a spirit. Her response was choppy and relayed in code, similar to that yellow car from *Transformers*. There were some things about possession that I would never get over; like the lack of privacy, the slight pressure on my back, and the constant paranoia of someone standing right behind me. I could turn in circles until I got dizzy, but she would always be behind me. Lilith: the ghost in the machine.

Suffice to say that I wasn't the only one involved in this little experiment. She was scared of me tampering with hazardous material, and I couldn't really blame her. Tobias had told me that Lilith would protect her host, but I didn't know how far she would go for self-preservation. Either way, it was unfair not to run this decision by her first.

"I know you're scared, but I need to know what's going on. If you can think of a better way to figure this out, I'm all ears. I'm not gonna hurt you or me. Trust—"

I didn't finish my sentence because I caught the feeling of being watched. A sense of unease came from nowhere. I knew that feeling, the icy chill of fear and the searing heat of stalking eyes. It drew closer, a menacing overcast of ill intent. Its energy wasn't human, that much I knew, and it seemed hell-bent on scaring the crap out of me.

My eyes stopped at a dark figure standing under a streetlight. Believing it was a fickle shadow, or perhaps a trick of the light, I tried to ignore it. The key word was "tried."

The inky shade unnerved me, not so much as its presence, but by its association with the lamppost. The light didn't bounce off the form as it should, but sucked into a vacuum of obscurity. I couldn't see the color or style of the clothes, just the basic silhouette, a void with the illusion of endless depth. Surrounding houses, cars, trees, the entire block was nothing more than an elaborate backdrop, and this thing, this chasm in the scope, was cut out of the frame.

When I drove closer to the lamppost, it moved. It happened so quickly, I wasn't sure I saw it. It moved again in choppy jerks, parody to a nervous tick or bad stop-motion animation. None of that prepared me as the thing leapt off the curb and stopped in front of my car.

I slammed on the brakes, but I wasn't fast enough. My heart bobbed to the back of my throat, the scream shredded my windpipe, and yet, there was no collision. A gust of wind hit the driver's side with such force that it rocked the car.

The rush of flying leaves plastered to the windows, darkened the interior, and blinded me from the street. The wind passed over the hood in a visible ripple, entangling debris in its path. Air shot from the heating vents and thickened the interior with a humid musk that I could almost taste. As quickly as it began, the light returned. The onslaught faded into a gentle breeze that brushed the windows clean, revealing an open stretch of road.

Watching leaves dance and flutter to the ground, I had no doubt what had caused this, or rather who. Loud, ragged breathing filled the car in an audible struggle for calm.

I stared at the street, not sparing a glimpse at what now sat next to me in the passenger seat. I just sat there for several moments until my breathing calmed, my hand wringing the steering wheel, wishing it was his neck.

"Drive," he ordered.

My foot, which seemed stuck to the pedal, lifted off the brake for the car to cruise along. Normally, I would have a witty comeback or a masterful cuss-out ready to go, but all rational thought had left me, and I had a suspicion that I was going to wet my pants.

We rode in silence for a few blocks. Five houses away from home, I risked a glance at him from the side. Tobias, in all his malevolent hotness, sat with his eyes glued to the road, panting in that strange canine fashion. Whether it was his body heat or the tangible proof of his anger, the temperature rose considerably and fogged the windows.

He must have felt my stare, and that one fleeting look was enough to get him to speak. "I tried to be reasonable, to give you time to accept the truth, but you insist on forcing my hand. I saw you drive to the hospital. You went to see *him*."

Not bothering to deny it, I said, "Caleb's in a coma and his spirit is starving. How else can Capone feed?"

"It's a waste. You're just polishing his coffin."

My head whipped in his direction. "You can't hurt him. I won't let you."

"I told you before, I have unfinished business. I warn you now, Samara. Stay out of my way."

"Or what? If what you say about you and Lilith is true, then you can't hurt me without hurting yourself." I paused as a burst of insight nearly struck me blind, a point so obvious that I scolded myself for missing it. "And if you harm Caleb . . . you'll hurt me . . . and by extension hurting yourself." His body suddenly went tense, giving me all the confirmation I needed. "That's it, isn't it? That's the *real* reason you haven't killed him already? You certainly have the power to do so, and you had a ton of chances, even before Halloween. You just *can't*, can you? Bet you didn't see that coming, huh? We really are *linked*," I sneered, the words leaving a sour taste in my mouth.

The sickened look on his face told me he didn't like the flavor of that truth either, or at least the part that involved Caleb. "Yes. But your mother is not. Your father, your friend Mia, her lover Douglas, your coworker Alicia—they have no connection to me whatsoever."

"You son of a—" My words were cut off as his fist slammed against the dashboard. The hatch to the glove compartment fell open; its contents spilled onto the floor. At the same time, the lights of the interior went off and the car jerked to a halt. My seat belt kept me from flying into the windshield and yanked me back against the headrest.

He shifted in his seat to make sure he had my complete attention. He had it—just not the good kind of attention. I stared at a face only made in Heaven, while Hell stared back at me through two glowing orbs. The contrast was simply terrifying, the ultimate deception.

"Already you forget who I am, and what I'm capable of, so let me remind you. I'm not human, and human life means very little to me other than food and pleasure. And it is my pleasure to take every ounce of life from the Ross family. The only reason they aren't dead now is because of you, but don't push me. Killing him might hurt, but I have a higher tolerance for pain and loss than you can imagine. The question is: How much pain can *you* stand?"

"Tobias, you're scaring me," I said, shocked to have confessed that aloud.

Instantly, he slumped back and looked out the window. His face scrunched up in a pout, and even with that very human expression, he could never be mistaken for a mortal. "Your car has a strange odor, like old lunch meat," he said, and I wasn't sure if it was an insult or an observation.

I didn't answer him and started the car again. A moment later, I pulled into the driveway and noted that Mom wasn't home yet. She had her group meeting tonight, so I wasn't too concerned; actually, considering my angry passenger, I was grateful. I consulted the clock, but 12:00 blinked on the dashboard as a result of Tobias's short temper. Great. I would have to reset all my favorite radio stations, but I had to handle business first.

Shutting off the engine, I turned to him. "If I stay away from Caleb, will you let him live?"

He hesitated for a moment before saying, "Yes."

"And his brothers?"

All I heard was crickets.

"Tobias!" I yelled.

"You ask an awful lot of me. But I promise, I won't make the first move. If they interfere in any way, I won't hesitate."

"Are you a man of your word? How can I trust you?"

"The same way I can trust you, and I'm not a man. You hold up your end of the deal and we'll be fine. I won't let you waste my energy on that demon mutt. It's for you and Lilith only. This is quite the betrayal, Samara."

"Then you'll think twice before you get all 'date rape' on me, won't you?" I snapped. "I haven't forgotten about your little scare tactic behind the bleachers, so forgive me if I'm not more considerate of your precious gift."

"I told you why I did what I did. My methods may be harsh, but they're effective. What I do is for food and survival. I don't allow any woman I take to suffer like humans do, so you can take down your feminist flag. While you're at it, you might want to take your hand off my leg."

I looked down at my hand and yelped. Unbeknownst to me, my hand was moving in slow circles on his denim-clad knee. I snatched it away as if I'd been burned, wondering how it had gotten there. It seemed that my body had a mind of its own, working from a separate directive.

With arms crossed over our chests, we stared at my house, struggling for composure. We were both pissed off, but neither one of us was going to move until we calmed down, so I broke the ice. "The energy I took from you was . . . weird. What was it? How many lives were there?"

"Dozens, finely coiled together and compressed—the best of the best," he said, his chest puffed out high and proud. "Think of it as a quilt. You take a piece here and there and stick them together to make one whole tapestry. I'm meticulous with the material I use."

"That's a lot of lives to store. How can you ingest all that?"

His smile thawed some of the frost coating the air. "I'm bigger than you think."

Against my better judgment, my gaze lowered to the front of his jeans, then looked away.

Noting my wandering eyes, he grinned wider. "You really do have a one-track mind, Flower. I'm talking about me, as a preternatural entity. I'm quite vast and heavier than I appear. Incubi can manipulate their body density so they can move with the air, defying gravity to an extent, expand and compress at will, just like spirits can. People think clouds are all light and fluffy, but the smallest one can stretch a mile wide and weigh over a million tons."

"So how much do you weigh?"

He cowered away as if repulsed. "Oh come on, you never ask a person that. That's just rude. But I'm happy to know that I fascinate you."

Words escaped me. Not only was he dangerous, but he was completely insane. I guess eternity would do that to a person. What made it worse was his correct assessment. He did fascinate me, made me feel things I didn't want to feel, like excitement and longing, emotions that should never be associated with an enemy.

"So, you're strong, can transform into stuff, look like a bunch of people, and live for a really long time. What *can't* you do? Do you have any fatal weaknesses?"

"You."

"Besides me?"

"No, that's about it. You're my Achilles' heel. But it doesn't have to be that way. In fact, you can have the same abilities as I have, and we could combine our powers if you choose."

He leaned closer, making me perfectly aware of how small my car really was. Only a wall of hot air and tension stood between us and Tobias had no problem with crossing boundaries.

His voice was a silk scarf caressing my skin. "Your human body confines you, anchoring you down with earthly limitations. Even as a Cambion, you've yet to tap into the power you have. There's so much of the world you haven't seen that's right in front of you, visions only your demon eyes can withstand. The things I could teach you, Samara, if you just allow Lilith a little freedom, if you just let go."

"No, thanks. I'll pass," I answered before I could second-guess myself. Oh man, the curiosity was there, and he had one hell of a sales pitch, but the asking price was too high. I had enough trouble getting Lilith under control as it was.

Moreover, the fate of Caleb and his brothers still hung in the balance, unresolved. Something deep down told me that Tobias would keep his promise and wouldn't go after them. But he was cunning enough to find a loophole somewhere. Right now, the best thing to do was to keep my distance from them. For Lilith's sake, he would never harm me, but everyone else was fair game.

Hating the silence, I asked, "Can you go away now? I'm sure Malik has a curfew or something."

"I've already checked in, and his family is fast asleep."

Feigning a yawn, I made a production of stretching and rubbing my eyes. "Yeah, well, it's late. I'm gonna call it a night. You should probably get some sleep too."

"You might be right. Too bad I don't sleep, though."

I paused with my fingers on the door handle. "You don't sleep? At all?"

"Not the way you do, no." Sighing, he threw me a look of impatience. "Samara, I'm inhuman, and by your estimation, quite evil. No rest for the wicked. That would imply some sort of reprieve, wouldn't it?"

"Oh. Good point." I opened my car door.

"Do you need help carrying your bags inside?"

"I can manage." I stopped for a moment as an idea struck me. "On second thought, could you carry my book bag? It's really heavy."

Hefting the bag over his shoulder, he waited by the passenger-side door while I grabbed the bags from the backseat. Keeping an eye on him, I dug into one of the bags and singled out the small bottle of oil. Lilith rattled my spine, taking the defensive, but I ignored her. She'd annoyed me enough for the night. I unwrapped the plastic tamper-proof covering and twisted the cap. I dipped my finger inside, expecting some burning sensation, but nothing happened.

"You okay back there?" he called.

"Yeah, just grabbing trash from the back," I said, then returned to my task.

The oil slid down my finger, warm and creamy, coating the digit in a shimmering gloss. It didn't hurt to touch, so it wasn't an irritant like silver supposedly is for werewolves. Maybe it had to be ingested. I wondered what effects it had on real demons. To my knowledge, their skin was like human skin, but pliable enough to transfigure into other forms. I poured a few more drops and slathered my hands in the oil. The sound of crunching gravel shot me upright. I made quick work of hiding the evidence, closed the door, and turned to face Tobias, who came around to my side.

His eyes darted to the backseat, then back to me. "You ready?"

"Yeah. Let's go."

We marched side by side down the walkway until we reached the porch. I opened the front door and dropped the shopping bag inside before turning to him.

He waited.

"You can't come in," I said and blocked the entry.

"Since when do I need an invitation?"

"Since now," I said, then grabbed his hand with my oily one. He flinched at the contact, loosening his grip on my backpack.

I snatched my bag, rushed inside, and slammed the door in his face. My back pressed against the door, my heart drumming a beat that Caleb would want to sample for his collection. Club Rib Cage: the panic remix.

As the band played on around my ears, I considered my counterstrike. It had worked. The oil had really worked. My victory didn't last long as a peculiar side effect came to my attention. It began slowly at first, but as the rush of danger drained away, it surfaced, a light heat on the same hand that had burned Tobias's.

The entry in Angie's journal warned me about how a linked pair could sense each other's pain, not the injury per se, but the echo of its effect. The feeling would worsen as the pair fed from each other, but the energy charging my system was enough to make my hand tingle from an unsighted sting. This was the least of my problems once that strange, odorless smoke crept under the door, tickling my ankles. Dry ice the color of pitch had begun to slither up the wooden surface, its outstretched fingers clawing its way in.

I dove into my shopping bag, recovered the oil, and let a few drops spill on the cracks around the door. The vapor drew back once it made contact. I moved to the living room and added oil to the windowsill, then followed suit with the one in the dining room. I'd finished painting the glass when Tobias appeared on the other side of the pane, looking winded and livid.

"You can't come in. Please just go away!" I yelled.

He chuckled to himself. "Where on earth did you find anointed oil?"

"It's not that hard to come by."

A tight smile stretched at his lips. "You did your homework. I'm impressed. Must have been a powerful elder, or several to cause this amount of damage. Good stuff." He regarded his burned hand, which had turned red and blotched with peeling skin and small white blisters.

"I'm not going to hurt you, Flower. I can't." His eyes pleaded for compassion, understanding. His brows knit together in pain, not for his hand but from my firm rejection. I felt his grief burning within my chest, Lilith whining and appealing on his behalf, my arms throbbing to hold him and make it all better, but I had to be strong.

Bright headlights caught both of our attention. Mom's blue Chrysler pulled into the driveway and parked behind mine.

Tobias's sullen expression morphed into one of menace. I looked to Mom, to Tobias, then back to Mom again. The headlights shut off and the car door opened. Her dark head appeared before leaning in to grab her briefcase. I looked back to Tobias and screamed.

On the other side of the glass stood my dad, dressed in a gray suit and tie, smiling down at me. I shook my head, knowing what he would do. Tobias had been in my house long enough to see photos of my family. As the heavyweight champion of mind tricks, he no doubt knew about Mom's unrequited feelings for Dad. This was bad, really bad, and I was helpless to stop it.

Mom's high heels clicked against the pavement, drawing closer. Telling by the evil glint in Tobias's eyes, she would never make it to the front door. I wasn't one to beg, but if it would keep my mother safe, I would kiss the ground he walked on. But the words refused to break free, nor did I have time to speak.

Tobias took one step forward, then stopped dead in his tracks. Horror distorted his features, and the dark brown tint of Dad's skin melted down his face like a runny watercolor. Tobias in his true shape appeared behind the fallen mask, terrified beyond words or movement. His breath caught, his eyes bugged out as he watched me, but more directly, the bottle of oil hovered dangerously close to my lips.

Meeting him square in the eye, I shook my head slowly. I wasn't sure what taking olive oil straight to the head would do to me, or Caleb for that matter. But the possibilities were enough to render Tobias motionless, and that was worth the risk.

Mom's keys jangled at the door and if he was going to make his move, now was the time. But he didn't budge. We stared at each other for a long, excruciating minute, communicating our stalemate with silence. His attention locked to my mouth and the lips that touched the rim of the bottle.

Taking a deep breath, he lowered his head, then nodded in a manner that declared defeat. He stepped away from the glass, retreating into the shadows as the front door opened.

"Whoop!" Mom yelped, followed by the thud of her briefcase hitting the floor. By the time I rushed to the door, Mom clung to its knob in an attempt to keep from falling flat on her butt. One foot shot out in front of the other as her left shoe flew off and landed by the stairs.

I raced to her side and grabbed her arm. "Mom, are you okay?"

Standing upright, she yanked and smoothed down her charcoal pantsuit. "Yeah, I must've slipped. Did you spill something by the door?"

"Um, yeah. I'll grab a towel to clean it up." I went to close the door.

Outside, Tobias stood on the opposite side of the street, that dark cavity cutting through the scenery once again. I may have won this round, but this fight wasn't over. His presence burned into me, waging a war that he vowed to win.

15

There was no way to downplay or diminish the temperament of my internal roommate.

Lilith was straight-up pissed. I'd expected as much—no one wanted to be used as a bargaining chip in a hostage situation. But it had gotten Tobias off my back for the next three days, so mission accomplished. Seeing as Lilith couldn't talk, she didn't voice her displeasure aloud, but boy, was it obvious. She made her disapproval known by doling out another bout of insomnia.

I'd endured sleepless nights before, but images of Tobias lengthened the hours between midnight and sunrise. I knew for a fact that I wasn't in love with him. I was more than certain I hated him, but that didn't prevent the explicit images from flashing before my eyes. My personal adult video library and we were the lead actors in every scene.

I'd pinch my eyes shut and count to ten to rinse away my filthy mind, but an ocean of water couldn't remove that stain. Only one thing could supplant the immediate need, only one body could replace another. Just thinking about him made me sick with guilt.

Caleb.

What would he think about me drooling over his potential killer, a jilted demon lover on the rebound? I imagined Caleb's bright eyes peering down at me in contempt, though at this point, I'd do anything just to see those eyes open. I missed having someone to confide in; I missed his goofy style and our verbal spars. Heaven help me, I missed his hands—large, strong hands that promised safety and comfort.

I kept my promise and stayed away from Caleb's room, technically. With help from one of the orderlies I caught in the parking lot, a few drops of oil protected the door of room 278. I hated using my abilities like that, but I needed to cover my bases.

Though I kept my end of the bargain, I called Haden every few hours for updates. Caleb remained unconscious, but seemed responsive to voices. I explained that I had too much makeup work for school to visit, and the brothers agreed to hold down the fort until I could think of a better lie.

After ending the final call of the night, I stayed awake, but fell into a trance of deep introspection. What a difference a few weeks could make. Or maybe I was the one who had changed? I used to have fun, joke around, and laugh until it hurt. Now, I was a good razor cut away from turning emo. I'd never needed to lie to everyone I cared about, but now lies followed each sentence like punctuation.

Pride demanded that I blame Lilith for flipping my world upside down, but what good would that do? There's no escape from one's self. No matter where I went, there she was: 24-7-52. She felt what I felt and likewise with me. No matter how much it annoyed me, Lilith was now my responsibility, and it was my job to sate her appetite.

That soon became a problem when I nearly passed out in government class the next day. The few drops of Tobias's energy I had kept finally burned off and my poor sleeping habits made the crash that much harder. I was a fiend for another hit, and what's worse, my dealer kept staring at me from behind his textbook, giving me the "sex me" vibe.

After the olive oil standoff, Tobias attended every class we shared, seeking my attention. He didn't dare sit next to me; I kept olive oil in a small body spray bottle in my pocket. This demon business was very much like training a pet. Whenever he misbehaved, I had to hose him down. In return, he sat across the room, using the Jedi mind trick to project his longing and employing Lilith to trigger mine.

I squirmed in my seat, gripping the edge of the desk while witnessing images of Nadine and Tobias. Vivid details crowded my senses: the sounds, the smells, the warmth of his skin. And Lilith, the little perv, did nothing but kick back and cheer them on.

It was wrong, yet I couldn't look away, even if I'd known how. The mating process fascinated me; it was very different from human coupling, not that I knew from personal experience. Some images appeared in split-vision, taking multiple points of view at once. I could feel not only what Nadine felt, but also Tobias, and his response through her. Signals passed through their private frequency, back and forth, moving faster, climbing higher until—

"Yo, Sam!" a voice called from the outside world.

I looked up and found Mia glaring down at me, her binder clutched to her chest.

"Class is over," she reported.

"Oh." I swept a glance across the now empty classroom and wondered where the time had gone. Mr. Frasier stood in front of the marker board, wiping away notes that I was pretty sure I would need for Friday's test.

Eyeing me in suspicion, Mia said, "I saw how Malik was staring at you. So are the rumors true? Are you two hooking up?"

"No," I answered and wiped the sweat from my neck and forehead.

"You sure about that? I've seen you two together. That's really messed up, Sam. Caleb's in the hospital, and you're sneaking around like this."

"I'm not sneaking around, okay?" I gathered my books and scooted out of my seat. "Look, there's more to this than you know. It's—"

"Complicated. Yeah, I know. That's what you keep telling me." Her upper lip curled and twitched. "Just do me a favor. Pick one guy and stick with it." With a swing of her ponytail, she stomped away.

What was Mia's problem? I'd never seen her so upset before, and it puzzled me to stand at the receiving end of her criticism, a position reserved for Dougie. Any other time, I would've been all over that, but now I had class and a hungry roommate who needed food.

It wasn't good to let Lilith starve or else force her to use her "mojo" to lure boys to me. Subtle signs of the draw began at second period, with boys grinning in my face, and again in gym class during warm-ups.

Mere months ago, no one was thinking about my pudgy ass, but now I had dudes—otherworldly and benign—drooling like bums in front of a hot meal. How was I going to deal with this when I went off to law school? Men were everywhere, lawyers, bailiffs, judges. I could sway the jury with a smile and I wouldn't have to work for anything in life—except integrity. Some girls might have reveled in all this attention, but it just left me bitter.

While doing crunches, I regarded the bleachers and what had occurred behind them. Memories of the thrill resurfaced—the fear, and the unspeakable pleasure of feeding. Boys stretched across the gym, muscles flexing, all that potent male testosterone pumping through the air. My body ached, my tongue burned for another taste, yet the energy wafting off the students was only a tease. I wanted the real thing, the whole thing. I needed a donor and I needed it now!

Tempted beyond human limits, I raced out of the gym to the locker room before the plot to attack my peers was set to action. Leaning over the sink, I looked Lilith square in the eyes. Her light flickered and swelled behind my brown contacts in an attempt to break free.

Mimicking my mother's best authoritative voice, I said, "We can't do this. That was a one-time thing and it's over."

She wasn't having it and showed her disobedience with more tingles.

I grabbed my book bag out of my locker and fished for the emergency candy hiding at the bottom. Sweets were just a temporary solution, but a great substitute in a pinch. My hand ran across the bottle of olive oil I tucked away. As though struck by an electric shock, Lilith jumped and cowered in her private little corner.

"That's it! I said I was sorry. What is your problem? I'm sick of you and your attitude. Either you talk to me or—"

Before I could finish, an image appeared before my eyes.

I stood in front of a steamy bathroom mirror, but it wasn't me. It was Nadine. Her wet blond hair rested in a tangled twist on one shoulder. Her skin looked almost translucent under the harsh light. Droplets of water ran down her neck, absorbing into the towel wrapped around her. Her green eyes glistened with tears, hooded under shadows that came with no sleep. She held a bottle of pills with shaky hands, and cried as if it was the answer to her prayers.

"This is for the best," she whispered as she poured out the tablets and swallowed one by one.

Lilith screamed inside her head—as much as spirits could scream—pleading for her to stop. Nadine ignored her and kept swallowing pills, washing it down with handfuls of water from the tap. The drugs worked fast, and each time she threw her head back, the surroundings blurred. Lines, shapes, and a filmy coat framed the edges. Lilith trembled within, worrying the spine to get Nadine's attention.

"I need to get away from him. You won't let me," she muttered.

Lilith whined and twitched, a servant tugging to the hem of her master's robe, begging not just for her life, but for her home.

"You want me to stop?" Nadine slurred. "Then you cut your connection with Tobias. Now!"

I blinked away the vision and welcomed the familiar layout of the locker room. Tears dragged down my cheeks, joining the wet trail down my neck.

Collecting my thoughts, I asked, "She tried to kill herself? To get rid of you? Because of Tobias?"

Lilith tingled in reply.

"And you think I'm trying to do the same thing with the oil?"

Another twitch cruised up my spine.

"Lilith, I'm sorry. I wouldn't do that. I admit I wish things could go back the way they were, for you to be with Nadine, but we can't. We're each other's now, and I promise I won't do anything to hurt you."

The sound of a toilet flushing stopped our little heart-to-heart. I'd checked the stalls earlier, and I hadn't seen or heard anyone come in. The door opened and the image that greeted me turned my blood to ice. I forced my mouth not to drop open at who stood there, plain as day and within earshot of my one-sided dialogue.

"Oh my God! Mia?"

16

I sat perfectly still, hoping immobility could somehow turn me invisible.

How much had she heard? How much could I explain away?

Mia sauntered out of the stall and breezed past me on her way to the sink to wash her hands. Instead of her gym uniform, she wore her usual jailbait couture, with not a stitch out of place. She fluffed and primped her hair, while her jaws worked on a thick wad of gum.

Before I could think up a good excuse, she spoke. "You know, Sam, you really shouldn't talk to yourself. People will think you're schizo."

When she looked at me through the mirror, I saw the gold glow in her eyes and realized who really stood there. It made perfect sense. Mia didn't have gym this semester and wouldn't have stayed in the locker room any longer than she had to.

Dumbstruck, I asked, "You can turn into girls, too?"

"I told you, I can be any person I see. You'd be surprised how many chicks are into that sort of thing," Tobias replied, matching Mia's pitch and cadence perfectly.

The outfit was also Mia's, which inspired an interesting question. "How do you change your clothes like that?"

"Who says I'm wearing clothes?" he asked in a low, syrupy tone, and speaking in Mia's voice made it that more disturbing. Watching me squirm, he said, "It's mind over matter, an illusion. Even as a Cambion, you can understand that much, can't you? So, are you ready to talk to me now?"

I dodged the question in exchange for another. "How long have you been in here?"

"A couple minutes. I heard you crying in class and came to check on you."

I wiped my nose with my shirtsleeve. "I wasn't crying."

Popping his gum, he leaned a hip against the counter. "I could hear your tears, Flower."

"Hear my . . . what do tears sound like?"

"Thunder, or like a heavy ball rolling across the floor. Kinda annoying, actually."

"Whoa, wait. Is it just my tears, or anyone's tears?"

"I hear all tears within an immediate area. That's why I stay away from weddings, funerals, and nurseries. But I'm attuned to you, so your tears are always the loudest, no matter how far you are." Seeing my astonishment, he went on to say, "The world you experience is completely different from mine. For example, did you know irony is a color?"

The question threw me completely into left field. "No, I didn't."

"Well, now you do. It's an iridescent tone too faint for humans to see, yet it's all around you. So, why are you crying?"

"I'm not talking to you, and could you change into something else please?"

"I think it's better I stay like this in case someone walks in. This way you can talk to Mia without talking to Mia, you know? I'm sure it's killing you keeping this secret from her."

This guy was too observant for his own good. Then again, stalkers were pretty thorough. But why did he care if I suffered when he was the cause of most of it?

He sat across from me on the bench and flipped back long dark hair, a gesture Mia made frequently. "Come on, girl, talk. What's eating at you?" He blew a bubble the size of his head before it popped.

"Just go away!" I slid to the edge of the bench.

He sucked the deflated bubble into his mouth. "Can't. You're hurting. It's not healthy for you to starve yourself. That's how accidents happen and dead bodies appear."

"Which is why I can't feed here. Lilith's out of control."

"She is who she is," he crooned in a haughty, I-told-you-so way. "You're the one trying to make her go against her nature. Nadine tried to leash her, but the spirit prevails eventually."

I shook my head, trying to reject his words, no matter how true they might be.

"Have lunch with me. I'll take you someplace safe where you can relax."

I cowered away from his outstretched hand. "I don't think so."

"You think too much. This isn't about you. Come on."

"I'm not going anywhere with . . ." was the last thing I remembered saying before a hand shook me awake.

It was barely a second in time, not even a full blink, and everything changed without natural transition. Shaking the cobwebs from my brain, I took in the new scenery, which didn't resemble the girls' locker room at all.

I was in a truck, Malik's new truck—telling by how high we sat from the ground—and parked under a canopy of trees. Beyond the trees lay a row of small colonial houses bordered by white picket fences. A horse and carriage trotted along the dirt road, and I briefly wondered if I had traveled back in time. Much like the grocery store incident, it took a minute to get my bearings.

Without conscious effort, I now sat in Merchants Square, the heart of Colonial Williamsburg, the place where bonnets and buckled shoes were considered casual wear all year round. But knowing my location didn't explain how I got there, or how I had changed back into my school clothes.

A low, velvety voice spoke close to my ear, too intimate for my comfort. "Come on, sleepyhead. We're here."

I lifted my head to Tobias, in his natural state, smiling from the driver's seat. His hair fell around his face in a soft, wavy curtain, daring me to touch it.

Fighting the urge, I asked, "What's going on?"

"We're having lunch."

"No, no, no. How did I get out of school? How did I get dressed? Did you drug me?"

He looked as calm and reserved as a doctor would while diagnosing a patient. "You have an overactive imagination. You daydream a lot; you let your mind wander to the point where you lose track of time. It's kinda cute, but I don't recommend you doing that while hungry. You're weak and Lilith can easily take over if she feels the need. So here we are."

Take over? Like possessed? Granted, she was a spirit, but to actually become possessed, to do things unaware, scared the hell out of me. I had endured that out-of-body experience before, but I had been awake for it, cognizant to an extent. This was a full-on blackout, and according to the clock on the dashboard, fifteen minutes of my life were unaccounted for. There's no telling what could've happened.

As if hearing my internal debate, Tobias affirmed, "Nothing happened. Although I'll admit, you're far more agreeable when unconscious."

What was that? The sex offender's anthem? I scooted closer to my door.

"Let me give you a demon lesson. Incubi have the power of suggestion, seduction. We tempt weak humans into making the willing decision to surrender, but we ourselves can't do it by force, especially if they're pure. Think about it. If all we had to do was jump a woman in a dark alley, then what would be the point of our draw, or our beauty? No one, not even our victims can say we forced them to do anything. It's a bit poetic in that regard—forbidden fruit and all that. Humanity is all about choice, good or bad. We simply tip the scales in our favor."

I took a small sigh of relief, but it was short-lived. "Does this apply to Cambions?"

"Cambions are primarily human, so yes. I may have Lilith's vote, but she has no say in the final verdict. It's your body, your free will. Your purity makes you a bit more resistant to my influence, but Lilith isn't as squeaky clean as you are. There's the rub. As long as that purity remains, not even Lilith can override it. Won't stop her from trying, though." He smiled.

I nodded and processed the new data. In the beginning, I'd gotten upset over how Cambions could sniff out a virgin in a crowded room, but my purity had saved me from a few scrapes in the past and was still going strong. As a Cambion, I now knew what they saw, that bright ring around the body while more experienced auras looked dim by comparison.

"Come on, let's eat." He climbed out of the car and went to my side to open the door.

I looked to the dirt path leading to the street, then looked back to him. "I—I can't."

"Sure you can. Feeding in crowds is safer than feeding directly. You need this, so come on." He caught my waist and hefted me out of the truck like I was a toddler. And much like a toddler, I kicked and squirmed while he carried me to a bench in front of the souvenir shop.

Setting me down, he leaned over me with a finger pointed in my face. "Sit and absorb."

Confident that I couldn't outrun him, he sat next to me and observed the square. My plot to escape faded once I locked eyes on the parade of tourists and locals. The heavy tourist rush was over, but charters and yellow school buses crammed the parking lot. The dry, chilly air carried smoke from wood stoves and the musky stench from where horses had left their business in the street.

Historical homes, taverns, boutiques, and apathetic livestock lined this one-mile strip of brick and cobblestone. Signs written in colonial language hung from iron hinges. Happy couples walked hand in hand, taking in the sights. Actors with cloaks and oil lanterns retold the tribulations of eighteenth-century living from firsthand experience. An elementary class huddled close, while their chaperones instructed them to stay with the group.

I'd never had a thing for children—my siblings had killed all enthusiasm—but now I was able to see them in a different light. And what light! Their laughter carried a tune of wind chimes in the breeze; their energy danced in the air like pollen. With my eyes closed, I breathed it in, gorging my lungs and spirit with nourishment.

We sat there for almost an hour, watching people come

and go, the centuries tangled together in cultural harmony. The distance made it difficult to pull the energy in, similar to sucking a thick milkshake through a straw. Our reward was worth the extra effort and damn if it didn't feel good going down.

Moaning in satisfaction, he asked, "Feeling better?"

"A bit." I threw my head back and let the sunlight warm my face. "Why are you being nice to me?"

"I'm a nice guy. When I want something."

At least he was honest. Across the street, a tall blonde girl in a green William and Mary sweatshirt left the college bookstore. My eyes followed her drifting through the crowd in the direction of the campuses a block away. It was weird how the smallest things could trigger memories.

"Why did Nadine try to kill herself?" I asked. Now that my appetite was sated, I could move on to more pressing matters. Lilith's vision bothered me, and Tobias was the only one in a talking mood right now. But he wasn't prepared for that question.

He looked to the candy shop as if the answer lay there. Anger lines altered his profile; his jaw flexed, straining to find the words. "Lilith wanted to be with her mate. Nadine wanted something else, but she couldn't resist me. She tried to end it for good, but the only way to do that is through death. To save the life of her host, Lilith promised to close herself from me. For years, I couldn't find her, I couldn't feel her."

"How does that work?" I asked.

"Why would I tell you that? So you can block me again?" He sniggered. "I don't think so. But that's the reason why Lilith couldn't sense me in town or while we were in class together. That kiss under the bleachers—"

"You mean your oral assault—"

"—was the first time Lilith fed from me since the barrier was created. My energy broke down that wall and now Lilith's getting that ol' feeling again. This is a fresh start. Nadine was a strict master, but Lilith was patient, waiting for a time when Nadine wasn't so depressed and guarded to reach out to me again."

"She was in for a long wait," I scoffed. "Of the years I knew Nadine, I never saw her smile. She was in love with misery."

"She wasn't always like that. She had so much light and optimism and—"

"You corrupted her," I cut in. When he didn't deny it, I asked, "What happened to the guy she was seeing, the married man?"

He caught my accusatory stare. "I didn't kill him if that's what you're implying. She was tired of being the other woman and ended that relationship on her own. Didn't go as well as I would've liked, but I offered her a distraction, a way out."

"A true knight in rusted armor," I derided. "Did you love Nadine, or was it just Lilith you were after?"

"I love *all* women. It's who I am." He grinned, displaying rows of even, white teeth. "Incubi don't love, Samara. We devour, and on those very rare occasions, become devoured. Love is far too light and frilly a word for what we feel. So no, I didn't just *love* Nadine."

My eyes met the ground. Caleb had once said the same thing about Cambions. Must be a universal principle. "If I'm the only thing in your way, then what's holding you back from killing me?"

He reared back as if struck. "Why on earth would I kill you?"

"Lilith will be free, and you can go off and do whatever the hell you creatures do."

He wore a pained expression, not sure how to form the proper response. "Samara, I can't hold something that has no body." Sensing my confusion, he leaned closer. "Lilith is a spirit; she has no life and no body. She uses you as a vessel, and feeds off the life energy you provide."

"Did she ever have a body?" I asked, trying to repel the warmth of his nearness and the smooth bass of his voice.

"No, but her source did many centuries ago. Lilith's ancestor was a full-blooded succubus. When she first possessed a body, she had to relinquish her own, much like shedding off a coat. She didn't return to the body in time, and it decayed, leaving her stuck with the body she now acquired. Passing down the generations through Nadine's bloodline was her means of survival, immortality."

"So demon spirits can leave their bodies at will? That's pretty cool, but why would she do that?"

"Many of our kind do that as a way to multiply our numbers. We can't reproduce in our true form, so we possess a human body and pass on a part of us through their children, hence Cambions. Once the Cambion child reached puberty, their spirit would take over. After attaining enough energy, they would transform into true incubi and succubi. None of us expected the human side to rebel. As a result, hundreds of Cambions and only a handful of incubi."

"You could do that if you wanted," I offered, avoiding his eager stare.

"I'm quite happy where I am, thank you."

"Malik!" a boy called and raced in our direction. He looked no older than eight, wearing baggy jeans, a red sweater, and a huge smile on his face.

I turned to Tobias, who must have transformed into Malik when I wasn't looking. I would never get over the chameleon routine. It threw one's sense of reality off-kilter, and I really didn't need any help on that score.

The boy reached our side and wrapped his arms around Tobias's waist. He was a bite-sized Malik, same dark complexion, haircut, and infectious smile. He would break hearts when he got older and probably had the girls in his class swooning.

"What up, little man? How's your field trip?" Tobias hefted the child in his arms and over his shoulder.

The boy giggled and rambled on a mile a minute. "It's good. We saw the Governor's Palace and horses and people making clothes out of cotton. Oh, guess what? I got picked for bus monitor this week. I get an orange sash and everything."

"Sounds cool. I'm proud of you." Tobias laughed, then waved to the female teacher who hovered nearby.

Settling to the ground, the boy looked up with wide eyes. "You picking me up early?"

"Nope. I got practice at four. I've got the truck today, so Mom will be home when you get there."

"Okay. Who's this girl?" the boy asked with frank curiosity.

"Marcus, this is my friend, Samara. Samara, this is my youngest brother, Marcus."

Struggling to get into character, I extended my hand. "Nice to meet you."

The kid had a killer grip for his age. "Hi. You Malik's new girlfriend?"

"Uh, no. We're just friends," I answered, ignoring Tobias's knowing grin.

Marcus frowned, and I could almost see his young brain churning at high speed. "Oh, okay. But you're a girl."

"You caught that too, huh?"

His stare bounced between his brother and me. "Malik doesn't have girls as friends."

Before I could think of an explanation, Tobias stepped in. "There's a first time for everything. You'll find out when you get older. All right, go back to your class. Don't wanna get you in trouble." Tobias pounded fists with the little man in a series of movements Marcus and Malik had probably practiced a thousand times.

"Okay, deuces." With a lopsided smile, Marcus dashed across the path to join his class.

Pushing back my amusement, I turned to Tobias. "He's adorable."

"He's a handful," Tobias corrected. "He can't keep still for a minute, always running around, talking back to people, tracking dirt all over the floor, bringing weird creatures into the house, and refusing to put his underwear in the hamper. I tell you, children were designed to be cute to keep you from killing them." He took a deep, relaxing breath, then smiled. "But he's bright, extremely smart. Top of his class."

I could relate. My siblings were the incarnation of all things evil, but I loved them just the same. It could've been the way his eyes beamed with fatherly pride or the warmth and joy projecting from his body, but I knew he meant every word. My question was, why? Why the kid, why the family? He'd said his kind could feel everything, but did that include compassion? The subtotal of the real Malik's existence now belonged to Tobias, and it continued to live through him vicariously. Memories were strange things.

"How can you turn personalities off and on like that?" I asked.

"The same way you do." He looked at me and chided, "Oh come on, don't tell me you act the exact same way with your white family as you do with your black side, the way you speak, your whole demeanor."

Again, this guy knew me way too well, and nobody liked being called out like that. I was about to explain, but he cut me off.

"You think Douglas acts like a thug around his parents or their friends at the country club? Doesn't make it any less a part of who he is. We all have a closet with many outfits, and we wear what is appropriate for the occasion."

Tobias certainly did his homework, and it disturbed me how much he knew about me and my friends, internal knowledge that should take years to learn.

"This charade can't last," I argued. "And you'll destroy an entire family with this deceit."

He shoved his hands in his jean pockets and led the way back to the truck. "I'm trying my best to avoid that, Flower. Trust me. They're a very happy family, and that joy is too good to let go."

"I have a name, you know. Why do you keep calling me 'Flower'?"

"Because I want to pluck you." He wagged his eyebrows.

That wasn't even worth a response, so I walked ahead toward the truck. I opened the passenger-side door when a hand pushed it shut again.

Leaning into me, he said, "Tell me, how do you feel when you're with me?"

"Bipolar."

"I'm serious."

"So am I. I live in a nation divided. Lilith desires you with a passion that can only be called psychotic. I can't get involved with you like that. As much as I hate to admit it, I belong with someone else."

If my answer hurt him, he didn't show it. "Sounds like an obligation."

"No more than it was for you and Nadine. Did you feel oppressed, burdened, or enslaved? No, because it was your own will that you were in agreement with. There's a type of freedom to have someone know you so well and love you regardless. I'm sorry for your loss, but I can only offer friendship, at best. It's yours if you want it."

"I'll take anything you give me, Flower." His lips pulled into a kind, easy smile as he helped me into the truck. "For now."

We didn't say much on the way back to school, which was cool with me because I had plenty to think about. This supernatural world was getting bigger, yet I felt more claustrophobic than ever before, and this episode with Lilith made the space even smaller. True, I zoned out and indulged in flights of fancy, but having Lilith play puppeteer was so far out of bounds, I couldn't see the field anymore. How long had this been going on? I definitely needed to have a talk with her when we got home.

Tobias, in his default form, drove in silence with a serene look on his face. So at peace he seemed, like all was right with the world, him behind the wheel and me at his side. What was worse was that I found it hard to dispute that arrangement. Tobias intrigued me. The things he said, his outlook on life, the ages he'd lived, had my mind whirling with questions. I still didn't trust him, but I would love to pick his brain.

I studied his hands on the steering wheel. The burn had healed, with only a fading red stripe across his wrist. My eyes drifted to his face and almost cried at what awaited me. It wasn't beer goggles, or Lilith's unquenched lust, but an undisputed fact for anyone with twenty-twenty vision. The man was *fine*, neither feminine nor masculine, but the best of both. A square, chiseled jaw, ridiculously long lashes, a plump, slightly pert nose, and masterfully carved lips defined sensuality. Not a scar, blemish, or zit in sight, but a smooth stretch of butterscotch skin that my hands burned to touch. I didn't dare look at his body; it would only break my heart.

He pulled into a parking spot and killed the engine before looking at me. As a man with all the time in the world, he waited for me to speak first.

"Um, thanks for lunch, or whatever that was," I muttered.

He bowed his head. "You're welcome. You need to take better care of yourself."

I looked away, dodging his piercing stare. "I appreciate your concern."

"I am concerned," he asserted. "You hold a very important asset and I need to keep it safe and healthy."

Before I could respond, a familiar song intruded into the silence. Though muffled, I knew the theme from *COPS* from anywhere.

"Where's my phone?" I searched around my seat.

Annoyed at the interruption, he hitched his thumb over his shoulder. "Behind your seat, in your book bag."

I reached behind me, grabbed my backpack, and dove inside, all the while cursing Tobias for bringing this burden on my head. I knew what waited on the other end of the phone and expected the harangue headed my way. No doubt she'd checked my location from my bracelet.

I barely put the phone to my ear when the voice on the other end yelled, "*WHERE ARE YOU? WHY AREN'T YOU IN SCHOOL?*"

I pulled the phone from my head, and winced at the blast of fury. I didn't need that right eardrum anyway. "Mom, I'm fine. I'm back at school now and—"

"Why did you leave? You've been gone for almost two hours! Don't you know there's a crazy killer on the loose?"

My eyes strayed to Tobias, who sat with his lips tucked and his chest quaking with laughter. At least one of us found this amusing. Friend or foe, it just wasn't cool to withstand a parental bitch-out in front of people.

"I'm sorry. I didn't mean to make you worry. I—I needed to feed and grab some fresh air. I didn't want to lash out on the kids at school. That would be a whole other problem."

A loud sigh shot through the phone. "Well, you should've called me. It's not safe to wander off. There's no telling what kind of lunatic is tracking you."

I glanced sideways at Tobias again. *You don't know the half,* I wanted to say, but I held my tongue. After several reassurances of my well-being, Mom began to speak in lower octaves.

"You come home after school! You hear me, Samara Nicole?"

I sunk lower in my seat. "Yes, Mom."

"I mean it! We need to talk."

"Okay." I hung up and stared out the window, not wanting to see the humor—or worse, pity—in Tobias's eyes. It was all his fault anyway.

"I'm sorry if I got you in trouble. I was only trying to help."

"Yeah, well, 'there is nothing either good or bad, but thinking makes it so.' "

He smiled and nodded in approval. "*Hamlet.* Nice."

He even found my random medieval speak amusing.

Disgusted, I climbed out of the truck and slammed the door.

By the time he caught up with me, he'd changed back into Malik, and I wondered why he didn't just stay that way. Maybe there was a time limit to shape shifting, but more than likely, he wanted to show off his mad skills.

He kept my pace as we passed through the back entrance to the empty cafeteria. "Your mom cares about you a lot," he said.

"Maybe too much." I pushed through the double doors leading to the main corridor.

"Are you angry with me?"

"When am I *not* angry with you?"

"Well, you haven't sprayed me with oil today, so I think we're making progress. Anyway, I don't think it would be a good idea for her to know about me. In fact, I highly suggest that you don't tell her."

I stopped in the middle of the hall and looked up at him. "She already knows what I am."

"But she doesn't know what I am. I'd like to keep it that way." He closed in on me, forcing me to retreat until my back flushed against the bulletin board.

"It would be safer for her not to get tangled in something so . . . complicated. Now, you promise you won't tell. Keep this between us. No outsiders."

My nod felt more like a twitch, but passed as a sign of compliance, at least enough to gain back my personal space. Subtlety was not his strong suit and his sudden "concern" for my family's well-being was a page right out the villain handbook, one of those don't-let-this-happen-to-you sermons Mom went on about.

Behind the creepy delivery, Tobias presented a good point. Mom had enough on her plate. She was one step away from a nervous breakdown, and this would only add to her sleep deficit. This was my dragon I had to slay, not hers, and I couldn't hide behind her skirt forever. On this one occasion, silence was golden.

I returned to class with my mission in my sights. I knew what I had to do for the sake of everyone, and for my own peace of mind.

17

"Hey, guess what, there's an incubus in town disguised as my classmate and he wants to bond with me and murder Caleb—true story," I blurted out.

Not smooth by any stretch of the imagination, but it was the quickest way to remove this Band-Aid.

There was silence on the other end of the phone, as I'd expected. I treaded the floor of my bedroom, waiting for Angie to find her voice. Our weeklong game of phone tag had ended when I finally caught her before she went to bed. She currently stayed in Amsterdam, procuring local artwork and God knows what else. As a second mother, Angie seemed more laid-back and equipped to handle supernatural drama than my mom.

Finally, she spoke. "Are you sure it's a real incubus?"

"Yup," I drawled, tapping my fingers against the first volume of her journal.

"How long has he been in town?"

I summed up the past month, leaving nothing out. She remained so quiet that I thought she had either fainted or hightailed it to the airport. Her stilted breathing alerted me that she was still on the line; her voice cracked under what I assumed was awe and fear.

"How long have you had these trances? Do they last long? You may need to see a doctor about that. Not all daydreams are innocent; it may be a symptom of absence seizures."

"Seizures? Like epilepsy?"

"Not as bad, but it can be if not treated."

"Tobias said that as long as I feed, Lilith won't try to take over."

"I agree. Our spirits don't become aggressive to us unless we don't feed. Or . . ." she paused.

"Or what?"

"Or when they need to mate."

I swallowed hard. "So, Tobias's presence is triggering this?"

"I have no doubt, but I believe it started long before Tobias. Have you zoned out around Caleb?"

I winced. "Sometimes."

"Samara, this is a very precarious stage in a Cambion's life. You're new to this and unprepared for the changes that are occurring in your body."

My upper lip curled. "Uh, Angie, I've already had this talk with Mom when I was like five and I still have nightmares from it, so—"

"I'm not just talking about puberty, but the changes with your spirit," she interrupted. "Adolescence is a very delicate time in a human's life. Your thought patterns and hormones are erratic and you're more susceptible to everything, especially the influence of a demon. This is a perfect time for your spirit to take over. Nadine already endured the changes, but this is a new body, and you have to suffer through the phase. Lilith is going into heat, she wants to feed and mate. Simple as that."

"I don't get it. Why is she acting this way now? I thought she loved Capone."

"Welcome to the animal kingdom, little one. This is also why Cambion males and females keep away from each other; the attraction is at its strongest at your age. Lilith desires a mate, and whoever is strong enough to claim her will win. She came to Capone because he was the only option, but now he has a competitor. The demand will drive you crazy, but you must appease her, so I suggest you increase your intake of energy until it passes, but not too much. That is, unless you wish to bond with Caleb." The statement hung in the air in anticipation.

"Uh, well, I . . ." This was awkward. I didn't want to talk about this with Angie. That invisible wall between parents and children existed for a reason.

"I never knew Nadine had a mate. She never told anyone. But she kept a lot of things private in her later years," Angie supplied.

"Did you know that she tried to kill herself?"

The dead air that occupied the line hurt my ears.

"I'm aware." Angie cleared her throat. "That was a dark time in her life that she dared not to repeat. Do you know why the bracelet was so important to her, why she never took it off?"

I looked down to the object in question on my wrist. "For her protection? In case she got kidnapped?" I guessed.

Angie laughed softly. "Hardly. This is my daughter we're talking about here. While it held that purpose, it was also a reminder to her promise. Every day, I would monitor the signal from her bracelet. Each motion vowed that she would never leave me by her own volition; that her love for me was stronger than her need to die."

Silence fell between us again, and though she spoke from thousands of miles away, her pain couldn't have felt any closer if we shared the same body. Blood may be thicker than water, but Cambion ties outlived the flesh.

Moving to a less depressing subject, I opened the journal and flipped to the page I'd bookmarked. "There's an entry about one of your ancestors who met an incubus. Going by this, the incubus can only bond with succubi or Cambion females. Since the Cambion is mortal, he'll share the life expectancy of his mate, and live for as long as *she* does. He may keep all his powers, but if his mate dies, so will he."

"That's sounds about right. Cambions intertwine the same way; their lives are each other's."

"There's no way to reverse it?"

"As you know, if a Cambion consumes enough life energy, takes enough lives at once, he becomes a full demon, becoming immortal. If his mate undergoes the transition, he might regain his immortality. This is theory, of course. I wish I could be more help, but I'm afraid my experience with incubi are limited."

"No, no. It's okay, it's a good theory; it explains a lot." I trailed off, my mind busy analyzing this new discovery.

If the accounts were true, then that meant Tobias should've died with Nadine. I'd known this beforehand, understood it, but hadn't quite grasped its significance until now. Lilith was keeping him alive. Similar to my connection with Caleb, I was his lifeline, but I was certain Tobias wouldn't allow me to die of old age. To be fair, what was a measly eighty-odd years to an immortal?

"Are you sure you don't want me to come to Virginia? I can be there in ten hours." Her urgent tone reclaimed my attention.

The thought of Angie swooping down and declaring war on my town made me cringe, but it was good to know she had my back in case shit went down. "No, it's okay. I just wanted you to know what's going on. I can't really tell Mom."

"You need to tell her soon. She has to be warned. Have you protected the house?"

"Yeah. I put oil over the cars too. I don't think Tobias would hurt my family. He's trying to get into my good graces."

"Be careful, he just might. Incubi are charming and irresistible, even to us. Remember that. But also remember that you have a sentient in your body. Above anything else, Lilith's vessel is her top priority. Nothing will invade her home without your consent. Don't let her take over. You will choose your mate, not her."

After another thirty-minute pep talk, Angie promised to drop by for Thanksgiving, but I wasn't banking on it. She had a family of her own, a husband, a son, and two other Cambion daughters to look after, and I didn't want her abandoning them to deal with my issues. At some point, I'd have to see her soon, for the connection with Lilith demanded that she reunite with her source occasionally.

I stretched across my bed and looked over Angie's journal, hungry for more words of wisdom from the past. The Petrovskys were the oldest and most esteemed Cambions in existence, springing those under their dominion into action by a single word. These entries not only followed the Petrovsky bloodline, but listed over fifty Cambion clans, stretching across East Asia, Europe, North Africa, and South America. Three major families lived in the United States alone, including a powerful family who ran the entire East Coast.

These chronicles also served as a Cambion rulebook, establishing codes of conduct far different from those of the outside world. One particular law brought a chill to my spine, ringing truth to Tobias's conviction. Killing your own kind was a big no-no in this dark society, and Angie would have been well within her rights to put Caleb and his brothers to death for their negligence.

Not only had they been spared, but they'd been adopted as extended members of Angie's dynasty. Caleb's family was beyond broken, with a fallen patriarch and a tarnished reputation. Bonding with Caleb would connect the families permanently, granting security and prestige. I just wasn't ready for that kind of power play, and I refused to be pressured into anything, no matter how sweet the temptation.

Thinking of Caleb reminded me that I hadn't harassed Haden and Michael for a good twelve hours, and I was overdue. I grabbed my phone again and bombarded the brothers with a new round of texts. Michael must've been bored keeping watch, because for the past week, he'd been dressing Caleb up and sent pictures of him to everyone he knew. Today's uploaded image included that blond elf wig, a pink bra (no doubt borrowed from one of the nurses), and bright blue eye shadow. Michael was one sick puppy, but he helped take the edge off of waiting for the unknown.

Caleb still showed no improvement and I knew he needed more energy from me. I could almost hear him crying out, dragging through the wasteland for one drop of water, but for his own safety, the energy from his brothers would have to make do until I figured something out.

The ring of the doorbell shot me to attention. I raced downstairs and peeked through the front window to find the last man I wanted to see. At first, I didn't recognize him due to his casual attire and the pleasant look on his face. David Ruiz paced back and forth on the front deck, appearing out of breath and out of time.

I pressed my back against the door and asked in a deep man voice, "What do you want?"

"Hello, Samara," he greeted cheerfully. "Nice to see you again. Is your mother here?"

So much for disguising my voice. "She ain't here." I moved to the dining room window and opened the pane by an inch. "I'm not allowed to have company inside the house while she's out." It wasn't a total lie, but he didn't need to know that. And where was Mom? She should've been home from work by now.

"She told me to meet her. She wanted to discuss a few things over dinner. I'm surprised she didn't tell you." He pulled a cell phone from the inner pocket of his blazer and began to dial. He waited a beat before he smiled at the voice on the other end.

"Hi, Julie. I'm at your house, but where are you?"

Julie? Had I missed something?

"Yeah. . . . Okay, that's fine. I can wait. . . . No, no trouble at all. . . . All right, hold on." He bent down and slid the phone through the crack in the window. "She wants to talk to you."

I put the phone to my ear and waited for Mom to tell me whether she'd lost her mind. Clearly she had—she ordered me to allow him inside to wait for her. Too distracted with chewing me out for ditching class, she'd forgotten to tell me that she'd invited him for dinner. She was running late at the office and would be home in fifteen minutes, and that was sixteen minutes too long for me.

I closed my eyes and called on the forces of the universe to get through this meeting. I had to act normal and not give away anything that might make him suspicious. A difficult feat, seeing as the man was a six-foot-tall accusation.

Cursing under my breath, I balanced my shoulders and opened the door. "Come on in." I handed him his phone.

"Thank you. I didn't mean to inconvenience you."

"Not at all," I assured behind a plastic smile. "You can wait in the living room."

"You have a very nice home." He strolled around the sitting area, perusing the knickknacks and figurines placed around the room.

I stood by the entryway with my arms folded, not daring to cross the threshold. "Thank you."

"You can relax, Samara. I'm off duty." He stopped in front of the fireplace and picked up a picture of me. "This is adorable. How old were you?"

I studied the photograph from where I stood. "Ten. It was Easter at my nana's house."

"Hmm. You shouldn't hide your natural eye color. You're prettier without contacts." His dark stare had a hardness to it, not quite human, but more of an android on a search-and-destroy mission.

I shrugged. "It's just a phase, I guess."

He returned the picture, then picked up another. "A sentimental gesture, I suppose. Because Nadine Petrovsky had green eyes as well, a very unusual shade, very clear and prismatic." He offered a plaintive smile. "I'm sorry. The pictures in her file are very precise, and the color is a very hard thing to forget—so vivid."

"Right . . ." I drew out the word.

"Tell me, how have you handled the grieving process? I'm sure it must be hard for you living within the same room the murder took place. Have you spoken to any grief counselors?" He stepped near the couch in the exact place where Nadine had taken her last breath, as if an X marked the spot for him to stand and mock me.

"No. I'm fine, although my mom is going to a group." I watched his feet, clad in Italian leather, tread over my friend's splayed arm and hair. The sofa hid the rest of her, so I was spared from seeing her face, her brows furrowing in pain at the foot crushing her hand.

Get off of her! Can't you see her laying there? Move! I wanted to say, but it would only prove what I already knew, what my parents feared, and what Ruiz probably suspected.

I was losing it. Fast.

Silence dominated the room. The seconds crawled along as we faced each other like a pair of gunslingers. Sweat beaded my forehead as the man began to take on a skewed, funhouse mirror impression. I looked around the sitting area, noting how the furniture seemed to look flat as cutouts in a pop-up book. Whether it was the room or my own disorder, I had to get out of there.

Remembering my manners, I turned around and asked, "Did you want something to drink?"

"Sure. What you got?"

I counted the list of options on my fingers. "Water, iced tea, soda, purple stuff, Sunny D."

"Tea would be nice, thank you." Still holding my picture, he took a seat.

My hands shook as I wiped the clamminess from my palms. I waited until I was in the privacy of the kitchen before I freaked out. What was I going to do? And what was taking Mom so long? This guy wasn't going to let the subject drop, and sitting at the scene of the crime didn't help my neurosis at all. Taking long, measured breaths, I wiped the tears from my eyes. While pouring the man his tea, something moved to my left. As if my day could get any worse, Tobias loomed at my back door in a cloud of bad karma.

I opened the door and lo and behold, my nemesis stood there looking good enough to eat, in a gray turtleneck sweater and designer jeans.

He leaned against the doorjamb and struck a pose. "What's wrong?"

"What are you doing here?"

"You're upset, and for once it's not my fault. I had to see why."

My gaze dropped to my sneakers. "I'm not upset."

"Again. Tears. Thunder. Loud. Annoying. So why are you upset? Better yet, what's Magnum P.I. doing in your house?"

"The second that becomes your business, you'll be the first to know," I replied.

"You know he's been following you for about a week now, right?"

"And you would know that how?"

"Because I've been following you, too," he answered with such coolness, as if violating a girl's privacy were part of a balanced diet.

"Well, at least now I know to request a restraining order." I tried to shut the door, but he held out his hand.

"I don't trust that guy. There's something off about him." Tobias craned his neck to see behind me. "He makes you uncomfortable as well—I can feel it. Why is he here?"

"He's still investigating Nadine's murder."

"I thought it was open and shut."

I shrugged. "Apparently not."

He frowned. "Let me talk to him."

"What? No. I'll handle this."

"Come on, Flower, I can get through his wall better than you can. I'm telling you, this guy is crooked somehow. He knows something, and I don't want him alone with you. Let me in."

I didn't want to be alone with Ruiz, either. Just the thought of going back into the living room made me throw up a little in my mouth. However, with Tobias here, my stomach churned for a different reason of which I didn't care to explore. I didn't own the courage to do this alone and Tobias, in his sick, self-centered way, was willing to help.

"Fine. Come in." Knowing this would come back to bite me later, I stepped back from the door and waited.

He studied the four sides of the doorframe, then took a deep breath. "There's oil on the threshold. I can't come in."

"But I just invited you in."

His eyes slowly rolled up to meet mine. "Wrong folklore, sweetheart. I need to cover the oil. Good thing I came prepared." He reached in his pocket and pulled out a Ziploc bag full of powder. "Here, pour some of this over the door."

Taking the bag from him, I examined the strange gray dust. "What is it?"

"It's a neutralizer that will counteract the oil. Now pour it down."

I did as instructed and spread it around evenly with my foot. Once done, Tobias placed one foot over the border, testing the area, then stepped inside. He sighed in relief, loosened his limbs, and cracked his neck. "Okay, where is he?"

"In the living room. Are you going in there like that?"

"Don't worry about me. You just make yourself scarce. You giving him that glass of tea?"

"Oh yeah." I reached out and grabbed the glass. When I turned around, I nearly screamed. Tobias had morphed again, in one of the most disturbing transformations yet. Precise from head to toe stood an exact duplicate of myself, right down to the outfit.

He took the glass from me. "If you want to listen, keep out of sight."

I just watched, dumbstruck, as he left the kitchen. No

mirror could capture the full detail of seeing yourself, and I had to pull my eyes away. This reflection moved independently and allowed me to take in the full dimensions of its form. However, from this angle, my butt wasn't as flat as I'd suspected.

This whole body-swap thing turned out to be a bad idea, and why I'd gone along with it was beyond me. I didn't know what bothered me more, that I had allowed an incubus in my house and let him impersonate me, or the fact that my mom couldn't tell the difference. One hug from Tobias had her grinning, all stupid and weak at the knees. He would make a fortune as an actor, because he rendered my smile, my hand gestures, and the inflections in my speech with haunting accuracy.

The party moved to the kitchen, where Mom unloaded groceries and prepared for dinner. As my life played out before my eyes, I hid from sight, a tricky exercise while trying to eavesdrop. If Mom wasn't zipping around the kitchen, Ruiz kept leaving the room to answer his cell phone every ten minutes. I ducked and hid around corners, mindful of the paradox of time travel: The past and the present can never meet and two of the same matter could never occupy the same space.

Of course, Tobias saw me and hid his smile with a cough, ignoring my signals for him to scram. I finally gave up and sat at the top of the stairs, listening to myself talk during the most awkward dinner ever. To add insult to injury, it was Taco Night and Tobias was eating my share.

I was a second away from revealing myself when Tobias stood up from the table. "Excuse me for a minute."

He made his way to me. His eyes, or more accurately, *my* eyes, grew wide with that have-you-lost-your-mind look that was my calling card. "What is wrong with you? You could've exposed the both of us."

"I can take it from here. Thanks." I tipped my head in the direction of the door.

"It was just getting good."

"Well, it's always good to leave a party early. Now get lost."

He eased me toward the kitchen, out of view of the dining room. Leaning in, he whispered, "I pulled some of his energy, but his memories are under lock and key."

"What does that mean?"

"He's blocking me. Takes years of practice to be able to do that. Which means he knows about us. He knows what we—correction, *what you*—are."

"What?" This was just great. "What do we do?"

"I don't know, but it's your problem now." He moved to the back door.

I pulled his arm. "Wait."

He turned to me with humor. "Stay, go, come in, get out. You really know how to play with a guy's head."

"What should I do?"

The smile melted from his face as he caught the fear on mine. "For one thing, act normal and stop looking guilty. You haven't done anything wrong."

Wow. That's a big help. Staring myself in the face didn't improve my mental health, either. Under closer inspection, I caught him peeking behind the eyes, making the color appear more hazel than green. "Yeah, great. You can go now."

My doppelganger grew an extra foot and a half and lightened in complexion. If I'd blinked, I'd have missed the morphing process. Tobias, in his cruel deliciousness, backed away toward the door with his bottom lip poked out. "Aw, so soon."

He wasn't moving fast enough for me, so I pushed his chest to help him along. "Get out and take your fairy dust with you." I handed over his personal effects, then snatched it back. "What is this powder anyway? Is it magic?"

"It's not magic nor powder. It's ash."

Holding the bag to the light, I examined it closely. "Ash? Like from a fireplace?"

"Something like that."

I didn't like the sound of that. Knowing I would regret it, I asked, "Where did you get it?"

He hesitated for a moment before saying, "Remember in the cafeteria, I told you I spent the night with a widow after I left your house?"

I struggled to recall. "Yeah. You slept with her and made her believe that you were her dead—OH MY GOD! These are her husband's ashes!" I dropped the bag on the floor and wiped my hands on my jeans.

This wasn't real. There was no way this guy had brought dead remains into my house. No one was that sick. For a moment there, I forgot who I was talking to.

"That's the only thing that could break the barrier. Your oil sanctified the entire house. I had to desecrate the dwelling to enter."

"With a dead guy?" I asked while trying to keep my voice down.

Snickering, he picked up the bag and tucked it in his pocket. "It's not a corpse, Samara. It's just the ashes."

My body shook in disgust, fighting the urge to cold-cock this dude straight in his grill. I'd seen enough death to last a lifetime, and even Nadine would agree that this was way too morbid. Oh my God, I actually touched it! There's only so much a girl can take, and I stood a breath away from losing my mind or my lunch, whichever came first.

"Get out!" I hissed through my teeth.

He had the nerve, the complete and utter gall, to look upset. "Calm down."

I nearly fell back in a dead faint; blood pounded around my temples. "Calm down? Really? What reason do I have to calm down? My boyfriend is in a coma, my mom's flipping out, my best friend hates me, I'm failing government and trig, I'm being shadowed by the cops, and now I've got dead man crumbs all over my floor. Get. Out!"

He had the inhuman strength to fight me, but he didn't, and one good shove sent him into the chilly night. Just when I was about to shut the door in his face, he said, "Oh, one more thing you might want to know."

"What?" I bit out the word.

"Ruiz has a crush on your mother. Huge. And the feeling is mutual. Good luck defusing that bomb." Whistling, he trotted down the back porch, leaving me stock-still by the door.

18

Welcome to Beat Up on Samara Week in Williamsburg.

First up to bat was Mom, and the lady was a heavy hitter. She didn't overlook the ditching school thing, but whatever charm Tobias had used on her cushioned the blow. Plus, she seemed too starry-eyed and dizzy over Ruiz to ground me. I didn't trust the man and was highly grossed out by their courtship, but I appreciated his help in dodging that bullet.

Mom seemed impressed by my new interest in housecleaning. After dinner, I dumped the ashes outside, buffed the kitchen floor to a shine, painted another coat of oil over both entrances, then soaked my hands in rubbing alcohol for an hour before going to bed.

Once again, Lilith added her two cents, curling, flipping, and practically digging a hole in my back. I didn't know if she was hungry or pining for Tobias, but whatever it was the result was another restless night.

The energy from Tobias made her spoiled, greedy for

more than what I was willing to give. We had both fallen off the wagon as far as food was concerned, and it was up to me to take back the reins and resume control. Tobias was a one-time trip to the buffet for Lilith and a lesson that I would never forget. I just had to get her to agree with me.

Things didn't improve in school. Girls gritted their teeth, sharpened their nails, and cracked their knuckles. Whispers grew louder behind my back. Jason Lao tried to keep the gossip under control, but the web was a lawless terrain with no conscience or master.

Tobias found any excuse to talk to me in the hall, but I kept ducking that fool as if I owed him money. On the day our class pictures returned from the studio, I was forced to look at him, by means of the wallet-size photo that landed on my desk. I peeked over my shoulder and caught Tobias passing out autographed pictures to the rest of his harem.

It didn't surprise me that my photo looked like a criminal mug shot, but Malik's senior picture had me wincing for a different reason. Perhaps it was due to the entire image casting a soft glow like those Glamour Shot photos at the mall. Or it might've been Tobias's dead-on impression of Derek Zoolander's "Blue Steel" pose.

"I know you saw it," he whispered in my ear. "You should have seen your face on Picture Day. It was priceless."

Time went still when he was this close to me, yet the world around me progressed in natural speed. Mr. Frasier went on with his lesson, students took notes and texted under the table, and Mia slumped over her desk, not even trying to stay awake.

"What exactly did I see on Picture Day?" I asked while keeping my eyes to the front of the classroom.

"Something only demon eyes can see. It only happens

in harsh light. No need to lose sleep over it, Flower. We have plenty of time to know each other." His breath, a light flame, licked at my earlobe, neck, and shoulder. I gripped the desk and rode out the wave of heat that reached down to my shoes. Each day, the fire took longer to die down and its burn left me exposed to the elements. I counted the seconds until class ended, not that it would do any good.

I wasn't the only one with problems. I caught Dougie at lunch, hoping to get friendly advice, but got another earful of heartache. His new plaything had decided to change schools, and he suspected Mia's harassment had something to do with the sudden transfer. He seemed to be pressed for time, eating half his food while still in the lunch line.

"Yo, SNM, you better get your friend. I mean it—she's friggin' crazy and I'm done!" he said, grabbing two slices of pizza from the warming pan. "I'm trying to be the bigger person here, 'cause this is just getting dumb. So I go over Mia's house and bang on the door until she talks to me. Next thing I know the door opens, and I get hit upside the head with a can of soup. Soup, Sam, soup."

I scooted closer, trying my best not to laugh. "Was it chicken noodle?"

"No. Cream of mushroom. Could you focus please? Anyway, I'm sick of it. You know how many girls would love to get some of this?" He rolled up his shirtsleeve and flexed his bicep to a rhythmic beat. "Check it out. Pow! Yeah, that's what's up."

I had to admit, it was impressive. I guess wolfing down protein shakes and rolling around on a gym mat with sweaty guys worked wonders.

Dougie took a bite of his pizza and slid his tray down the line. "But girls around here are too scared to approach me now. I gotta step up my game. Enough about me. How's Caleb?" he asked. "Does he know about you and Malik Davis?"

Oh, great. Not this again. "There's nothing going on."

"Sam, I may not be an honor student, but I ain't stupid either." He looked at me with narrowed eyes. "You've been all kinds of shady, don't deny it. We're in the same lunch and you never sit with me. Who does that?"

"I know, I just . . . look, there's a lot going on."

"And we mere mortals are too dumb to understand, right?" he replied. "Because we don't notice all the guys that follow you around, or why you never talk about that girl that died in your house this summer. We're just too stupid to notice how your brown eyes look real fake." He inched closer. "I can see the tiny rim around the whites of your eyes. You never wore contacts before."

I stood frozen in shock. Was my transformation really that obvious, or had I been underestimating my friends? "I'm sorry, Dougie. I wish I could tell you what's going on, but . . ."

"Nah, it's cool. You got your reasons. Just don't get too caught up in the bullshit and forget the people around you, is all." He handed the cashier a crumpled five, then turned to me. With a mouth full of greasy cheese and crust, he said, "Listen, I gotta go. I need to meet the coach before lunch is over." He snatched up his half-empty tray, and in a moment, he was gone.

That afternoon, my report card came in the mail, confirming that I was, in fact, failing government and trig. Not wanting to be left out of this communal stoning, Dad rolled up and threatened to hold my new car for ransom.

"It seems only fair that since you no longer want to attend Howard next fall, you won't be needing the car I spent my hard-earned money on." Dad treaded the kitchen floor, clutching a copy of my transcript, which Mom had faxed to his office. Snitch.

Mom usually played "good cop" during these interrogations, but she was slacking on the job big time. She was parked in front of her laptop, chatting with her new squeeze about live ammo. Only Mom would agree to a date at the gun range and find it sexy.

"Don't argue with your father, sweetie" was all she offered to the conversation.

Knowing I was on my own, I tried to reason. "Daddy—"

"Don't 'Daddy' me!" he barked. "You know how important education is. You're ruining any chance of a future running around behind some boy."

I almost fell out of my stool. "Whoa! How can Caleb be a bad influence while in a coma?"

"You spend all your free time with him and it's interfering with your schoolwork."

This debate was going nowhere, so I cut my losses and did damage control. "I'm sorry you feel that way, but unlike Caleb, at least I'm awake to apologize. I don't know if he will ever open his eyes again. Besides, I haven't been to the hospital in a week!"

Whatever he was about to say had been cut off and he lost all his steam. "Samara, I know how you feel about him, but take a moment to see things from where I'm standing. I just wish . . . I . . . Just talk to me, baby girl." He wore that look again, that confused mask of unfamiliarity, struggling to match the face with the name. The longer he stared at me, the sicker I felt.

"I don't know what to say. I'm still trying to adjust to everything." I shook my head and swallowed down what I really wanted to say. "I can take a makeup exam and do some extra credit. I have until Christmas break to pull my grades up."

He knew I was hiding something, but didn't say a word, and it was almost a blessing when he left. I could hear his heart breaking, see the fumes of frustration and helplessness waft off his skin. That defeated look hurt worse than any possible slap or strike with a belt, and I bore every lash in silence.

Thinking I would get a break from my troubles, I pranced to work on Saturday. All merriment flew out the window when the store manager called me into her office. I knew I wasn't employee of the month, given all the sick leave, but I didn't expect Linda to whip out a chainsaw on my work schedule. She assured me that it was just until the Christmas run began, but I wasn't getting my hopes up.

Alicia gave me the cold shoulder during our shift. Between busy rushes, she kept herself occupied with odd tasks and rereading the latest edition of *Specter*. From what little I got from her, she believed the rumors of Malik and my romantic tryst, and was ready to stamp a scarlet A on my forehead. I had never known this, but apparently she supported my relationship with Caleb, and held a personal investment in its staying power. I wished I shared her optimism.

I had never felt so lost, so overwrought, so alone in my life. I craved my Cake Boy. Though only a week had passed since I'd last seen him, it felt like a millennium and each minute lasted a year. I needed to see his face, touch his hair, smell his skin, hear him breathe, just a few crumbs of his presence to keep me going.

The last straw came the day before Thanksgiving break when I caught Mia by her locker. She'd been evasive as ever during class, pretending I didn't exist. When that didn't work, she delivered her famous death-ray glare that turned living objects to stone. I was used to that look from the other students, but getting it from Mia hammered the final nail on my coffin.

"Would you please talk to me?" I begged. "I don't get why you're acting this way."

She loaded books into her locker, not bothering to look at me. "I'm not acting like anything. You're the one who's forgotten who your friends are. I'm curious, how is Caleb doing? Or are you so far up Malik Davis's ass that you forgot about him, too?" She lifted her eyes to a spot behind me.

Tobias stood by the wall, wearing his Malik suit, some faded varsity sweats, and a secretive smirk. He watched attentively as if he could read lips from the thirty-yard gap. It appeared that he could, and he clung to every word and the spaces in between.

"Mia, I'm not cheating on Caleb. I may be a lot of things, but I'm not a cheat. Again, always jumping to the wrong conclusions; no wonder Dougie dumped you." The words just flew out of my mouth, their venom going straight for the heart. I had no idea where they had come from, but as soon as they reached daylight, it was a wrap.

Mia slammed her locker, the noise drawing an audience. With one hand on her hip, she crowded my space and unleashed the dragon. "Look, I understand you've become male catnip for some inexplicable reason. But in case it escaped your attention, the world doesn't revolve around you. You're not some sacred vessel; you're not God's gift to the world. You're the same girl who snorted a packet of ramen seasoning in eighth grade on a dare, so get off your pedestal."

"Mia, I—"

"No, Sam, you forget yourself, but I know you. Don't be that girl who's too caught up in attention to make up her damn mind. If you want Malik, cool, go be with him, but don't string them both along. You're better than that, and I refuse to be another groupie in your fan club."

I stood with my mouth open as she marched up the

hall. Trust Mia to serve it up raw, and the hurt in her eyes told me this had been a long time coming.

I turned, ready to go after her, but stopped on sight of Tobias. He stood against the wall, thoroughly entertained by the spectacle. To add to my disgrace, he lifted a finger to his lips, tracing the tiny dent at the top. His eyes twinkled as he mouthed, *Shh*, before disappearing around the corner.

Only then did I realize how much of my life Lilith had taken, a pendulum swinging to the beat of indecision. Her obsession was making me soft, letting me go quiet into that good night like a punk. If Mom knew that I'd allowed some dude to bully me, I really would be grounded. I had to take Angie's advice and handle business, demonic treaty be damned. This was my house, not Lilith's, and this dance had to end before the music stopped altogether.

19

Thanksgiving wielded a type of magic that comple-mented the ever-changing foliage.

Nature and tradition conspired, performing works deemed impossible, except this time of year. The enchant-ment held healing properties, a warm salve in the form of hugs, laughter, and comfort food. Relatives traveled long distances, arms full of goodies and well wishes.

This was the only occasion where the fridge exceeded its storage capacity, yet everyone starved until that Thurs-day. Even then the torment continued, because no one could enter the kitchen when my nana was throwing down. Equipped with her own ingredients and cookware, Nana toiled over her concoctions, sending thick clouds of pep-pery spice to tease our empty stomachs.

Family members—mostly from my dad's side—rattled the walls with laughter, howls, and clinking silverware. The festivities took place at our home since Nana's house was too small for large parties, Dad lived too far away, and everyone wished Grandpa Marshall would die in a fire. My house became neutral territory where everyone behaved themselves, though not like in the family get-togethers usually seen in movies. The feast itself was much like dinner theater, with a parade of oddball characters who resembled me to some degree.

Dad came by with his wife, Rhonda, and the twins. Prim and proper as she pleased, my stepmother wandered around, forcing small talk behind a tight, condescending smile. I withstood every thinly veiled insult she slung at me, while my brother and sister ransacked my room and terrorized the guests.

When Rhonda wasn't turning her nose up at everyone, she voiced her conspiracy theory on how Mom's parenting skills had caused my "bad juju." The rest of my family didn't discuss my sudden transformation, but Rhonda tried to expose me to anyone who listened. If she only knew just how close her assessment came to the truth, these greetings would be far less hospitable. It took all my willpower not to drain her dry.

David Ruiz made an appearance during dinner, bearing cheesecake and a bouquet of roses for Mom. The next hour was a tense affair, for both the investigator and investigated. Dad shifted in his chair, gritting hard at Mom's new companion. A few of my uncles cleared the room for fear of Ruiz digging into their shady pasts. The women circled around the detective, crooning at his northern accent and forgetting that their men were in the house.

I still didn't know Ruiz's motives, but he made Mom happy. Most of all, he wasn't a Cambion or any facsimile thereof, which was a plus in my book. Mom was a cautious woman, and with good reason, but I couldn't help notice how she came alive when Ruiz was around. I wasn't the only one who noticed and Dad got all in his business, making such a stink that Rhonda pulled him aside to have a "talk."

After the big meal, the guest list dwindled in size and I could now see the floor and the trash left behind. Children ran everywhere, women gossiped in the kitchen, and the men gathered in the living room, screaming to the television at the missed touchdown. Everywhere I looked, people lounged around like beach seals, giving in to the drugging effects of the Itis.

> *Itis [i-tus] noun*
> *A chemical reaction when too much blood rushes to the stomach in order to help digest large quantities of food. Symptoms occur frequently during holidays and gatherings that involve pork, poultry, or Chinese takeout. Symptoms include: light-headedness, fatigue, laziness, indigestion, bloating, sudden weight gain, and a propensity to repeat the gorging cycle an hour later.*

I sat on the other side of the kitchen island as I had done every year since I was five, watching the best entertainment in town. My legs swung under the stool while I listened to the women gossip and talk smack about the men in their lives.

Things were quiet on the paranormal front. Tobias hadn't made any effort to contact me and if he knew what was good for him, it would stay that way. I didn't want to entertain any negative vibes today. I was surrounded by chaos, warm, loving chaos, and I savored the flavor.

My peace crashed and burned when Mom opened the

door and Haden stepped into the house. My aunts and cousins swooped in to appraise the merchandise. The Ross brothers may be ladies' men, but none of them could handle the wanton females in my family.

Squirming from the throng of pinches and petting, he pulled me to a secluded corner. "Samara, I need you to come with me."

"Why?" I asked with a mouthful of pecan pie.

"Caleb's gone."

I froze mid-chew, unsure if I heard him right. "What do you mean gone?"

"He's not in the hospital. I went to grab a bite to eat. Michael popped out to use his phone for a moment and when we came back, he was gone. Three nurses on duty were taken to the emergency room tonight. Heart complications."

His words, though simple, held deadly connotations pertaining to our kind. A donor experienced stress to the heart and could die if too much energy was taken, and the severity of the news forced me to set down my plate and take action.

"Do you think it was Caleb?" I asked.

"Well, it wasn't us," Haden snipped. "Are you really shocked that he'd go to this extreme? You haven't been around and he's starving for energy. Why did you abandon him when he needed you the most?"

"I didn't abandon him," I said, not wanting to see the resentment on his face.

"Caleb must've taken it that way and decided to take matters into his own hands. I'd assumed this would be the first place he would go, but I guess not. Two possibilities are at play here. If he left on his own, he's running about somewhere, desperate for energy. But if he was taken . . ." The sentence went unfinished, but the words poisoned the air.

I didn't want to think about the possibility of someone abducting him. "Where do you think he is?"

"I don't know. That's why I need you. You can sense where he is, can't you?"

"I'm not sure. I've been out of whack after all that's been going on." I looked around for anyone listening. Good thing Ruiz had left an hour ago—he would've loved to walk in on this conversation.

"I don't mean to ruin your celebration, but this is important. Can you please come with me?"

"All right, but I need to tell my mom." Julie Marshall was a woman of compassion, the defender of the underdog with warm, maternal instincts. Surely, she of all people would understand my plight.

"Absolutely not!" Mom threw her head back and laughed, the red wine swooshing around her goblet. "This is a holiday. You need to be at home."

So much for sympathy. "Mom, Caleb is missing and there's no telling what's happened to him. He needs me."

"If he needs you, then he can come here. And if he's in danger, then you need to call the police."

Okay, this was why parents shouldn't know about otherworldly happenings in their children's lives; they always interfere with lectures about safety.

"Mom, Haden is coming with me. He'll protect me. He just needs me to track where Caleb is, nothing more. When we find out, he'll bring me back." I looked to Haden, who confirmed with a nod.

I saw Mom's resolve wavering and I moved in for the kill, doling out my best sad-puppy face. "Their family is broken, Mom. All they have is each other. Imagine if I was the one missing. You'll know where I am." I waved my bracelet in front of her.

"All right, fine. Keep your cell phone on and call me every hour on the hour, you hear me?" When I nodded, she moved to Haden and caught his chin between her fingers. I knew that wide-eyed, innocent look that turned manic as she devoured her prey.

Her voice tingled with perverse glee as she spoke. "Mr. Ross, you cannot truly comprehend the horror that awaits you should something happen to my daughter. Just know that I'll find you. I have heavy connections, impeccable aim, and my family owns a pig farm in Smithfield. It will not be quick. You get my meaning?"

Haden's Adam's apple bobbed as he gaped at the small woman in front of him. "Yes, ma'am."

"Good," she chirped with a wide smile, then turned to me. "Grab a coat, sweetie. It's chilly out."

"You're one hell of a woman, Ms. Marshall," Haden commented. "You remind me a lot of my own mum."

"Yeah, your father seemed to think so too," Mom replied from over her shoulder, the icy delivery putting Haden in his place. I giggled under my breath, savoring the moment of raw pwn-age.

I gathered my stuff and slinked out the door while Mom distracted the company, namely Dad. As soon as I stepped outside, my body screamed to race back into the warmth of the house. Frost capped over the lawn and on the cars lined around the driveway. Music blared from houses nearby and Christmas lights glittered through the naked trees.

Haden leaned against my car, rubbing his cold hands together. "I took a taxi here, so we'll have to use your car. It's better that I drive so you can concentrate."

I played with the keys in my hand, reluctant to offer up my firstborn to a commoner. "You're fortunate that these are dire circumstances, 'else your impertinence would come at the cost of your head," I said with theatrical flair.

"My car doesn't know you, and we drive on the right side of the road in this country."

"So I hear. Now I see where you got your warm personality," he mused. "Does your family really own a pig farm?"

"That's confidential information, Mr. Ross. If all goes well, you'll never have to find out." I smiled and tossed him my keys.

We cruised down the main strip through this ghost town with its closed shops and vacant parking lots. People were home with loved ones while we drove in the cold in search for the lost. The repetition of the road, black and slick as night waters, held me in a trance.

This thing living inside me, this growing connection, was better than any GPS in existence. In truth, it was more of a wire cable that pulled me in whatever direction Caleb moved. This would've been a handy little tool if it actually worked when I needed it. I centered my thoughts, even stuck my head out of the window to get a better signal, but there was nothing.

Perhaps my connection with Tobias had muted it. That sneaky pest gnawed at the cable's protective covering, splitting some of the wires and scrambling the frequency. I shuddered at the thought. If Tobias had kidnapped Caleb, there was no telling what he would do. Caleb could be in danger and I couldn't find him. Panic grew by the second, and that malignant tumor fed from every negative thought. I had to cut it out before it rotted my brain.

Our phones lit up with calls from Michael and Mom wanting updates, but the news stayed the same by the second hour. Michael combed the area around the hospital and came up empty-handed. He agreed to meet back at my house to compare notes, so Haden decided to end our scavenger hunt for the night. I stared out of my window, watching the sleepy city speed by in long streaks of light. I wouldn't let this get to me. I couldn't.

Confusion, rage, and excruciating hunger filled my senses out of nowhere. It came in waves, making me rock and sway with motion sickness. I'd been too distracted, too preoccupied, to even notice, or maybe the feelings were so familiar I'd mistaken them for my own.

"Turn around!" I ordered.

"What's wrong?" Haden asked with his eyes still glued to the road.

"I feel something. Head toward his place again."

"You sure? We've driven by there twice already."

"I'm positive. Go back," I insisted.

Haden veered to the left shoulder, crossing two lanes and busting a U-ie in the intersection. We doubled back and made our way to Caleb's neighborhood.

The houses in the subdivision displayed a model of suburban life, but they were as coldly artificial as a movie set. As we drove closer, the vibe grew stronger, and hunger like I'd never felt before overwhelmed me. The feeling worsened as we reached his street. The only one who seemed cool with any of this was Lilith.

Haden parked a block away to keep from rousing any suspicion. He killed the engine and turned to me. "You sure he's here?"

I nodded. "I feel him."

He climbed out of the car. "Wait here."

Was he serious? That's how people got killed in horror movies. "Mom said that I'm not to leave your sight. I'm going with you." I jumped out of the car before he could argue.

Strolling up the quiet street toward the walkway, I kept

watch for landmines that might appear within the un-marked terrain. Neither of us knew Caleb's current men-tal state or whether he was alone, so our approach had to be handled delicately. Even more so when we found the front door unlocked. Pushing the door open, Haden and I stared into the dark interior—two kids forced to enter a haunted house on a dare.

"You sure he's here?" Haden asked again, not moving a muscle.

"Yup." Instinctively, I patted the spray bottle of olive oil in my pocket, hoping I wouldn't need to use it tonight.

Haden went inside first and turned on lights as he in-spected each room on the bottom floor. He pulled out his cell phone again and wandered into the kitchen. A few bags lined the hall leading to the stairs, items the brothers had brought with them while they watched over the place in shifts. Old newspapers, junk mail, and empty cereal boxes lay in the green recycling bin by the door.

Caleb's townhouse was spacious with a high ceiling, crown molding, and hardwood floors. However, the li-brary of music piled in every available space distracted the eye. Somewhere within the pillars of vinyl were a couch, an entertainment unit, and an old-school turntable where he mixed his music. Every square inch of the house, each stain, each piece of furniture, told a story. But the deserted atmosphere now reminded me of a tomb, an airtight vault preserving Caleb's treasures.

I smiled at the weird weapon collection mounted on the wall: swords, daggers, crossbows, double-sided axes, all handcrafted in precious metal. My eyes fell on the longbow he'd used on Halloween, a time as ancient as when the weapon had been in fashion. It felt like ages ago, a waning dream I strained to recall, and this artifact produced memories of a past life.

A noise came from the second floor, creaking floor-boards above. Haden was still in the kitchen, likely raiding the fridge.

I couldn't trust my eyes or my own judgment, so I asked Lilith, "Is Caleb here?"

She hummed and danced up my torso, a similar reaction to the one she had whenever she fed from Capone. The image of Caleb's face smiling down at me appeared behind my eyes. The feeling put me at ease for a moment and supplied me with enough nerve to proceed.

I crept up the stairs and inched toward the first room on the left. A light issued from under the door, an eerie glow that seemed to be the basis of every ghost story. Purple shafts of light speared through the cracks, putting me in the mindset of alien abductions and little green men. The noise that followed made the impression worse.

Babysitting my brother and sister had introduced me to that particular sound, the nimble pitter-patter of racing feet on the floor above. But there was no floor above, not even an attic space where a bird or squirrel could escape the cold.

I sucked in a deep breath, gathering both air and courage before opening the door. No sooner than I turned the knob, the brightness disappeared, casting me into darkness, save the soft light pouring from the window. My hand fished around the walls for a light switch, and found one that didn't work. The same was true for the light in the hall and the bathroom, but those on the bottom level guided my way up until this point. It could've been a short circuit or some other valid explanation, but paranoia ensured that logic had no business in this house.

I'd scarcely seen Caleb's room, and truth be told, I wasn't missing much. A dresser, two nightstands, and a wooden sleigh bed filled the space between the bare white walls. I tried my luck on the lamp on the small table and struck out, which forced me to rely on night vision. A ripped hospital gown, blackened with dirt, was slung over the footboard. I fingered the soiled material and noted how the body heat still lingered.

Muddy footprints on the carpet led me to the other side of the bed, ending in front of the window. Jumping out at the last minute would've been impossible, if the latch locking the closed sill was any indication. Unless he could dissolve through glass all of a sudden, this was a dead end. Nothing stirred outside, yet movement and activity hummed around me. He was here, but where? And why was he hiding?

"Caleb," I called to what appeared to be open air.

I studied the footprints again and noticed more trailing up the walls. The heel and toe marks pointed upward, creating a walking pattern that defied gravity and reason. I followed the tracks, which faded upon reaching the ceiling.

"Didn't take you too long to find me," he said. "It's not safe for you to be here."

His voice left a delayed echo in the room, bouncing from one wall to the other. The light from the window didn't reach as far as I'd hoped, barely outlining edges of furniture. My eyes dragged across the dresser, the bed, the window, to a man squatting in the corner by the closet.

Perhaps squatting was not the right description, seeing as his feet by no means touched the floor. Instead, he perched catty-corner to the wall like a large bird; his head mere inches from the ceiling. His relaxed position told me he'd hung up there the entire time, watching me wade through the dark as an owl would a juicy rodent.

I should've been out of the house and halfway home by

now. I should've raced downstairs, told Haden to pry his brother off the ceiling, gotten in my car, and dipped. But I couldn't take a step until I saw his face.

"Caleb?" I whispered.

The purple nimbus returned, operating as a searchlight sweeping up and down my body. Those high beams radiated the room, obscuring his face and blinding me in the process. Never before had I seen his eyes so bright and alive, not even while angry, but it removed all suspicion of disguise. Though Tobias could impersonate any human on earth, he could never replicate that signature glow.

"How did you get up there?"

"I climbed up here," he stated matter-of-factly, the words coming out in stereo around the room.

"Why did you leave the hospital?"

"Excuse me for not wanting to die in a hospital gown. If I'm gonna go, it'll be at home with some decent clothes." He pointed to his jeans and thermal undershirt.

His dirty, scabby feet flushed to the wall as if a nail pinned them there. He didn't appear to be in pain, and barely seemed to be aware of anything but me.

"You blame him for Nadine's death. Don't deny it! I felt the hate in you—I could taste it. I can still taste it, bitter like spoiled milk. Just know if I go, you're coming with me."

"What are you talking about? I didn't come after you. I haven't seen you in a week." My mind raced, seeking meaning behind his words and the situation at hand. "Did someone attack you in the hospital? Is that why you left?" I took another step. "Caleb, are you all right?"

He didn't answer but his eyes drifted around the room, looking for something in the shadows. "That noise! I can hear you, you sad little puppy. You think I wanted this? She shouldn't have died that night, but her spirit is mine now. You can't have her! I won't make it easy, I promise you that. Come on, you coward!"

It's hard to evaluate specific thoughts while in a state of shock. But one detail filtered through, screaming louder than the rest: Caleb was scared out of his mind. And that mind, diseased and distressed as it was, had ventured to some dark, nightmarish place that I couldn't follow. His fear was real, but what caused it left me standing stupid.

"What happened to you?" I asked.

"You shouldn't be here when it happens, but he won't come otherwise. He'll follow you to the ends of the Earth if need be." He leapt off the wall, landed on his feet, and stood before me in one collective movement. His stiff, imposing stance threw off his natural posture, a suit that didn't quite fit. Neither did that intense heat shooting from unfamiliar eyes. "But he needn't travel that far. My door is wide open."

I reared back, mostly to avoid the glare of those eyes. It hurt to look directly into them, and they left an inverted image behind my lids when I blinked. What little I could see dropped a weight in the pit of my stomach. Not only had his pupils expanded to the size of quarters, but his irises had taken over the whites of his eyes. They were the eyes of an animal.

Tobias and his costume play had taught me to distrust external appearances, but this was not an outward deception. No, this was Caleb's real body, but as some darker rendition. Though the answer had been staring me in the face since I entered the room, I had to hear it from him. "Who are you?"

His head tilted to the side, studying me as if I were a new species. "Don't you recognize me? After all, you named me."

My body shook from the terror of knowledge; a host of explanations played in my head, countless opportunities that ascribed to this new dilemma. This was what Caleb feared most, the overthrow, the mutinous role reversal between master and subject. No matter the catalyst, the crisis remained.

Capone had been unleashed.

20

I'd always been a fan of horror movies, zombie movies in particular, those scabby, half-dead creatures shuffling toward their next meal.

There's always that scene where one infected person has kept quiet until the last minute and the survivors have to make the crucial decision to kill them. But there comes that moment of pause where the camera zooms in on the actor's expression of disbelief and turmoil before he pulls the trigger.

That's kinda how I felt right now, but far less entertaining. The only difference was I didn't have a gun. I could grab one of Caleb's weapons downstairs, but the fierce light darting from his eyes suggested that I could barely breathe without permission.

He ambled to the nightstand and clicked on the light, which suddenly decided to work from his touch alone. Everything about him and this situation was wrong—from attic to basement, hitting every floor in between.

And just like those people in the movies, I experienced

that moment of pause, frozen beyond shock or denial. Sure, I could fight and scream loud enough for Haden to come up here—where was Haden anyway?—but I couldn't leave by my own will. If a part of Caleb was still here, still alive, then I had to find him. I had to save him, if only from himself.

Capone knelt down and pulled a pair of high-laced boots from under the bed. He bounced on the mattress, slung a leg over his knee, and slid on the footwear in a method of ceremony. He applied heavy concentration to this act, a sacred ritual before going into battle. Caleb rarely wore those boots, known throughout the punk-rock circle as "ass-kicking boots"—and ass kicking seemed to be one of the events scheduled for this evening.

"Someone's been sleeping in here. Caleb doesn't make the bed this way." Capone sniffed the air. "I smell licorice, so it must be Michael. They ate all the cereal in the house too—that had to be Haden's doing. I hate when they use his stuff. They always take and take and he gets what's left." He whipped his hair back and caught my gaze. "Except for you. He doesn't have to compromise or split you five ways like clothes, toys, and attention. He can have all of you. Do you have any idea how much joy that brings him, or how much energy that joy creates?"

He dragged his tongue over his lips as he recalled some past flavor. "Oh, I've never had it so good. I've been sucking on misery and fear for almost two decades. Imagine eating cold soup every day with no variety. But you, Samara, the joy you bring him is warm and sweet and spicy like cinnamon. He won't go back to cold gruel and neither will I."

I just stood there, stone still, as I tried to make sense of his ranting. Finally, I found my voice. "Where's Caleb? Is he dead?"

"If he was dead then I wouldn't be here, now would

I?" Capone replied, sliding on the next boot. "Your lover is safe. He's not in any condition to drive, as it were, so I'm taking the wheel."

"Caleb and I aren't lovers, not technically," I groused.

"Which shows your ignorance of the word and its true meaning," he returned nastily. "That's part of the problem, am I right? You're too concerned with the physical when it's just a means to something more profound. We'll deal with that later. Now, I have bigger obstacles." Capone reached his feet and roamed around the room, staying close to the walls, listening to its secrets. His smooth gait worked the floor, bidding the shadows to come forward.

Again, where was Haden? He should have been up here by now. I was sure he could hear all the commotion up here. Or was something keeping him downstairs? Was he hurt?

Manic laughter intruded my thoughts. Capone stood by the door with his ear pressed to the wall, giggling.

"I hear you," he singsonged. "Come on, fight me. That's the only way you're getting what you want."

"What's going on?" I asked.

"He's coming, and he's not happy." Capone pressed his face against the wall again, his hand stroking the chalky white surface affectionately. "Shh. He's coming. Don't you hear him—that poor little puppy, crying for his lost mate. Well, he can't have mine. Here, puppy, puppy. I've got something for you. Who's a good boy?"

I didn't need to ask who he was referring to. No one else I knew cried like a dog, and the way Capone was egging him on, I had no doubt Tobias would answer the challenge. I pleaded with Capone to stop, but he ignored me and continued antagonizing the walls.

He paused and glanced at me over his shoulder. "Ah, I see. He needs a motive, an extra push." Capone scooped me into his arms before I could protest. He trapped my face in one hand and crushed his lips against mine. I pushed and squirmed, but he was too strong. The kiss, greedy and punishing, initiated a response from Lilith. She didn't appreciate being manhandled either and rushed to my aid.

Capone leapt back with a yelp and wiped his lips. "Dammit, Lilith, you didn't have to bite me! Just having fun."

"Fun time's over," I replied.

He backed away, his chest rumbling with more inhuman laughter. Just before he was about to run into the wall, he used his heels to begin a backward climb that disobeyed the laws of physics.

"You think he didn't follow you?" he asked as he climbed. "You think he doesn't know where you are right now? He doesn't like me touching you. Not one bit."

While Capone continued to play Spiderman, I heard it, the shrill whine that abraded my ears and hurt my heart. The sound traveled faster like a soaring jet overhead, almost deafening upon approach. Capone just giggled at this, elated to get the game started.

"Capone, please, we have to get out of here."

Squatting, he leaned at a ninety-degree angle, perpendicular to my stance. His face drew closer as if ready to kiss me again. "No. I told you, we won't share you. He started this and I'm gonna finish it. He needs to know what he's dealing—" His eyes lifted to a spot just over my head. "Get down!"

A firm shove sent me to the opposite side of the room, my feet kicked from under me. During this unplanned flight, a shadowy tube whooshed past me, tunneling its way toward Capone. The air cracked in a burst of sound as it struck Capone in the chest. His body slammed against the wall, almost driving him completely through it. Plaster crumbled and chipped, raining dry clumps on the floor.

That's when I realized that the man of the hour had arrived, and what an entrance! Tobias squatted on the headboard, gold rays shooting through the black strands covering his face.

Capone pushed from the crater in the wall and charged after him, using his hands and feet like a large monkey. Tobias followed suit, springing off the headboard to meet Capone halfway. The two collided in midair, wrestling their way to the floor. The wood cracked and bent under their weight. Capone broke from the hold and raced to the opposite side of the bed.

Tobias stood and wiped his mouth. He looked at his hand, surprised at the smudge of blood on the fingers. "You're pretty strong for a demon mutt."

"Must have been something I ate," Capone sneered and looked to me.

Tobias's hurt and resentful gaze fell on me crawling on the floor.

It took me a minute to understand his meaning, but a lightbulb clicked on in my head when it did. That was why Tobias didn't want me feeding Caleb his energy. Whatever power he had would pass on to Caleb, making them equals in combat.

Again, that contradiction about time travel came to mind where two of the same matter could never occupy the same space. By fighting each other, they were fighting themselves and the attempt would backfire in a really bad way. But I was the only one in the room who seemed to care.

The lamp flew across the room, hitting Tobias in the shoulder and drowning the room into semidarkness again. A battle cry echoed the walls; footsteps pounded the floor as two dark components rammed into each other. The impact was a bomb with no fire, two atoms clashing in an explosion of power. Everything after that occurred with unnatural speed, while the pair performed acrobatics only seen in Cirque du Soleil.

My screams went ignored by the brawling men as bodies flew over my head. I curled into a ball in the corner, ducking sailing furniture, and cringing from every blow delivered. This couldn't go on forever and if they kept it up, they would destroy the house in the process. I got to my feet on shaky legs when a gust of air knocked me over.

One push sent me airborne again, barreling through the door and into the hallway. The more I fought, the more the force pushed me back. I tumbled and rolled, hitting walls and objects soaring in the upheaval until I landed in the tub in the hall bathroom.

Lights flickered around my eyes. I couldn't breathe, let alone scream. Every blow and hit struck my body with remarkable strength. Yet I felt no pain. Though numb to the sting of each assault, I felt its pressure, the strike across my ribs, stomach, and jaw. Angry scratches dragged along my neck, but didn't break the skin.

I didn't know who hit who at this point, but it became apparent that I could feel both of them at once. It could've been from the energy we shared or the ever-growing link, but I was a third party to this brawl and I wasn't even in the room.

This was a bad situation, not conducive to tight quarters such as a bathroom. Though I didn't feel the punches, the effects threw me against the wall, hurled me into the sink, slammed me against the mirror, and shredded my forearm in broken glass. Before I could scream, I was thrown upward. I scrambled for the edge of the sink, the towel rack, but nothing could slow my ascent to the ceiling. I hit the surface with a sound thwack; my back lay flat as though magnetized to the roof.

Catching my breath, I looked down at the destroyed area below. The ripped shower curtain hung on its rod by two rings. The broken toilet cover lay cracked on the floor. Shattered glass glittered in the sink. The bathroom door, dislodged from its hinges, canted against the wall. Yellow and purple flashes shot from the hallway, turning the house into a discotheque.

There was no time to evaluate this new turnabout. I kicked out my feet and tried to drop down, but all efforts left me pressed against the ceiling, withstanding an indirect beat-down. I managed to roll on to my stomach and crawl on my elbows toward the door. I grabbed the doorframe and pulled my body into the hallway.

It looked as though Haden had decided to join the festivities at some point; he now lay unconscious near the stairs. Part of a bedroom door—what was left of it—had landed on top of him.

"Haden!" I yelled and got no answer.

Air rushed in every direction, howling in my ears and tangling my hair over my face. I crawled across the ceiling until I floated directly above him. "Haden, wake up!"

Haden's head floundered from shoulder to shoulder as he came to. He sat up slowly and shoved the door off his chest. He shook his head, shedding the cloud of dust and rubble from his hair.

"Sam? Sam, where are you?"

"I'm up here," I called.

Seeing my predicament, he sprang to his feet with one of Caleb's daggers shaking in his hand. No doubt, it was the first weapon he'd grabbed from downstairs. "How the hell did you get up there?"

"Long story. We have to get Caleb. He's in the room

with—" My words were cut off by another violent impact that sent me tumbling to the end of the hallway.

Haden tried to follow, wading through the jungle of furniture and fallen wires.

Something caught hold of my feet and dragged me from one wall to another. With only a split-second glimpse into the bedroom, I caught Capone sailing from wall to wall in a similar fashion, our paths crossing in a synchronized dance in midair. My body ricocheted off each surface in a bad game of pinball until I flung through the entry of Caleb's bedroom. I hit the floor hard and slid across the carpet to home plate, and the friction burned my jeans. I planted my feet down to stop, but lost my footing and plunged downward.

The back wall and the window disappeared into the night. The furniture had either flown outside or fallen through the great crater in the floor from whose edge I now dangled.

My feet rocked to swing my legs up, but I couldn't manage a grip. All the while, Tobias and Capone continued to scrap in the corner. Capone served a heavy right cross, which sent Tobias flying over my head and into the wall. The bedroom in the apartment next door came into view.

"Take my hand!" Haden yelled above me, reaching over the edge.

Just as I reached out, movement came from above and knocked my helper off his feet. Tobias towered over him and delivered a sound kick to Haden's ribs. Capone wrapped an arm around Tobias's neck, giving Haden time to get to his feet. With dagger in hand, Haden lunged forward with deadly purpose. Capone and I seemed to reach the same conclusion as we saw what he was about to do.

"No. Stop! You can't!" Capone warned.

"Haden, don't!" I screamed to no avail.

The blade burrowed into Tobias's stomach as far as it could go with only the handle sticking out. Tobias fell to his knees, doubled over in pain. Capone soon followed, clutching his abdomen from a sightless injury. In that same instant, fire ate at my torso, burning my insides. Haden paused, stunned at our joint reaction, a realization that arrived too late.

Tobias wrenching out the dagger was the last thing I saw before my hand slipped. Gravity pulled me downward, my arms flung over my head as the second floor drew farther away from me. I landed on my back against broken wood planks, albums, and soft couch cushions. It wasn't a hard fall. Plus, the stabbing pain below my right rib kinda blotted out all other injury. But the drop itself left me stunned with tiny starbursts and dust coating my vision. Beyond the light show stood two men looking down at me from a hole in the floor. Behind them lay a ruptured roof, exposing the burnt night with moving clouds.

"Samara!" Tobias's frantic screams accompanied footsteps and low grunts of pain that seemed to shake the remaining walls. If the deep, guttural roar was any sign that I had outstayed my welcome, the growing cracks snaking the ceiling made it clear.

"Samara, run! Get out of the house and take Haden with you!" Capone shouted down to me as the second floor began to crumble under heavy pressure.

I rolled on my side, stumbled to my feet, and raced toward the front door, which now stood in triplicate. More rumbles and yells aimed at my back, but I trained my focus on the exit, and chose the door in the middle. Neighbors in bathrobes held cell phones, gawking at the sleigh bed and dresser scattered across the lawn. Yells and accusations rent the air as people huddled around the demolished yard.

I took off in the opposite direction, cutting through the row of bushes that divided the next cluster of houses. My feet ate up the dirt and grass, my thighs burned, my throat felt like sandpaper, sweat and drywall prickled my face, and yet I kept running. My hand pressed into my side, staving off the gush of blood that wasn't there. I had to remind myself that it was mind over matter, and my feelings couldn't be trusted. Not anymore.

I must have reached four blocks when I realized I'd left my car. And Haden. I wasn't about to go back for either of them, even if Haden still had my keys. I decided if I got far enough, I would call Mom. Haden was larger than I was and well able to handle himself.

But I couldn't stop, not now, not while the fear of pursuit remained fresh. Whoever it was, he gained on me fast, shrinking the distance between us with each second, until I could almost feel his breath on the back of my neck. I pushed my legs out, pumping faster, running harder, but my limbs wouldn't cooperate.

Something heavy knocked me to the ground. I rolled on my back, fists swinging. My screams were no more than whispers, but I fought without sight.

"Sam, it's me." I heard his voice, but I didn't want to believe it. My body was shutting down, its adrenaline wearing thin. I was too far gone to weed out the Caleb imposter, but I had to try. To my knowledge, Tobias never fed from Caleb. Our link may allow Tobias to feel Caleb's emotions, but he didn't have his memories.

Between breaths, I asked, "You told me you loved me once. Where were we?"

"In your bedroom," he answered without pause. A lavender glow filled his eyes, silhouetting his face and body. "But Caleb gives you quarters every day in case you forget."

And that's when I broke down. I laid my head back against the chilly grass, trembling with each sob. My breath fogged the air, making little smoke signals in the night.

Capone took my hand and pulled me up. I lay limp against his body, which seemed to hum with vitality. I would've killed for just a drop of that energy now, because I'd been torn into three pieces: Tobias, Caleb, and whatever was left of myself.

Capone wrapped his arms around me and stroked my back. "It's all right, Samara. It's me. Caleb is safe. But we have to get you out of here." Capone winced at the pain in his side, as our twin wounds throbbed in the same rhythm.

"I feel it, too," I said. "I'm not bonded to either of you, but I feel pain."

"We feel his response to the pain, nothing more. If you were bonded, you'd be bleeding all over the place, so be thankful." He paused for a moment as if in thought, then said, "I think it's starting to go away. That means he's healing, and he'll be coming after us soon."

"Come with me," I begged. "I don't know how long that energy I gave you will last." I wiped my tears on his shirt, then looked around. "Where's Haden?"

"He took your car and is looking for you. We need to get on the main road."

I patted my jean pockets for my phone. "I'll just call him."

I was relieved that it hadn't been damaged in the fight and that I had two good bars left on my battery, but I paused at the time on the display. 11:46? Only ten minutes had passed since I entered Caleb's house? Ten minutes, two lifetimes, and a leap year was more accurate. I called Haden, who sounded as weary and terrified as I felt.

"Where are you?" he barked.

I searched the area until I spotted a street sign.

"We're just five blocks away. Head toward the highway. We'll meet you there in a minute." I shoved the phone in my pocket as a hand yanked me forward, almost giving me whiplash.

"Run!" Capone yelled.

Running was the last thing I wanted to do right now. That was, until I sensed the danger storming behind us. At first, we only heard it coming, the bending and cracking of branches, the swooshing of leaves.

"Come on!" Capone held firmly to my arm, dragging me along like a child with a kite. He moved more quickly than I could; my feet barely touched the ground. Capone's movements appeared locked in counterpoise as the surroundings blurred around us. The wind stung my face, my legs ached, but I kept moving.

We cut through a small wooded area, the trees spaced far enough to see the road and houses on the other side. Just like those chicks in the movies, I made the foolish mistake of turning around. Tobias had warned me of what he could do, but I hadn't been prepared to see it. Not then, not ever.

A storm burrowed behind us, eating all in its path like a dead star. Lawn furniture, shrapnel, and particles swirled in the eye of this cyclone. Streetlights, even the glow of the moon absorbed into its vacuum, but the beast craved the taste of flesh. Unsatisfied, it spat out debris around our heads. Splinters and glass scraped our skin. It plowed forward, moving as we did, echoing its rage with inhuman howls and cries.

We made a sharp left in an attempt to confuse it. I lost my footing, stumbled, and righted myself again without missing a beat. Making up for whatever adrenaline I'd lost, fear tapped into hidden reserves, and rebooted my system once again.

I didn't know how fast we were going, but I could never have achieved this mileage by my own strength. The green glow tinting my vision answered that riddle, but why was Lilith helping? Wasn't it her plan to be with Tobias? Or maybe survival trumped romance at the moment? Either way, now was not the time to refuse aid.

Trees and brush zoomed past me as the world was set on fast forward, and I no longer needed Capone's hand. We raced side by side, hurling over brush and logs to get to the finish line.

Leaves and wet earth gave way to paved road. I stopped to catch my breath, watching the houses and more forest sitting across the empty street. Capone rested his hands on his knees, his breath coming out in puffs of steam.

"Where is Haden?" he asked.

Before I could answer, a pair of high beams blinded us. The driver leaned on the horn, trying to get our attention. Shielding my eyes, I ran toward the car. Whether it was Haden or an angry commuter, it was worth the risk to get him to stop. The car slammed on brakes and spun in the middle of the road as the driver's window rolled down.

"Get in! It's coming!" Haden yelled.

The warning was unnecessary. We could feel Tobias snapping at our heels, his heat at our backs. We didn't need to see what lurked behind us; the wide-eyed terror on Haden's face told it all.

He opened the back door. "Come on!"

Capone kicked from the ground and leapt inside head-first. He misjudged the landing, slid across the seat, and struck the opposite door.

I hopped inside with better care, while Haden floored

it before I could close the door. The cloud enclosed the car, bouncing off its veneer, causing as much harm as vapor. Again and again, it rammed against the open door only to fan out behind an invisible screen. Nothing but two inches of empty space separated us from harm, yet that was enough to deny him entry.

Not pressing my luck, I slammed the door shut and rolled up the windows. Relieved to be out of harm's way—if only for two seconds—I regarded the narrow road stretched before us.

It was a miracle we didn't crash on the way back to the interstate. Haden veered from lane to lane, dodging the shadow that chased us down. It was hard to tell what caused the motion sickness, Tobias playing bumper cars with the fellow commuters, or Haden's daredevil driving. Each turn flung me from one side of the car to another, and I scrambled around for my seat belt.

"You mind telling me what the hell just happened back there?" Haden yelled from the front seat.

"I'll explain when we get someplace safe," I promised.

"And where would that be?"

The answer at once solved the riddle of the strange shield. I didn't know why I hadn't realized it before. "My house. It's protected and he can't get in," I said. "He can't hurt us there or while we're in this car."

Haden turned his profile to me. "Protected?"

"Olive oil protects the house," I explained.

"Olive oil? Are you telling me that thing back there was a . . ." The statement went unfinished when my cell phone rang.

I reached in my pocket and answered the call. "Mom?"

"Samara, where are you? You said you were coming back home; you should have been here by now. I was about to call the police. Where are you?"

"I'm fine, but Caleb is hurt. We're on our way home now. Is Michael there?"

There was a pause before she answered, "He just pulled up in a cab. Samara, what's going on?"

I ignored her question and asked, "Is there anyone else there?"

"No . . . why?"

"We'll be there in a few minutes. When we pull up, I want you to open the door."

Mom stammered, "O-okay? Why do you sound frantic? What's going on—"

I hung up. Too many questions; not enough time.

The car traced the warped curve toward the shadow of trees up ahead. As luck would have it, I only saw one cop car in the area, empty and parked in front of a minimart, but not even the threat of arrest could lift Haden's foot off the gas. My free hands clamped down on the back of the driver's seat as I held my breath. All we had to do was get there.

While Haden auditioned for NASCAR, I tended to Caleb, who remained unconscious next to me. I held his head on my chest and tried to wake him. Blood leaked from the growing knot on his head.

"Capone? Caleb? Either of you, come on, wake up. Please, wake up." I ignored the pain in my own head and rocked him in my arms, hoping my nearness alone could revive him.

Apparently, Haden felt that the use of the driveway was merely a suggestion. The car hopped onto the curb, barely missing the mailbox, and charged over the grass toward the walkway. Dirt and grass kicked from under the tires, and tracks of bare earth marred the landscape. He would've driven through my living room if I hadn't yelled for him to stop. He honked the horn and the front door swung open. Mom stepped out of the house, rubbing the chill from her arms.

"Get back inside!" I yelled as I opened the door.

Haden went around the car and helped me pull Caleb from the backseat. Michael rushed from the front door to help. The olive oil I'd used protected the house and the inside of my car, but not the few yards in between. Caleb's dead weight was slowing us down and Tobias was getting closer.

The brothers hefted Caleb across the lawn.

"What is that?" Michael pointed to something just beyond the trees. I didn't look and neither did Haden. We moved faster as the wind picked up and the leaves swiveled around our feet.

"Come on, hurry," Mom coached from the doorway as the darkness surrounded the lawn and blackened the security lights. Slowly, she retreated into the house, cowering from the image that had produced that horrified look on her face. Unable to look away, she nearly tripped while holding the door open for us.

Twelve feet had never been such a far distance. While moving backward, Michael stumbled on the second step, causing a chain reaction of clumsy maneuvering. My hand held firm to Caleb's leg, using his jeans as a handle to pull him along.

The shade followed us across the grass, up the stairs of the porch, and stopped short at the threshold just as I slammed the door behind me. Leaves and papers fluttered in the foyer and settled to the floor. I leaned against the door, absorbing the central heating and the promise of safety.

Mom hurried to my side and touched my cheek and dust-covered hair, flinching at every new injury she came across. Her bun had fallen loose and brown tendrils cascaded down her round, angelic face, but her greeting was anything but heavenly. I heard her speak in that high-pitched screech of alarm, but I couldn't register her words.

Something large moved outside, loudly enough to pull me out of my trance. Metal creaked and ground together, then pried apart in some industrial demolition. I searched for the source of the noise, and my heart ripped in two when I looked out of the window.

Trash, lawn furniture, and Christmas ornaments overran the yard, dancing to a chaotic beat the wind commanded. The dark funnel twirling along the grass burrowed underneath the wheels of my car.

The vehicle rose in the air as though it were no more than a Matchbox toy, then plummeted back to earth. Closing my eyes didn't mute out the crash, the shattering of glass, the clatter of fallen hubcaps. I knew what was happening, almost expected it, as if "what more could go wrong" was the theme of the evening.

The rules about keeping a low profile didn't seem to apply to Tobias, and his temper tantrums were spectacular. I had to respect my opponent. He sure knew how to hit below the belt and knew all my weaknesses. I schooled my emotions, trying to trick my mind to not give away my reaction. My breath shivered, my body trembled, but no tears fell. I wouldn't allow it. He would hear them if I did.

21

One question people ask in traumatic situations is, "How did this happen?" As if the mind has rejected the message the eyes delivered.

That question kept repeating until I got an answer, and only a good one would get me to move again. I stared out of the window, my face pressed against the glass, waiting for the chemical stasis to wear off. Everyone handled shock differently, but I opted for an approach that involved the least effort.

My pride and joy, not new, but still new to me, lay on its back in the pebbled driveway. The wheels pointed skyward like the legs of a dead insect. White coils of steam shot from the crushed engine as the roof and floor sandwiched together and met the business end of a trash compactor. Tobias was just a large child taking his anger out on his toys.

After his epic hissy fit, Tobias called it a night and left us with the check. I knew this had been a sample of the damage he could cause, a warning shot. The next confrontation wouldn't be as friendly, which made the prospect of returning to school that much more thrilling.

A howl came from the couch and shattered the tension. I leapt back a few steps and clutched my pounding chest. Mom pulled me behind her, but I caught a glimpse of what had caused the noise.

Caleb had returned to the conscious world, kicking and screaming on the living room floor. Color leached from his skin, all but the puffy red folds around his eyes.

The brothers scrambled for a good grip on the swinging arms and legs. Michael and Haden hefted him back on the couch. I didn't know who was at play here, Caleb or Capone, but both suffered in tandem and dragged me with them. Tobias's energy ran its course and left Caleb stranded. Capone may have imparted superstrength and agility, but Caleb was still human and endured the hangover from his comic book antics.

Though this wasn't my pain, my body, those grunts and tears were definitely mine. I'd heard stories about amputee patients who could still feel their missing limbs years after their procedures. It was the phantom limb, a shadow without an object to draw from. I could now appreciate its effect and dreaded how bad it could've been. I braced the wall for support, counting the seconds until the throbs went away.

"Fire! Feels. Like fire!" Caleb growled between breaths. Sweat drenched his body and soaked into his clothes.

When Haden touched his feet, Caleb went stiff; the veins rose in thick ropes on his neck. He thrashed against the pillows, pleading for relief that no one could give.

"We have to remove his shoes," Michael advised while fumbling with the series of laces. The simple gesture made Caleb jerk and twitch. Slowly, the boots peeled from the feet, exposing swollen flesh caked with mud and scabby blisters.

"What on earth?" Michael covered his mouth, his face turning green with disgust.

"He left the hospital on foot, literally," Haden commented. "We need to clean this up before it gets infected."

That was Mom's cue to take action. Judging by her haste to leave the room, she needed an occupation. She always kept a level head, even in distress, but this was out of her element. Her house had become a hotbed for otherworldly dealings, which was bound to rattle anyone's nerves. She returned shortly with more bandages and a pan of soapy water. The brothers pulled Caleb to sit straight and directed his feet over the pan.

As soon as his feet hit the water, Caleb and I engaged in a screaming contest. The pain shot a lightning bolt up my spine, locking my joints and straining muscles.

I centered my thoughts, focused on my own feet and wiggled my toes. If I could feel Caleb's sickness, then he could sense my health. It was a good theory. Too bad his pain canceled that program. Heads lobbed back and forth, confused over which one of us to treat first.

"Sam, are you all right?" Haden helped me to my feet.

"No." I pushed him away. "Don't worry about me. Help Caleb!"

"It burns!" Caleb battered against his brothers' weight. "I swear I'll kill him when I see him!"

"Calm down. Get yourself patched up and think about killing later," Michael said while the others tended to Caleb's feet.

Caleb's body quaked under his restraints. He looked rabid, truly possessed, yet Capone had no input in this behavior. It wasn't physical pain from his injuries, no cuts or scrapes, but uncensored rage. Only then did I grasp the intensity of a Cambion's nature.

What lived in us fed from life energy and emotion, and

therefore, experienced everything to the extreme. All this time, I stood in the company of pure torment, which materialized into solid matter. I half expected it to pull up a chair and start talking to me, for its presence was very much alive.

"We need to get him calm." Ducking the stray blows, Mom placed a cool towel over Caleb's swollen eyes and pressed down. "This should soothe the burning. Cambion light can get very hot after a while," she murmured to no one in particular, but we all heard it and froze to the spot.

"What did you say?" Haden asked.

"Something I read. Let's focus please," Mom instructed and flipped the towel over.

The seconds crawled by as the men continued to pin down their brother. Slowly, the pain began to dissipate, all but a dull ache that left me stiff. I moved to the couch and reached for Caleb, but he shrank away from me. The distress in his eyes hurt worse than any external injury.

Mom leaned over and trapped Caleb's face in her hands. On contact, he stopped fighting and stared at her, his eyes wild with implicit terror.

"Don't get too close," Haden warned, but Mom shrugged him away.

"It's all right, Caleb. It's all right. You're safe," she whispered. "I'm not afraid of your power. I feel it pulling me forward, but you won't hurt me, will you?" It wasn't a question, but an affirmation of what she already knew.

The rest of us weren't so sure, and we waited expectantly for Caleb's reaction. He was hungry, scared, and unstable. There was no telling what would set him off.

To our surprise, Caleb just watched her, his chest heaving as he strained for understanding. The two locked eyes while Michael dried Caleb's feet and wrapped them in bandages.

Mom stroked Caleb's tear-stained cheeks. "Where else do you hurt?"

"Everywhere." He gulped. "But more on the inside."

Mom frowned and pushed the sweaty strands from his face. "May I hold you?"

Caleb nodded keenly; his lips trembled as he whimpered, "Please."

Mom clutched him tight to her chest, rocking him back and forth as she had done with me countless times. And like me in that position, he clung to her quiet strength. Maybe it was a maternal thing, or her kind nature, but she projected a warm halo of safety that kept the monsters at bay. They hovered in the shadows, skirting the border, but dared not enter the sanctuary of such light.

Caleb stopped struggling and surrendered to the steady lull of peace. The even rise and fall of his chest told us that Mom had worked her magic, and I'd never been more proud.

The brothers stood and witnessed the display in quiet awe. This woman in all her human frailty achieved what no supernatural being in the room could do. I couldn't ignore the presence of irony, but I did wonder if it possessed a color.

Just when the night couldn't get any weirder, any more chaotic, another issue dropped into my lap. One would think I'd be used to it, have developed a tolerance somehow, but I felt just as green as when I'd first learned Cambions existed.

From the doorway, I searched the room and met a familiar yet clean setting. The party favors, dishes, bloody bandages, and trash were cleared away and the furniture set to rights. Cleanup would have taken hours, indicating a substantial lapse in time between Thanksgiving dinner and this point. It felt surreal, and in my sedate hindsight, no one could convince me that I had left the house tonight. However, the wailing of sirens outside the house begged to differ.

Red and blue police lights swept over the lawn, marking it as ground zero for yet another crime scene. Heads peered behind drawn curtains, while more daring onlookers came outside in coats and fuzzy slippers to view the spectacle.

"Must have been a freak storm. This wasn't the only area hit. Damages stretch from here past I-199. Damnedest thing, too. The weatherman said it would be clear skies 'til Mundee," one of the officers relayed to Mrs. Sherwood, a weasel-looking woman two doors down.

Her raggedy gray poodle shivered under her arm. The poor thing, used as an alibi to spy on the neighborhood, looked as miserable as I felt out in the cold. Mrs. Sherwood wasn't the only one with an ear for scandal. Locals picked this particular time to defrost their cars and take out trash.

Twice in one year, the police had interrupted this quiet, unassuming block in the middle of the night, a disruption certain to bring down the neighborhood's property value. Just another stigma my mom and I had to live down.

I chuckled bitterly at the murmurs and failed attempts at reason. People tend to adhere to clean-cut facts, never mind that the pattern of said storm was so erratic, it appeared the weather held a motive. Or that the wind path seemed to concentrate on one area before dispersing. Despite the nods, suspicious eyes glared at my ugly white house with its chipped paint and the crushed soda can that resembled a car.

The tow truck guy successfully and loudly flipped the car back on its proper side. The chains clanked as the belt lift hoisted the crumpled wreck by its axel. Pulling up his sagging jeans and hawking a loogie on the driveway, he propped himself against the side door of his truck. He was dragging away two years of scraping and saving like something he'd shot in the woods. And that was his show of condolence, this sloppy mortician, jaded by the constant presence of destruction. Nadine would've liked him.

My eyelid began to twitch, causing the entire right side of my face to pulse. I kept watching this crude funeral march until a warm hand touched my shoulder. "Sweetie, come sit down. We need to talk," Mom said.

I turned away from one devastation to face another.

Mom led me to the couch, where I met an awkward, albeit polite interrogation. The police had questions about a disturbance in Caleb's neighborhood. Witnesses identified me and two other men running away from the property. Someone had taken down the license plate to my car, which had led to this lovely house call. I wasn't under arrest, but I had a lot to answer for. I kept my responses precise and used my draw to smooth over the rough edges. If there was ever a time to exploit my powers, it was now.

Mom held my hand the entire time, while dabbing wet cotton balls on the scratches on my arm. Blissfully numb at this point, my eyes played on the weird shapes forming around the room. I strained to keep focused, or else get sucked into the dark vortex that the living room controlled. Now was not the time for panic attacks and hallucinations, not with this many witnesses.

"And you say you have no idea where Caleb Baker is now?" Officer Rolland leered at me, trying to read some hidden code in my face. He squirmed in the seat across from me as if waiting for something to jump out and attack. I recognized him and a few of the others littering the foyer. More importantly, they remembered me and what had happened in this house last summer.

"No. I tried to look for him, but the storm hit and I had to get home." I steeled my expression, curbing the instinct to lift my eyes to the second floor.

It had been Mom's idea not to bring Caleb out into the open. He was in no shape to go back to the hospital. There had to have been a good reason for him to have left wearing nothing but a paper gown, and this latest incident guaranteed that no one was leaving the house anytime soon.

"Was there anyone else at his residence?" the officer asked.

Keeping with the script, I shook my head. "No. Just his brother and me."

Officer Rolland scowled and jotted something on his notepad. "Hmm. I understand that his brothers are in town looking after him. Do you know where they are?"

"No. But they're worried about Caleb, too. They believed he might've been poisoned, which was why he was in the hospital. Sir, is Caleb in trouble?" I asked.

The officer's face was unreadable. "We just need to ask a few questions, is all. Mr. Baker reported that his car was vandalized a month ago and now his townhouse has been destroyed. There were no explosives, but whatever caused it started from inside. Do you know anyone that may have a grudge against him?"

Boy, did I. "No, not that I know of."

Much to my relief, Mom intervened. "Um, gentlemen, is there a way to continue this in the morning? She appears to be in shock and unable to make a proper statement right now."

"Quite all right. I think we're done here. If we have any more questions, we'll let you know." The officer left

the room with the unofficial threat of his return, although his rush to leave suggested this was the last place
he wanted to revisit.

I held my head in my hands and closed my eyes, trying
to block out the world. Maybe my stepmother was right
and I really did own bad juju, more than the standard
Cambion quota. People sensed it, but had the good manners to keep quiet. But this was only the beginning of the
questioning. Mom would want to know the truth and
there was no way to get around it now.

"Samara?" Mom stroked the top of my head.

I looked up and soon regretted it. Everything in the
room turned into a Salvador Dali painting—melting pictures and leaking chairs. Mom's features drooped like
hot wax, smearing on bland custard-tinted walls that
suddenly lost their depth. Nadine still lay dead on the
floor, her hair tossed across the rug like scattered hay. I
was desensitized to all of it, as this, too, had become
freakishly normal.

"Michael is sleeping down here tonight," Mom said,
her voice a slurred and warped record played backwards.
"Caleb and Haden have your room, so you'll have to
sleep with me. Come up when you're ready, okay?
Samara?"

I snapped my eyes shut and took a deep breath before
following her out the room. As soon as I crossed the
threshold, the second my foot touched the wooden foyer,
it stopped. Someone opened a sealed jar and let out the
pressure in my ears with a loud pop. The house fell quiet
again and I could hear myself think.

"Mom?" I called from the bottom of the stairs.

"In the morning. We will talk in the morning." Mom
climbed the stairs, holding a shaky grip on the banister,
an old brittle woman sapped of strength. I could only

imagine what was going through her head. As the only normal person in the house, she'd been drop-kicked into a world she'd never known existed, and probably wished for ignorance to return. I went to the alarm by the door and checked the setting. It was a small comfort, if anything.

"Tomorrow is another day" rang as the closing sentiment of the evening. I'd expected a flood of accusations, but no one wanted to talk. No one wanted to look at me either, and kept their distance in case my juju was contagious. The brothers took over my room, not letting anyone, mainly me, enter. Haden stood guard like a bouncer checking IDs at the door.

"Go to bed, Samara," he ordered gruffly.

"You can't tell me what to do," I said. "It's my house!"

"It's my brother," he countered with equal annoyance. "He's in a bad way right now. He needs to remain calm, and you might spark a negative reaction. Go to bed. We'll deal with this in the morning."

He wasn't going to budge on the matter. Sulking, I went to Mom's room, took a shower, and allowed the hot jets to beat me into submission. Try as they might, nothing could truly keep me from Caleb, the burning ache attacking my body made that point clear.

I was the last to hit the sack. Mom was already asleep, but she whimpered a lot and I knew the night's excitement had crept into her dreams. To be honest, I was feeling a little creeped out myself. Much like in the living room, bad memories clung to every shadow in her bedroom as proof that the dead weren't really gone. That was reason enough to sleep with the lights on.

I slipped to the left side of the bed, then snuggled close to my mom until the noises stopped. Turning on my stomach, I felt something hard and cold under my pillow.

My fingers traced along the barrel, and I didn't need to see what it was. I smiled at this shred of normalcy, relieved that some things would never change. It figured she would keep a weapon in her bed, and I just hoped it wouldn't go off when I rolled over.

22

The smell of coffee and bacon woke me the next morning.

My one good eye glared at the alarm clock on the nightstand, which revealed the approach of noon. I didn't remember falling asleep. No dreams supported this seven-hour blink, and the bands of light shooting through the curtains made it clear that said blink was all I was getting. I rolled over and found Mom already gone, the blue quilt on her side of the bed tucked and folded smooth. The world carried on without skipping a beat, and it was up to me to keep pace.

Gravity was a worthy adversary today; it kept weighing me down and tripping my legs. My head played nothing but reruns of last night's excitement, and I wished to return to the quiet abyss that came with sleep.

I poked my head out of Mom's room and found my door wide open. Steam from the bathroom leaked into the hallway. I made a mental note to disinfect the area of all the boy germs, and check the medicine cabinet for anything missing. Laughter from the first floor told me where everyone had disappeared to, so I followed the voices downstairs toward the dining room.

A picture of family splendor stood before me—the proud mother tending to her sons. The scene was a reen-actment of the precious gems in Caleb's memory bank, one of many I'd stolen while feeding from him. The brothers ate up the attention, wrapped in the memories of their mother. I felt like a guest in my own house, in-truding on a special moment.

"Here you go, Caleb. Now I want you to finish every-thing on that plate. You need to build your strength back." Mom set down a serving tray full of pancakes, eggs, and leftovers from Thanksgiving dinner.

The brothers leaned in and ogled the spread but drew back when Mom spoke again.

"And you two, don't you dare touch his food. You just wait until I bring out the rest."

Haden offered an innocent smile, while Michael—as usual when in a woman's presence—averted his eyes.

"Thank you, Ms. Marshall. You didn't need to do all this." Caleb reached for the bandage taped on his fore-head, but a light swat on the hand stopped him.

"Hush. I love men with healthy appetites." She ruffled Caleb's hair, then went to the kitchen.

Mom was in for it with these guys. Across the board, the Rosses were greedy sumbitches. As soon as her back turned, the brothers dove into Caleb's plate, snatching the bacon and honey biscuits.

Poor Cake Boy didn't stand a chance and he ate what was left of his meal slowly. The fork shook in his hands, trying to aim the food to his mouth. It would take a while for him to regroup completely, but his laughter promised a quick recovery. His dimpled grin made me homesick, and I wanted to taste the lips attached to that smile.

Without lifting his head, Caleb asked, "Why don't you come join us, Sam?"

The room got quiet in record time; silverware clattered against plates. My heart fluttered at the sound of my name. Of course he knew I was near. There was no concealment from him for very long.

I stepped from my hiding place and entered the dining room. "Morning."

Avoiding the three sets of purple eyes on me, I took a seat at the far end of the table.

Mom returned with another platter of food. "Morning, sweetie. How are you feeling? Get enough rest?"

"Yeah, Mom." I looked across the table to the only eyes not fixed on me. "How are you, Caleb?"

"Could be better, but glad it's not worse." He took a bite of his pancakes, while I shook off the chill of his answer.

Michael slapped Caleb on the shoulder, which almost knocked him out of the chair. "Don't worry; I gave him some painkillers that will set him right. He won't feel a thing in a bit."

Caleb didn't appear to feel anything now.

"Well, since we're all refreshed and coherent..." Haden paused and looked at Caleb teetering in his chair. "Close enough to it anyway. We can now discuss what happened."

Haden, Michael, and Mom waited for me to let it rip. I took a long, deep breath before speaking. I wasn't sure if any of it made sense, but I had to get it all out. On and on, I spat my tale, my chest heaving, hoping my audience could decipher the word-vomit. When I finished, I buried my head in my arms. I could feel them staring me down in allegation; worst of all was Caleb.

Michael spoke first. "Are you taking the piss?"

"Take what?" I checked the front of my pants. If I'd had an accident, last night had supplied a good reason.

"I meant, are you joking?" he rephrased. "You're saying that thing outside mated with Nadine? Ew!"

"Samara, how long have you known about this?" Mom asked from the doorway.

"Since that day I got detention in school." I rehashed the events, every sordid detail. When I mentioned going to the hospital the following day, the brothers lost their shit. More plates and silverware rattled the table as four reddened faces—including Mom's—closed in on me.

"Do you have any idea how dangerous that was?" Haden erupted. "A demon's energy is volatile."

"Yeah, but it's powerful enough to revive Caleb," I replied.

"Powerful enough to turn Caleb into a monster!" Haden pointed to his ailing brother. "Have you learned nothing from this summer, what Caleb had to go through?"

I looked to Caleb for aid, but his eyes fell on his plate again. "I just wanted to help him. The same thing could've happened to me. I figured dividing the amount between us might, I don't know, dilute the potency or something."

"Samara, why didn't you tell me?" Mom asked, clearly hurt by my secrecy.

"So you can have more reason to stay awake at night? Right."

Slamming his hand on the table, Haden shot from his seat. "I can't believe this! You put all of us at risk! If that thing can turn into a black cloud or any other bloody thing it wants, what kept him from entering Caleb's hospital room? He could've disguised himself as a doctor and killed Caleb in his bed. Better still, he could've murdered me or Michael while we slept. You should have told us, given us some warning so we could protect ourselves. But no, you'd rather take the empty promise of a demon? Tell me you're not that stupid, Sam."

I leapt to my feet. Blood rushed straight to my brain, but I gained enough clarity to tell him off. "Don't blame this on me. I didn't ask to be linked to Caleb, I didn't ask for Lilith, I didn't ask to get Nadine's baggage, and I sure as hell didn't ask for a psychotic demon to call dibs on me."

"Samara!" Mom admonished, but I was on a roll.

"No!" I yelled at her before swinging around to glare at Haden and Michael again. "Believe it or not, I was trying to protect you and Caleb. I had his room door covered with oil and I gave him as much energy as I could—good or bad. Tobias won't kill Caleb, and I've done everything to keep it that way, because I don't want to share the same fate as your father! So yeah, I made a deal to keep quiet and to stay away from the guy I love, but I'm not stupid! Don't think that my silence hasn't cost me anything, because it has. Everything I care about is being destroyed, including my car!" I fell back in my chair and returned to my sulk. The brothers went quiet while I continued to weep against the table.

Mom rubbed my back in a wasted attempt to console. "Honey, calm down. We'll figure this out."

"I used your shampoo, by the way. Good stuff. Smells like coconuts," Michael announced.

I lifted my head to Michael, who lovingly stroked his wet braid. All activity in the dining room paused at the random comment from its craziest occupant. It stood to reason that Caleb wasn't the only one at the table who was medicated, but Michael had succeeded in melting some of the tension.

Haden dismissed his brother and turned to me. "I'm sorry you had to go through this alone—quite a lot to

take on for someone your age. We heard of incubi growing up, legends and whatnot, but I'd never seen one until
last night. They're extremely rare, you see, almost extinct
to the point of myth. And if he's connected to you somehow, he'll be even harder to destroy."

I wiped my tears on my shoulder. "I don't think we
can. You saw what happened last night—Tobias and
Caleb are connected through me. They can't hurt each
other without hurting me, which hurts themselves."

"This is completely, absolutely mental," Haden raved.
"How can you be linked to two people at once? Do you
truly know what a link is, Sam?"

I narrowed my eyes at him. "I know what it is. I'm living it."

"Then you know that you can only have one mate.
Why don't you seal the bond with Caleb and be done
with it?"

"Because I'm not comfortable with the idea. Plus, I
don't know if that will work."

"My daughter is too young to be making these kinds
of decisions," Mom interjected.

At least someone had my back. There would never be a
shortage of people trying to dig into my junk drawer.
Was nothing sacred? This was no better than an arranged
marriage, and I would be damned if the most important
moment in my life turned into a business transaction.

"Be that as it may, the best for all involved is for
Samara and Caleb to bond immediately," Haden decided.

"It's funny how you think you have say over what happens to my body," Caleb finally spoke. He dropped his
fork, reclined in his chair, and stared down his brother in
defiance. "You can't make that call, and what we decide
is no one's business but mine and Sam's. This is our fate

we're talking about here—not yours. Our lives depend on the choice we make and we will make that choice when we see fit, so back off!"

I sat amazed and quite impressed. Caleb may have been the youngest, but he'd outgrown the bullied stages of his upbringing. Time and separation made him stronger, harder, something the brothers had trouble accepting, so Haden tried basic reasoning.

"Don't you realize if you two bond, Tobias can't interfere, and we can kill him?"

"We don't know that," I argued. "You said no Cambion can be linked to two people at once, and bam! Check me out. Now what makes you think there isn't another loophole for me? My whole situation is a freak occurrence and this may open up new issues."

"It'll at least buy us time to kill him," Haden said.

"Okay, great. If—and it's a very big IF—you defeat Tobias, then what? Caleb and I would be stuck like that. Forever! It's a quick fix with long-term penalties. I don't want to be responsible for anyone's life but my own."

"She has a point," Michael said, balancing his braid over his top lip like a mustache. "I think the worst thing they could do right now is mate. In fact, they should stay far away from each other to avoid temptation."

All eyes moved to Michael, who now addressed the wall and red curtains. This was a complete about-face for the man who had all but taken my measurements for my wedding dress. For him to reconsider us jumping the broom meant there was something seriously wrong.

"You have to think about this from every angle and not jump to the obvious conclusion," he began. "Sam is the common variable. The three of you are keeping each other alive, neutral at this point. So if you two bonded, it would sever her connection with Tobias. What's to stop Tobias from killing Caleb then?"

"He can't," Haden answered. "The separation would kill Sam. She couldn't live without her mate."

"If Tobias wants Lilith as badly as we think he does, he won't let that happen," Michael said. "If Caleb dies, the competition would be eliminated, but Sam won't die immediately. She'll have a brief window of opportunity to bond with Tobias. That is, if she doesn't find the idea of death before graduation agreeable. She'll be vulnerable, unchaste, and no longer immune to his draw. Grief and fear can make you desperate, and there's nothing more desperate than a Cambion with a broken heart."

For the head case of the group, Michael dropped some serious knowledge, and the room went quiet to let it sink deep. Tobias was manipulative, but would he go to that extent? The conversation we'd had at Merchants Square returned to memory. He said as long as I remained chaste, his influence wouldn't work, not even with Lilith's aid. Things might be different if I took the plunge, which explained how Nadine had fallen victim to his whims. Had he planned this all along? I wouldn't have been surprised if he had.

"So, we agree that the bonding idea is off the table— good," I said before anyone could object. "Now what? We still need to figure out a way to get rid of him. He's mortal now—sort of—and as you saw last night he can be harmed. We just have to find a way to do it without hurting me."

"Right then," Haden said. "First, I need you to tell me everything you know about this incubus. Where did he come from?"

The story was even worse the second time around. Haden sat patiently, taking mental notes and nodding at the appropriate times. When I got to the topic of Malik, he lifted his hand to stop me. "You said he attends your school? Disguised as a former student?"

"Yes. Malik was killed in an accident and Tobias has been passing himself off as him. No one knows he's dead but me," I clarified.

Haden rested his elbow on the table and pinched the bridge of his nose. "I just have one question—"

"Just one? Really now?" Michael chided with a shake of the head.

Haden's brows puckered together when he asked, "Where is the real Malik's body?"

That was a good question, and it was a shame that I didn't have a good answer. After all, the James River was pretty big with a lot of hungry fish.

After brunch, the brothers adjourned to the living room to plot a combat strategy. They huddled close, whispering in conspirators' tones, only to cut their eyes at me when I walked by. They'd made it clear that I wasn't to get involved, but I was too old to still be sitting at the kids' table. I may have been getting a taste of my own medicine, but I had the right to know what they planned to do, so I had to be sneaky about it.

"A forty-five might be a bit messy. I don't think bullets will work on him. Another thing, if we get him out in the open, it might make too much noise. A silencer maybe . . ." Michael turned to Caleb. "You still got your crossbow, right? Been keeping up with your aim?"

"Yeah. But if bullets won't work, how do you think an arrow will?" Caleb asked. "He can heal pretty quickly."

"I think we can improvise. Just a few alterations, maybe replace the arrows with—" Haden stopped when Caleb touched his shoulder. The brothers grew quiet and looked up to where I hid behind the entryway.

"I know you're there. Go find something to do," Caleb ordered, sounding way too much like my dad for my taste. This internal link thing killed all element of surprise, which sucked when you were trying to spy on someone. And Caleb's standoffish attitude didn't make it any better.

His silent treatment dripped lemon juice on my open sores. He hadn't said more than two words to me all morning, and it took all my will not to cry. I might have thought painkillers played a part in his flakiness were it not for the raw emotions polluting the air: dread, hunger, and pent-up hostility. I felt it when he brushed against me to leave the room. I saw it in the deadened stare that never quite met my eyes.

After I was rudely dismissed, I searched for Mom, the one person who didn't look nauseous at the sight of me. She worried about the brothers going off alone, so she called Ruiz to meet them at the station, and I was none too pleased that she had his number on speed dial.

At that moment, I caught a peek of what Dad had seen in Mom when they were young, back when love wasn't so complicated. A strange personality shift took place, one of those Freaky Friday moments where I was the concerned parent and Mom was the carefree teen.

Having seen enough foolishness, I cornered Mom in the kitchen. "What's with you and the Cuban Necktie?"

She covered the mouthpiece of the phone with her hand. "Nothing. We're just friends, that's all. I think he can help us."

"You're aware that he knows about me, right? He knows Cambions exist."

Her smile fell away. "How do you know?"

I balked. "Uh, I just do. He's been asking a lot of personal questions about Caleb. Who knows, he could be a hired hit man trying to kill him."

She rolled her eyes. "Samara, I think you're overreacting."

"Says the woman who sleeps with a gun under her pillow. Just be careful, okay?"

"I will." She put the phone back to her ear. "Okay, so what were you saying? No, I can't today. I have to take care of a few things here, but can I get a rain check?" That coy smile reappeared as she began playing with her hair.

Before my gag reflex kicked in, I left the kitchen, and ignored the sickening chorus of "Go on, David, you hang up. . . . No, you hang up. . . . I won't hang up until you hang up."

Sitting at the dining room table, I mumbled, "It's official; everyone in my life is insane."

"It's called hormones," Michael replied behind me, driving his knuckles over my skull.

I swatted him away and smoothed down my hair. "Yeah, well, there should be a warning label on that thing. Villainy, thy daughter is Lust, and her sister is Madness, which makes their father Foolish."

Not really listening, Michael plopped in the chair beside me. His thumbs sped across his razor-thin phone. There were very few moments when that contraption wasn't in his hand or propped to his ear.

"So, are you gonna tell me what you plan—"

"No," he cut me off. "It's best that you don't know. You're a liability, and we can't have Lilith somehow leaking information to Tobias, can we? In case something *does* happen, we don't want you lying any more to police than you need to. Caleb's not as soft as people think. Takes a lot to get him riled up and takes twice the effort to cool him down. I think you know that already." Not looking up from his phone, he continued, "Finding a Cambion mate is remarkable. We usually stay clear of each other out of fear, but desperately want that deep connection. A part of me is a bit jealous."

I laughed without humor. "Don't be."

"Oh, I don't envy your situation now. But your link

with Caleb has its advantages," he said. "You may not survive without the other, but you rely on each other for strength, making it twice as hard for you to die."

Put in that perspective, the burden of having a mate lightened in weight, but only ever so slightly.

"What's your spirit's name anyway, if you don't mind me asking?"

"Doesn't have one."

"What's with that? These are intelligent beings. Why don't they have names?"

He stopped texting to look at me. "Well, our spirits are descendants, pieces of a bigger entity. With each new Cambion comes a new spirit. My mum named my dad's, Brodie's wife named his, and you named Caleb's. It's a bit of a tradition to have our lovers name them."

There was that L word again. It kinda grossed me out, a sign that I wasn't cut out for all this romance stuff. Capone had told me that it meant more than it implied, something deeper.

Capone. It was a silly name, I had to admit, but it suited him. I remembered the day that I'd named him, a privilege that I'd never appreciated until now, a declaration of true devotion. Had Caleb known that day that we would be joined at the hip? Would he still make the same decision now?

Their ride showed up before I could learn the answer. A van waited on the curb with a white TAXI sign on the roof. Haden climbed inside the cab, leaving only seconds before Caleb disappeared with him. As I dashed out of the house, he turned and faced me with a blank expression. Every jerky limp and shuffle tested his endurance, but he was determined to walk over hot coals to reach me.

I met him halfway and caught my breath. "Caleb, I—"

He lifted a hand to silence me. "Don't take this the wrong way, but I gotta get the hell away from you."

The reply delivered a sucker punch to my stomach. "How can I not take that the wrong way?"

With a glazed, half-baked stare, he replied in a flat monotone, "I need to lay low for a while until this poison gets out of our systems. Capone's opened something dark in me, something violent that I don't want to acknowledge. He's restless and I need to rein him in—though I might need to use him again to fight."

Fight? Caleb was too weak to walk, let alone engage in mortal combat. "You can't. Capone's unstable and who knows how long it will take to get your control back next time."

"I can't defeat Tobias by my own strength." He rubbed his bandaged forehead to show his point. "If that means I have to up my food intake, that's what I'll do. Don't let my lassitude fool you, Sam, I know what's going on and I'll protect what's mine. Every woman in my life leaves— my mom, my sisters, Nadine—and I'll be damned if you follow."

"You don't have to do this. We can find another way," I pleaded. "I heard what you guys were plotting, and let me be the first to tell you that it's stupid. This ain't Dungeons and Dragons! Arrows and medieval swords can't kill him. I'm not even sure if he can die naturally, and you're just gonna piss him off more. I just got you back and now you're ready to return to the hospital, or worse."

"It's better than what's going on now." He tapped his temple. "Visions are flickering around in my brain; I don't know what's a dream and what's real. But I sense him in you, squirming around like a hungry maggot. And then there's Lilith, and I'm not even gonna go there."

"Speaking of Lilith, why didn't you tell me that olive oil was poisonous to us? Why do I always have to find things out the hard way?"

He closed his eyes for a second, struggling for the right answer. "I'm sorry, Sam. There are so many rules that come with being a Cambion; I can't keep track. I've never had to explain what we are to anyone else. We're born like this and we have a lifetime to get accustomed to how things work. I'm surprised Lilith hadn't told you." His stare settled on my shoulder, not really seeing it, but using it as a focal point as his mind wandered off. He shook himself out of it, then dismissed the subject with the swipe of his hand. "I'm checking into a hotel until all this gets sorted out. I'll give you a call when everything's settled. Might be a while, though."

"So that's it? Just . . . nothing?" When he didn't respond, I shoved his chest. "I can't believe you! After all I've been through with you, you're bailing on me? How can you push me away for something I have no control over?"

"I think control is our number-one problem, don't you think?" Without another word, he slid into the backseat.

I stood quietly for a moment, logging this new information away, but some details just would not compute. Did I just get dumped, or did I blink? It couldn't end like this, with no "good-bye" or "kiss my ass" to seal the deal.

During Mia's many fights with Dougie, she often used a term called "time-out," a suspension I associated with misbehaved children. Was Caleb punishing me?

"No worries, Sam. It's only temporary. Soon as we handle this demon business, you two'll be back on, you'll see." Michael scooted past me while stuffing Mom's red napkin rings into his trench coat. What he needed with them, I didn't know, and I was pretty sure he didn't either. With a parting smile, he climbed in with his brother. In minutes, the cab rolled down the block and disappeared around the corner, hauling the huge chunk of my heart in the backseat.

Mom and I didn't say much that afternoon. We had our own separate wars taking place and talking would disrupt the battle. For the rest of the day, she stayed busy on the phone, haggling with insurance companies and distracting Dad until this all blew over. Ducking the line of fire, I hid upstairs and played catch-up.

In light of all the chaos in my life, I still had a GPA to repair. Dad's threat over my car no longer held weight, but my acceptance into Howard stood in jeopardy. I needed the preoccupation, the reminder of who I used to be. I whipped out my syllabus, highlighted the list of extra-credit assignments, and redirected my energy to something useful.

For English, I had to read *Canterbury Tales* and dissect a story of my choice. *The Pardoner's Tale* of the three thieves struck a personal chord with me. Three men found bags of gold under a tree and, consumed by greed, murdered each other for a bigger portion. It brought to mind one of Ben Franklin's famous quotes I'd heard in history class: "Three may keep a secret, if the other two are dead."

Would that be the case for my sadistic triad? Tobias, Caleb, and I were braided together by empathy and secrets that would cost dearly if revealed. Would our ambitions destroy us, or would one walk away empty-handed for the sake of the other? I guess I'd find out on Monday.

I finished my essay and two math worksheets before sleep could no longer be avoided.

Caleb's use of my room granted a small relief and made the cavity that less hollow. I wondered if he'd done the same things I did while here: smelling the pillows and clothes, taking stock of every item moved, and touching each piece, hoping to feel the lingering body heat. To my surprise, I found three quarters in my bed when I pulled back the blanket. Out of habit, I recounted the coins in the jar on my dresser, and added the extra seventy-five cents to the collection with a renewed sense of hope.

Trapped in his scent, I rolled into a Caleb burrito under the covers and stared at my cell phone on the nightstand. He'd said he would call as soon as he checked into a hotel, but my voice mail showed no new messages. Though spite told me not to answer the phone, I just wanted the ring, just to know he was safe. I watched the tiny apparatus, checking for the slightest vibration or glow on the display. My eyes fixed, barely blinking, as if my will alone would make it ring at any minute. . . .

Any minute now . . .

23

There must have been a bug going around, because Caleb had come down with a bad case of Cambion fever.

It served him right for leaving me waiting by the phone, stealing hours from my life that I could never get back. If he'd suffered half the sleep deprivation that I had, it was a sound victory.

I never did get that courtesy call, but Caleb returned to his menial post at Buncha Books to do everything except work. Wherever I turned, there he was, pouting at me like someone had stolen his Big Wheel. He'd always had a peculiar side—it was just his eccentric nature—but he laid it on thick on Sunday. It began at customer service when I clocked in.

"Hey." Caleb blocked my path, wearing a heavy winter coat and a pale mask of discontent. He shuffled his feet and his hand stayed busy inside his pockets.

"Oh, hey." I sidestepped him and went to the computer, projecting my inner diva.

He bent close to my ear. "How've you been?"

The question blindsided me, but I played it cool. I couldn't let him see how he'd gotten to me. Of course, he could feel it, so no need for visual aid. "If you'd called like you said you would, you would know by now."

He peered around the store a few times as if ashamed to be seen with me. His demeanor was sketchy, a nervous collection of tics just before some back-alley transaction.

"I'm sorry. I've been busy," he said. "I don't mean to be difficult, but it's not a good idea for us to be around each other."

"Okay." I left him at the desk, no further explanation needed. If isolation would speed his recovery, who was I to delay progress?

The holiday sales made the bookstore busier than usual, which kept my mind from traveling to the music department. Between customers and restocking the baked goods, I had no time for drama. Even Alicia was too busy to trash talk. She didn't hide her excitement when she saw Caleb prowling around the aisles, but kept the giddy commentary to a minimum.

In case he hadn't been clear the last time, Caleb approached the counter to buy a brownie. "So, are you being careful? You know, in case he shows up again?"

"Yeah, Mom's got me on lockdown. She even has Ruiz playing bodyguard."

Caleb didn't see that coming. Leaning over the counter, he whispered, "How can you trust him? He's investigating me and my family."

"Yep, and he knows what we are, and I have no idea who he's working for. But he's offering protection, and I'm taking it for Mom's sake. At least he doesn't run from problems."

Caleb stiffened for a second until the verbal sting ebbed away. "It's nothing personal. I just feel that it's better that I don't see you, that's all," he replied, but it seemed more for his benefit. Maybe if he kept rehearsing those lines he might start to believe them. As it stood now, our mutual need was as strong as iron, welded together by heat and pressure.

"Sure." I handed him his food and resumed my cleaning task. The exchange was over, but he lingered for a good five minutes, watching me with shameless longing. The heating unit and the blazing oven made my shirt sticky with sweat, yet he still wore his coat, another sign that he wasn't operating on all cylinders. The torment in his eyes rendered me speechless, but I refused to offer help unless he asked.

He must have felt the third time was a charm, because he followed me to the magazine aisle during my break. "I don't think you understand how dangerous it is for us to be together."

"Dude, what is your problem? I'm not deaf. I heard you the last three times you told me. How about you follow your own advice? Stop chasing me around, quit spying on me from across the store, and take your emo ass home! You're not even scheduled to work today. Why. Are. You. Here?"

"I needed to see you," he answered simply.

I crushed the magazine in my hand before resting its crumpled remains on the shelf. My molars ground together, my palms tingled, aching to karate-chop him in the throat. Caleb was not going to infect me with his strain of crazy. I would take the high road and walk away with my dignity intact.

At least, that was the plan.

He caught my arm before I could leave the aisle, his face a testament of unspoken agony.

I lifted my head to the ceiling and groaned. "What's wrong with you? Have you fed today?"

"Around the clock."

I looked to him in surprise. Sizing him up, I asked, "Then why do you look like death warmed over?"

His gaze searched my body from head to toe, its intensity seeping into my pores. "It's not the energy I crave. It's the person it comes from."

"I wish I could feel sorry for you, but you've decided to martyr yourself for no reason. You know where I live, you have my number, and yet you continue to deny what you need."

"It won't stop at feeding, you know that. Capone's territory has been challenged and he wants to claim you. I can't trust myself to be near you."

Should I have been flattered that I'd been reduced to a piece of real estate? I understood the possessive nature of the beings inside us, but I planned to keep that lonely grain of self-respect I had left.

"Then this conversation is pointless," I said. "So, I'm going to enjoy what's left of my break." Holding my head high, I brushed past him.

"Sam."

"What!" I spun around with both fists clenched at my sides.

"I—I should leave. I've tried for hours, but my feet won't let me. Hell waits for me outside and everywhere you're not. I can't leave you. I don't think I ever can."

He'd done that on purpose! Knowing my weakness, he always uttered something random and sweet to expel the sound cussing that was his due. Why was he doing this to me, on my break, no less?

His eyes pleaded for understanding, but they also

glowed with hunger, a freak exhibit unfit for the public. I glanced to the book floor for witnesses.

"Come with me." I marched to the small recess by the front of the store that led to the stockroom. I punched my employee code into the keypad, not checking if Caleb followed me. I knew he did, so I opened the door and stepped inside. Surrounded by boxes and columns of yet-to-be-stocked books, Caleb stood by the wall, trembling from chemical withdrawal. His hands fidgeted at his sides; his blunt nails dug into his pants.

"You have to feed from me—Capone demands it. Let me guess, you've been sniffing behind me all day, taking the traces of energy left in the air." When he didn't deny it, I continued, "Is this what we've been reduced to, sneaking around like criminals? Why settle for crumbs on the floor when you can eat at the table?"

He drew deeper into the room, meandering through the maze of inventory. "I don't want to need you like this. Wanting you is bad enough. This feeling is running our lives and I can't have anything rule over me like that. I thought we'd have more time, but now, I don't know." He stopped and pressed his forehead against a bookshelf; his hands gripped the metal framework.

"No one's stopping you from living your life. I've got plans of my own, but that doesn't mean we can't be together." I crept behind him, noting how his body tightened in strain.

Sensing my approach, he looked at me over his shoulder. "Do you love him?"

I didn't need to ask who he meant, and bringing him up in conversation killed and buried the mood. "No. He's a monster, and if he had his way he would try to make me just like him."

"How so?"

"He will live as long as I do. He's gonna want to extend his shelf life. The only way to do that is to make me a demon as well," I explained. "Maybe that's why Nadine wanted to get away from him. She knew what he wanted her to do."

"That doesn't stop Lilith from wanting him," he disputed. "She's indecisive, but it's a woman's prerogative to change her mind. Isn't that what they say?"

Oh, that did it. I got right in his face. "Caleb, I don't care what she wants. She might get a kick out of suitors fighting over her, but I'm sick of it. No one wants me, not even Tobias if you think about it. It's all about Lilith. You are the only one who wants me, short, chubby, loud-mouthed, bossy me. As crazy as you are, you keep me sane. I love you and no one else."

His hand slid from the support bar on the shelf, revealing the hand-sized dent in the metal. There was no way Caleb could've done that without "inside" help, and I realized this private party was getting crowded. I looked to Caleb for an explanation, but paused at the blast of violet light. His injuries ran deeper than I'd thought, and Capone was trying to make a break for it. Mr. Baker was one wounded creature, a malady he hid well from the outside world, but not from me.

I reached out and tucked his hair behind his ear. "Stop fighting. I'm right here. I'm not going anywhere."

He closed his eyes and leaned into my touch. "Don't you see this is what he wants? It's a trap. No one is going to manipulate me; nobody will run my life but me. I won't let Tobias win."

I pulled back my hand. "Is this some sort of male ego thing? You gotta see which one of you can beat the other? Or are you so caught up with Lilith that you can't see me anymore?"

Silence met my question. I could feel the war waging within him, but his face lay dead to emotion, his eyes cold.

Lost for words, I grabbed the ends of his collar and pulled him to me. My arms roped around his waist under his coat. His heart drummed against my ear, his chest expanded under my cheek. My eyes closed, shutting out the world, centering myself on his touch and the hot, shaky release of his breath.

Caleb didn't fight as I'd thought he would and instead stood limp in my embrace. "Do you feel it?" he asked.

I nodded. The draw was strong, his hunger intensified to the point of pain, and being this close to him made it a thousand times worse.

"If you can feel it, then you know what I'm dealing with. It's not because of Capone, not some base need for satisfaction, but you. What I wouldn't give to go back to how we were this summer, to have just a few moments alone with you. But even now in this empty room, we have no privacy. Our wires are being tapped and monitored by the enemy. I can't go on like this." The tips of his fingers trickled down my arms, and I fumed from the unfairness of it all. The smallest of caresses, sentiments meant only for me, now required censorship. This was no way to live.

"Caleb," I began, but stopped at the finger to my lips.

"Samara." He rarely said my full name, but when he did, it always sounded like the only word he knew, the soft prayer of a dying man. His body pressed into mine, knotted with tension as he deliberately avoided my mouth, but took his fill on the rest of me. It was infuriating, but the gesture was kind and therapeutic, a soothing balm for my injured pride.

"Don't abuse your influence and be careful how you

tempt me," he warned against the hollow of my throat. "I'm weak, beat up, and in no shape to deal with what you're offering. You're stronger than I am right now, so go before I do something we'll both regret." He pulled away and turned his back to me.

For both our sakes, I granted his wish and went back to work. This tug-of-war was cramping our style, but we had to play by the rules until we found another strategy. At this rate, Tobias wouldn't have to lift a finger; the separation would kill us first.

Though it was Sunday, Buncha Books was staying open until ten for the holiday rush. However, Samara Marshall was clocking out at six on the dot and not a second later.

After standing outside for ten minutes, I realized that my daring escape had been for nothing, and waiting for Mom to pick me up was a lesson in humility. At least now I understood why Caleb had worn such a big coat, though he'd looked like he was about to steal something from the store.

Christmas music chimed through the speakers outside. Window shoppers strolled past me, herding around the surrounding shops while I shivered under the awning in a flimsy jean jacket, looking homeless. Maybe Mom was stuck in traffic. I was ready to call her when a heavy cloth draped my shoulders.

Caleb drifted beside me. "You look cold."

I adjusted the ends of his coat so I could slide my arms through the sleeves. The warm interior thawed my skin and I hummed at the familiar smell of vanilla and sugar. "I thought you left."

"I had to make sure you got home safe. Is your mom picking you up?" he asked.

"Supposed to, but she's running late," I answered through chattering teeth. "God, I miss having my own car. It's weird. I have keys, I got my bag; I step out of the building, and there's no car. My pattern's broken."

"I could give you a ride. Finally got my Jeep back from the shop," he offered.

I considered the option for a moment. The idea was hella tempting given the subzero climate, but sitting alone with him for any length of time was bound to end badly. "Nah. Mom would freak out if I'm not here when she shows up."

"Your call." He gathered both my hands in his and began rubbing the icy digits. "Your hands are freezing." He lowered his head and blew hot air between my palms. My thumb grazed his soft bottom lip while his hands ventured lower, stopping at the pulse on my wrist. My fingers curled to cup his chin and he stopped to look up at me under thick lashes. The world froze again and this time I wanted to stay locked in this moment. No words were spoken, but I knew he felt the same kinetic energy, the mystical force pulling us further into madness.

The sound of a throat clearing caught our attention. Caleb and I looked up at the same time, identical expressions of annoyance on our faces.

David Ruiz stepped out of the crowd and touched my arm. "Are you all right, Samara?"

Caleb took the defensive position and pulled me behind him. "She *was* fine until you came along. What are you doing here?"

"I came to pick up Samara," Ruiz said curtly, still looking at me. "Your mother's not feeling well and she asked me to pick you up."

"Is she all right? Is she hurt?" I asked, punching numbers into my cell. I didn't remember exactly when I'd taken out my phone, but fear made the body work on autopilot.

"Not in any way that I can see. But she's safe at home, resting and taking some medication," Ruiz explained.

The phone rang four times before Mom picked up. She sounded groggy but calm, a sign that the anti-anxiety medicine was doing its thing. She confirmed that Ruiz was my escort and instructed me to do everything he said.

I passed him the phone to report to Mom. I couldn't help but notice the worry in his voice as he kept asking if she was okay, making sure she ate and drank plenty of juice. The energy fanning off him was pure and sweet, a familiar vibe I often received from Caleb. He assured Mom that I would be home soon, then ended the call.

Caleb glared at Ruiz with distrust. "It's a good thing you came when you did—a bit convenient, even."

"I do what is required," Ruiz said. "I need to get you home. Don't want to worry your mother."

I took a step back. "If it's all the same to you, I'd rather ride home with Caleb."

"I'm afraid I can't allow that. I'm under strict orders to protect you."

"From who? Who the hell are you?" Caleb demanded.

Ruiz loosened his cuffs and rolled up his sleeves, revealing two strong and hairy forearms, a clear prelude to a throw-down if I ever saw one. "Who I am is not important. The main concern is why I'm here. I told you, I'm here to investigate the happenings taking place in Virginia. The Ross family ruffled a lot of feathers in the Cambion world, what with Nadine Petrovsky's murder, Nathan Ross's death, just to name a few."

And the truth finally comes out, I thought. I'd known he had inside knowledge of our existence, but to hear him say it aloud didn't make it any better. The big mystery, however, was why Caleb froze up all of a sudden.

Before my eyes, he turned pale, even paler than usual. At the moment, he seemed more angry with himself, as if there was some key element he'd overlooked, a dark secret coming back to haunt him. I gave him a hard stare, though I wasn't surprised that he would keep this tidbit from me. I just added it to the list of vital knowledge that *conveniently* slipped his mind.

Ruiz enjoyed Caleb stirring in the hot seat, and this entire ordeal seemed better suited for an interrogation room. "I advise that you go home, Caleb, and remember what we discussed at the station. Stay close to your brothers; make sure they don't leave the country. I'll contact you if I need further information, and I expect your full cooperation. I suggest you use an alternative method of feeding until further notice. If there are any more reported accidents before then, our next meeting won't be as civil. Are we clear?"

"Crystal." Caleb turned to me and pressed his forehead against mine, his anger made apparent by the trembling hands locked around my arms.

Our cold noses rubbed together while our lips danced around each other, never quite meeting. The second they did—that gentle ghost of a touch—he pulled back and walked away in a tight knot of frustration.

"Caleb." I reached out for him, but he escaped my grasp and disappeared into the swarm of shoppers. I didn't need an empathic link to tell that he was furious, and it was probably a good idea for him to cool down. He would get cool in no time seeing that it was thirty degrees and I still wore his coat.

"Come on, Samara. The car is this way." Ruiz extended his hand.

I dug in my heels, refusing to budge. "I'm not going anywhere with you until you tell me what's going on. What did you discuss with Caleb? Who sent you here to look after me?"

He looked at me as if the answer was as plain as day. "Evangeline Petrovsky—who else?"

24

Though I only lived a few minutes away from work, it was the longest road trip of my life.

I didn't look at Ruiz during the drive home, and sharing breathing space with him made me sick. An army of thoughts hijacked my brain, and I was too busy trying to reach Angie on my cell to talk anyway. I'd had a feeling she wouldn't leave well enough alone, but how could she betray my confidence like this? How much had she told the detective?

After the third call that went straight to voice mail, I gave up.

"You probably won't catch her for a few days," Ruiz said behind the wheel. "She's in New York now, delegating with the Cambion family. I believe Broderick Ross is with her, interceding for his brothers. Not sure what good that would do, but it saves us from hunting him down."

I sat in a deadened state, too burned-out from this screwed-up world to be shocked anymore. I heard the words, the information knocked at my head, but no one answered. But at least I knew where Brodie had disappeared to. While Haden and Michael looked after Caleb, Brodie was working behind the scenes to bail them out.

The detective kept his eyes on the road, his thumbs tapping the steering wheel. "I'm not explaining myself very well, am I? I keep forgetting how little you know. Let me begin by introducing myself. My name is David Manuel Ruiz, emissary and inquisitor for the Cambion family of New York. I'm sure you've heard of them."

I nodded. Haden had told me about a Cambion authority and how older families governed the smaller ones on their turf. "This family has dominion over all Cambions on the East Coast," he explained. "They never interfere in the lives of their subjects unless abnormal behavior catches their attention. The events in this town fall under that category, don't you agree?"

I leaned in with intrigue. "That's great, but what does this have to do with me?"

"Samara, you're a new Cambion under a different name, a new strain who could begin your own lineage should you choose. Since you're still a minor, you're under the Petrovsky title. On the same note, you were born within the family's territory, so you're under their protection and authority as well. Nadine's death occurred on this family's soil, under their watch, so they're obligated to investigate and document the event. And considering your . . . conversion, you've incited an interest with my employers. You are the first self-made Cambion to come along in centuries."

Fabulous! Not only was I a sideshow attraction, but I had more rules and protocol to deal with. Yay. "Who are you to this family, their messenger boy?" I asked.

"Again, who I am is not important."

"I think it is," I countered.

He said nothing until he rounded the corner leading to my neighborhood. "Believe it or not, I'm here to protect you, Samara. Your involvement with Caleb is dangerous, what with his history with women and all."

Whatever argument I had crumbled at once. "What are you talking about?"

"For centuries, the major Cambion families have set out to eradicate all incubi from the Earth. They're an abomination to human existence, as are any Cambion on the verge of transformation." Ruiz looked at me. "Caleb and his brothers knew that their father was on the brink, yet they failed to report him. The accidents this summer make the Cambion family of New York believe that Caleb's following in his father's footsteps."

My eyes grew wide with horror. "He's not."

He lifted a brow in a challenge. "Do you care to explain why three nurses went into cardiac arrest the very night Caleb went missing from the hospital? He's lucky he didn't kill them. I have to wonder how far he's willing to go before the conversion starts."

"He's not converting. He doesn't want to turn into a demon. He's a good person," I argued vehemently, but there just wasn't enough evidence to support my case. And after the Caleb-Capone mash-up on Thanksgiving night, I didn't have a leg to stand on, and neither did Caleb. The only leverage we had was that Ruiz didn't know about the mishap. At least I hoped he didn't.

"That may be so, but he's unstable, and I have the right to report this and take the Ross brothers back with me to New York for trial," Ruiz said.

"You can't!" I cried. Caleb may have been irking my nerves right now, but there was no way this guy was taking him away. If it meant kidnapping—or worse, calling up my grandpa to pull some strings—I'd do it.

"Caleb and I are linked. If something happens to him, it happens to me, and we wouldn't want to upset Evangeline, would we?" I said. He wasn't the only one who knew how to strong-arm people around here.

He pulled up to the curb in front of my house and cut off the engine. The leather seats squeaked as he turned to me. "I'm aware of your entanglement, Samara, and I truly sympathize. But this cannot continue and risk harming innocent women. Think of your mother. This is a highly sensitive situation and I can't afford to have this leak to other Cambion families. As I said, Mrs. Petrovsky is meeting with the family, trying to straighten things out. If all goes well, no one will be harmed, but we'll have to see. In the meantime, no one is allowed to leave town until I receive word."

I fell back in my seat, swaying from a sudden head rush. I'd known Angie had connections and influence, but to have her pull rank like this was creating more problems than solutions. This world was so complicated, and if Ruiz's convictions were true, Caleb would need a good lawyer. If he ever decided to talk to me again, I might even do it pro bono.

Did Ruiz open the door and tell me to tuck and roll? No, he escorted me to the house and came inside as if he lived there. I was too concerned with Mom to care. I found her upstairs, nursing a mug of herbal tea and covered in a blanket.

"Mom, you okay?" I sat next to her on the bed.

"I'm fine. I'm just overwhelmed. There's so much going on and too little time to process it." She stretched her stiff muscles and adjusted the sleeve of her frilly nightgown. "I talked to your father and told him about the storm. I hate lying to him; I was never good at it. He always said my nose twitches when I do, so it's a good thing he didn't stop by. We need to tell him soon, baby. He can't be left in the dark forever. He's worried sick about you."

"I know. Just a little longer," I promised, though I wasn't sure it was one I could keep. Dad was set in his ways and I was terrified of how he would react.

"But we finally got the insurance issue settled," she continued. "We can try to get a used car on Tuesday. It may not be the one you want, but it's transportation for school." Mom offered a weak smile.

Of all the things to worry about, she fretted over if I liked a car. Granted, I was still butt-hurt over losing my whip, but in the grand scheme of things, it was just a car. A few months ago, this would've meant the end of the world as I knew it. I couldn't believe how self-absorbed I had been, yet I still grieved in a way, for the innocence of that time had died with the leaves. Childhood was truly over.

I took the mug from her trembling hands and helped her lie down. "Come on, you should go to bed."

Mom didn't put up much of a fight and allowed me to tuck her in. She curled into the fetal position, clutching the pillow tight to her chest. I watched her toss and turn under the covers for a good twenty minutes until her body stilled. There was no way she was sleeping alone tonight, but I had to lock up the house.

Trotting downstairs, I realized Ruiz was still here—I had completely forgotten. It was kinda sweet how he stuck around, but it didn't excuse all the secrecy.

He hovered by the entryway and appeared dignified in light of the circumstances. He tilted against the wall, watching my descent with a furrowed brow. "How's your mother?"

"How do you think?" I snapped, then dragged my free

hand through my hair and gripped the root. I wanted to cuss this dude out so bad, I could taste its poison on my tongue, but it wouldn't change anything.

Ruiz waited patiently as I tried to keep my temper in check.

I opened the door for him, hoping he would take the hint. "Tell me something—was Mom and this dating thing just a means to an end? It's not cool to get played like that."

"No. Everything I told her was true, but she's forever asking questions. It's not easy to lie to her," he murmured to himself.

What did that mean? I stared at him for a moment before it finally hit me. Disgusted, I held the door frame for balance. "That's the real reason she's upset. She knows why you're here, doesn't she?"

"She knows Mrs. Petrovsky sent me for protection. Your mother is a cautious woman, one who wouldn't allow just anyone to bring her daughter home. But I couldn't tell her about my mission with the Ross brothers. Outsiders can't know about Cambion politics."

"She's my mom, not some accident or a pawn to be used in your little spy game."

He rounded on me with cold eyes and that no-nonsense persona that was all too familiar. "I have an obligation to not just one but *two* Cambion families, and I can't jeopardize my position for anyone, and that includes personal affiliations. Just know that this wasn't my intention." He stepped outside, then stopped and looked at me with a pensive expression.

"So what now?" I asked. "I'm under the impression that you care about her a lot. If so, you need to make this right and tell her everything. Secrets will ruin any relationship. Trust me."

"I know." The cold air fogged his breath as he sighed in frustration. "At some point, I'll tell her, but right now it's just . . . it's complicated."

"Welcome to my world. Enjoy your stay." I closed the door, leaving him standing on the porch.

25

Of all of my twelve years of school, including kinder-garten, no day had comprised as much fail as this one.
But that's what I got for believing things could go back to normal on Monday. What had I really expected? To go to class and pretend that the holiday from Hell had never happened? Luck didn't work that way, not for me anyway.

Mom drove me to school extra early and recited the list of safety precautions I'd already memorized. Aside from that, she didn't say a word, not about her relation-ship with Ruiz, her take on the weekend, or her two-hour conversation with Haden this morning. She looked se-verely to the road ahead, making the proper turns and stops and dropping her speed to twenty-five once we reached the school zone, but all this was done as some mechanical response brought on by habit.

She seemed distracted, troubled—proof that she was never meant for a life of crime. Somehow the Ross boys had dragged her into some covert scheme that was not only implausible but probably illegal. But she kept firm in the decision of me returning to school, insisting that we go on with our normal routine. I agreed, but I couldn't shake off the feeling of being used as live bait.

Sharing classes with the enemy didn't settle my nerves, and I counted the minutes before Tobias kick-started another round of harassment. But he didn't. He didn't show up for first period, he didn't lurk around the halls, and his presence was nowhere on campus. Relieved as I was, I stayed on guard. He was prone to materialize when I least expected it, and it would take more than a Cambion beat-down to throw off his rhythm.

Between classes, I tried to call Caleb, but got nothing but voice mail again. He was taking this separation thing seriously, determined to keep me out of his plan, out of his life. That was one bruise my ego wouldn't allow to heal. At least Angie had taken the time to leave a message—though a short and ominous one.

"I'm in New York on business. I'm sure you know what manner of business by now. I was hoping to explain this to you when I came to visit, but there's an emergency that requires my immediate attention. I'll explain everything when I arrive."

Yeah, very vague, and her tone gave me a chill of foreboding. It was the prologue of imminent doom, similar to whenever Mom said, "Wait until your father hears about this." Translation: I was so screwed.

On my way to the cafeteria, I took a moment to observe the chaotic scope of my academic environment. The color scheme of the main common area had gone from orange and brown to red and green overnight. Cutout pumpkin and pilgrims were replaced by paper snowflakes and cotton balls on the bulletin board.

Dougie leaned by his locker, chugging down a protein

shake and flexing his biceps to a squealing freshman. More girls walked around wearing those hideous *Specter* T-shirts. That annoying couple still made out in the middle of the hallway, and Jason Lao chatted in my ear about the latest news.

"Yo, there must be something in the water—people are wiggin' out. I can't post it fast enough," he said, his thumbs clicking away at his BlackBerry. "You know Alicia Holloway, right? Well, rumor has it she's got some dirty pictures of the Courtneys, but she's mad that I won't post them because they look Photoshopped. I'm a journalist and all about integrity." He popped the collar of his white shirt.

"Since when?" I asked while watching Mia hurry to her next class. She continued to ignore me, sitting in the far row in class and not returning any of my calls. I thought it best to wait her out for a few days, plus now I had to wait for my new ride to conduct a proper stakeout in front of her house. The complete turnaround of my life was still hard to process. I'd managed to push away every single person I knew. But I would get them all back. I had to.

Jason still chatted away, unfazed that I was only half listening. "Then there's a kid in my French class who said he saw a tornado or something on Thanksgiving night and it wrecked up all these cars on the freeway. Oh, and word's going around that Malik Davis ran away from home."

I turned to him, completely thrown off by the last statement. "What?"

"Yeah, he had a run-in with the law or something during the break and no one's seen him since." Jason tucked his phone behind his back as the rent-a-cop walked by. "Listen, I gotta go. I need to update my blog before lunch is over."

I sat with my rogue lunchmates and let Jason's words digest. Was Malik really missing? Why hadn't Tobias returned to the Davises' house? Maybe some fisherman found the real Malik's body and blown his cover. I would give anything to know what was going on, but no one, not even my mother, would give me a single crumb of information.

Students ambled through the back entrance from the parking lot, shaking the light rain off their coats and umbrellas. An icy breeze rushed into the toasty cafeteria whenever the double doors opened, forcing me to look up. As if on cue, as if a single thought had conjured him there, he stood just beyond the doors with his head bowed and his eyes fixed on me. Not Malik, or any other pretense, but Tobias in all his devastation.

The doors closed again, but as more students entered, he stayed locked in place. This continued for another five minutes, him playing peekaboo with the door, willing me to come to him. I obeyed, with no true conscious effort on my part, only the sole objective to reach my target.

I pushed open the door and stepped outside to find him gone. I turned to go back inside, then spotted him tucked into a small alcove off the side of the building. His back pressed against the brick wall and he watched me with what I could recognize as restrained anger.

"It's disconcerting the connection we share," he said. "I can feel him, you know. I could always feel him—his hunger, the burning in his chest whenever he looks at you, the tingle up his spine when he touches you. Makes me sick to my stomach."

"Tobias—"

"I thought I could trust you," he interrupted. "I thought you could keep a secret. Why did you give them Malik's address?"

I shrank back. "What? I don't even know where you live—I mean Malik—I mean, whoever," I stammered.

"Then why am I being blocked?"

"Blocked?" I looked to the cafeteria doors then back to him. "You mean you can't get in the school?"

"The school, the bookstore, my fucking house!" he hissed.

Now was not the time to point out that it was actually Malik Davis's house and that Tobias was getting too caught up in his method acting, so I kept quiet. The guy was outraged, and rightfully so. I wouldn't want someone changing the locks on me, and who had that kind of spare time? Who else knew about Malik and incubi repellant? The answer arrived before I could complete the question.

Caleb.

I wondered how he'd managed to pull this off, and why I hadn't come up with the idea first. This would've saved me weeks of torment.

"You ran away?" I asked, returning to the discussion.

"Didn't have a choice, did I? You look surprised. You said so yourself, this had to end eventually. I won't forget this slight, Samara."

I cowered away from his critical stare. "Don't look at me like that. I didn't grease down Malik's house or the school. You brought this on yourself. You don't know the meaning of 'No,' and you managed to piss off a whole family of Cambions."

"I couldn't care less about those demon mutts, and these stupid frat-boy pranks are hurting a lot of innocent people," he said. "You don't think I expected this? You think I didn't have a plan B, or C? Samara, there aren't enough letters in the alphabet for what I have planned. I came too close to losing what matters most and I won't do it again. No matter what they do, the outcome will be the same. If you bond with me, Caleb will die. If you bond with him, he will *still* die. I told you, I always get what I want."

"And I told you—" I drew closer, my courage building with each step. "You don't know me. I hold grudges for years and will risk self-destruction for payback. If that means taking a knife and carving Lilith out, it will be worth it to get rid of you. You might morph into whatever women want you to be, but the only thing *I* want you to be is *gone*."

The bell rang in that instant, and I stormed away before he could catch me. I felt his advance, but I tangled in the crowd, shoving my way to the entrance.

"Samara, wait," he commanded. When I ignored him, his voice broke, edged with desperation, "Lilith!"

I stopped. Slowly, I turned around to face him standing in the entryway. Raindrops spilled down his cheeks, creating tears he would never make on his own. I took one step and then another until I stood with only the door frame and the cold air separating us. Still not satisfied, he crooked his finger and willed me to come closer.

I had become a paraplegic learning to walk again. Basic mobile skills failed me at the moment and every step required effort. Something pulled against me in resistance, my shoes weighed down by lead, my legs bracketed by rusty hinges in need of oil. By the time I stood in front of him, sweat and rain dotted my forehead.

Tobias appraised my unsteady approach. "You're stronger than last time. I underestimated you, Flower. I won't make that mistake again." He reached behind my head and pulled me forward, allowing our mouths to meet in a rush of violence.

He traced the seam between my lips, coaxing them

apart. Unable to resist the warmth, I gave in and enjoyed his tongue working its evil spell. It swirled against the soft palate of my mouth, causing my pulse to race and tiny hairs on my neck to stand straight. A bolt of lightning pierced my heart, recharging nerves and reviving dead cells.

This was the kiss of life that I knew all too well, but this wasn't like any life I'd ever tasted. Gold and green fireworks exploded behind my eyelids and my center of gravity melted away. Power. Unbridled power coursed through me in silken ribbons, weaving around the fibers in my muscles and fusing to the pulsing tissue.

"Do you love me?" he asked against my lips.

"Yes." It was my voice, the breath pushed from my mouth to form the word, but it seemed foreign.

"Then prove it. Things didn't go as planned last time, but we can go forward. I've been wronged and it's up to you to make it right. Now, I've wasted too much time here and it's no longer safe. I'm leaving and I want you to come with me. It will be just us. No family, no friends, no rules. We can feed as often as we like without guilt. We still can have our chance. Come with me now, and I can give you forever."

"Okay." Again, the voice was still mine, but I didn't remember uttering the word. What was going on?

"Good." He leaned in and whispered something in my ear. The low rumble of his voice made me drowsy, but I had to focus on what he was saying. I could barely follow it, but every syllable made me greedy for more, a drop of rain after a long drought.

He took me by the hand and led me to the parking lot, and I followed in a drunken daze. My head felt ten times larger than its normal size and my ability to walk still remained a mystery. Everything in the outside world was set on fast-forward. Cars, trees, and orange Driver's Ed cones rushed by me in a blur while the dead weight of my brain lagged behind.

Wasn't I supposed to be in class? I had a report on Chaucer to turn in. I'd worked hard on that thing and it was worth a quarter of my semester grade. My class was on the other side of the school. Where was I going anyway?

It didn't take me long to find out as we stopped beside Malik's silver Toyota in the very last row. Tobias reached over the back of the cab and pulled out a rusty toolbox with chipped red paint. Setting it down, he began rummaging through the compartments until he found a pair of cutting pliers. He stood and gently took my hand in his again. His thick fingers felt warm against my wrist, which looked small and dainty by comparison. He seemed fascinated by my hand and I half expected him to slip a ring on my finger at any minute.

"One more thing before we go. Hold still, I don't wanna cut you." He slid the thin chain of my bracelet between the pliers' dull blades.

One quick snip was all it took to give me freedom. My shackle fell to the wet concrete with a strange note of finality that relieved and frightened me at once. I didn't have to worry about the all-seeing eye of my mother. I could go wherever I wanted. I could visit Caleb anytime I pleased. But I wasn't sure why I would want to see him right now. The faded image of his face drifted behind my eyes, losing focus until there was nothing more than a mirage—better still, an empty black shape cut out of the scenery.

Something was missing, yet I had never felt so free, so empowered. It was a yummy feeling, a long languorous stretch that reached all the way to my toes. It felt good to let go, to just sit back and say "screw it." And I would enjoy this high for as long as it lasted.

With a warm smile on his face, Tobias helped me into the truck, then climbed into the driver's side. He took his time, adjusting the seat and mirrors, even changed the radio station with the ease of a man on a daytrip. He backed out of the parking space, changed gears, then drove off of school property in the middle of the day with one distinct destination in mind. I just wished I knew what it was.

What about my clothes? Shouldn't I have packed first? I thought of what Mom would think about me skipping school again. Technically, I was still in school, according to the bracelet lying in the parking lot. But she would worry if I wasn't waiting for her when she picked me up this afternoon. I considered calling her, but I realized I'd left my phone in my book bag, which was trapped inside my locker. Talk about bad timing.

I looked out the window to survey the town I knew and loved with an appreciative eye. I doubted whatever city we traveled to would hold the same charm. True, I complained about its simplicity, and the colonial weirdoes roaming around, but this was my birth home. Drinking in the landscape, I recalled how it had been nothing but woods and cornfields when I was a kid, and now strip malls and fast-food joints obstructed the sky-line.

Was I supposed to go to work today? I forgot to check my schedule. I was sure Alicia could cover for me, but how would I call her? I didn't have my cell phone. This was very inconvenient, no notice whatsoever. It wasn't as though we were running from the law; he could've at least allowed me to grab my bag.

God, were there enough hotels in this town or did they need to build more? I wondered where what's-his-name was staying. Wait, what was his name? That's odd; I'd just had it a second ago. Caleb! Yes, I wondered which hotel he was staying at. Knowing him, he'd probably booked the one with the biggest room service menu. I was going to miss my Cake Boy, though I wasn't sure why. He was coming with us, right?

Thinking of room service reminded me that I was hungry. I hadn't gotten to finish my lunch before Tobias picked me up. Again, bad timing. He really should have planned this better. He was the one who kept going on about me not eating properly and—

My eyes lit up at the sight of a small yogurt shack in the middle of the shopping center. Its green and white striped sunshade flashed at me like a beacon of hope. I wondered if Tobias would make a quick stop for a slushy, though I doubted it.

But Samara loved slushies, and she could use some cheering up right now. She wasn't in the best of moods; I could feel her wiggling around inside trying to get out. Such a strong one for her age, a true warrior worthy of the succubi legacy. I couldn't have picked a better host, but her temper was no laughing matter.

If this little scheme was going to work, Tobias needed to get us out of town. Fast.

BURNING EMERALD

Jaime Reed

ABOUT THIS GUIDE

The following questions are intended to
enhance your group's reading of
BURNING EMERALD.

Discussion Questions

1. The story is told through an outspoken character. Does the narrative voice enhance or detract from the story?

2. Samara deals with a lot of difficult moments at home and in school. Are there situations in her life you can identify with? If so, how?

3. Though overprotective, Samara's mom tries to support her daughter. If you were in the same situation, would you trust your parents with that secret?

4. Being a Cambion takes a great deal of responsibility, and there's a constant challenge to maintain one's humanity. How do you think you would handle it?

5. Samara made several choices that had moral implications. Would you have made the same decisions? Why? Why not?

6. Samara and Caleb share an empathic link where they can sense each other's emotions. What would you do if you shared a similar connection with someone?

7. Lilith and Capone have personalities of their own. If you had a sentient being, how would you think he/she would behave?

8. Tobias has the ability to turn into any human he sees. Who would you turn into? Would you use that power for good or evil?

9. Samara's book, *Shh,* is mentioned several times. What is its symbolic significance?

10. Caleb, Samara, and Tobias have an unusual dynamic. Would you consider it a love triangle? If so, how is their relationship different from other love triangles?

11. Life and death is an ongoing theme in the story and they affect the characters in different ways: grief, insanity, depression, revenge. Are the reactions justified? Do they make the characters more sympathetic?

12. Tobias referred to Cambions as "demon mutts," establishing a type of classist view regarding his kind. How is this idea relevant in the real world?

13. If irony really had a color, what shade would it be?

Don't miss the next installment in the
Cambion Chronicles:

Fading Amber.

In stores January 2013!

In stores now:

Creeping with the Enemy

by Kimberly Reid

Using skills learned from her mom, an undercover cop, Chanti Evans has already exposed lies and made enemies at her posh new school, so she's no stranger to the games people play. But she's learning the hard way that at Langdon Prep, friends can play more dangerous games than any enemy.

The line in the Center Street bodega is five deep because it's Freebie Friday and the tamales are buy one, get one. I don't mind the wait—the scent of green chili reminds me how lucky I am to live on Aurora Avenue, just two blocks from the best tamales on the planet. Seeing how it's smack in the middle of Metro's second worst police zone, there isn't a lot to appreciate about the Ave, so that's saying something about these tamales.

Since they only let you get one order, I always find someone to go along who doesn't love them like I do so I can get one extra. Today my tamale pimp is Bethanie—we're numbers six and seven in line—and she's calling me some choice words for making her wait for a free tamale when she can afford to buy the whole bodega. I'm trying to explain to her that there's no sport in being rich (not that I would know) when a guy walks in from a Ralph Lauren ad and becomes number eight in line.

I don't know how a person could look so out of place and seem completely at ease at the same time, but this guy is pulling it off. He's also checking out Bethanie so hard that even though he's a complete stranger, he makes me feel like I'm the one who crashed the party.

"Did you lose something over here or what?" I ask the dude since Bethanie doesn't seem to mind him staring at us like we're on the menu with the tamales.

"Chanti, that's so rude," Bethanie tells me, never taking her eyes off Preppie. "Pay her no mind. She simply gets out of sorts when she's hungry."

First off, it's none of this complete stranger's business how I get when I'm hungry. It doesn't matter that he looks like a model, I pretty much don't trust anyone with my business. You never know how they might use it against you, even something as minor as your eating pattern. No, I'm not paranoid—I'm speaking truth. Second, why is she talking like that? *Pay her no mind. She simply gets out of sorts.* Bethanie's still working on her old money, rich girl impersonation, so maybe she thinks the girls Preppie hangs around talk that way.

"What's so good in here that people are willing to wait for it?" he asks Bethanie. He pretty much ignores me, so I almost laugh when his line goes right over her head.

"Supposedly the tamales are," she says, "but I've never had them."

I'm no pro at the flirty thing, but I'm sure he wasn't expecting her answer to be *tamales*. I move forward in the line, ignore their small talk and study the five-item menu as though I don't know what to order. Now there are only two people in front of me. Some Tejano music and the smell of cooking food drifts into the store from somewhere behind the clerk. I imagine somebody's grandmother back there wrapping corn husks around masa harina and pork. Yum.

I check out Preppie Dude like I'm not really looking at him but concentrating on the canned peaches on the shelf behind him. Cute. Not so cute he couldn't at least say hello to me before he starts fiening for my friend. He's still the last person in line even though tamale happy hour starts at four o'clock and the line is usually out the door until five. Weird, because it's only four-thirty. I'm about to mention how weird that is to Bethanie, but she's finally figured out Preppie is flirting with her and has apparently forgotten me, too.

Now there's just one person ahead, Ada Crawford, who lives across the street from me and who I'm pretty sure is a prostitute even though I don't have any proof. If we lived in a different neighborhood, I might say she was a call girl since her clients come to her. But we live in Denver Heights, so she doesn't get a fancy title. Luckily, she hasn't noticed me behind her because I'm not supposed to be here and I wouldn't want her to tell my mother she saw me. Not that Ada ever has much to say to my mom.

Still no one else has come in. Even more strange is the fact there's only one person working the counter on busy Freebie Friday, a man I've never seen before and I'm a regular. Along with the new clerk, maybe they've also changed the cut-off time to four-thirty. I suppose the owners would go broke if all people did was come in for the Freebie and not buy anything else. Or worse, get a friend to pimp an extra Freebie. I place my order—feeling slightly guilty—when I hear the bells over the door jangling a new arrival just as Ada walks away with her order. I look back to see a man holding the door open for Ada. He stays by the door once she's gone, and just stands there looking at the three of us still in line. He's jumpy. Nervous. He looks around the bodega but doesn't join the line and doesn't walk down the aisles of overpriced food. His left hand is in the pocket of his jacket.

My gut tells me to get out of the store. *Now.*

Just as I grab Bethanie's arm, the man brings his hand out of his jacket. It's too late.

"All right, everybody stay cool. Don't start none, won't be none. Just give me what's in the drawer," he says to the clerk, pointing the gun at him.

I'm hoping the clerk won't try to jump bad and pull out whatever he has under the counter. Every owner of a little mom-and-pop in my neighborhood has something under the counter. Or maybe it's in the back with the tamale-making grandmother. But no one comes from the back and the clerk isn't the owner. From what I can tell, it's his first day and he apparently doesn't care about the money or the shop, because he opens the cash drawer immediately. Bethanie pretends she's from money, but I know she's a lot more like me than she lets on. She knows what to do in a situation like this. Stay quiet and let it play out. We steal a quick glance at one another and I know I'm right. Either she's been through it before, or always expected it to happen one day.

I'm trying to stay calm by thinking ahead to when it will be over. Ninety seconds from now, this will just be a story for us to tell. The perp will be in his car taking the exit onto I-70. Hopefully I will not have puked all over myself by then. Or worse.

But then the cute guy speaks.

"Look man, just calm down."

What the hell? *Just shut up*, I want to scream. The clerk has already put the money into a paper bag and he's handing it over right now. This will all be over in thirty seconds if Preppie will just shut up.

The perp turns the gun in our direction. I lock eyes with him even though I know it's not the smartest thing to do. He realizes I can identify him; I can see him thinking about it, wondering what to do next. Suddenly, the smell of tamales sucker punches me and my stomach lurches. The wannabe-hero turns his back to the perp and shields Bethanie, pushing her to the ground and sending the contents of her bag all over the bodega floor. That move is like a cue for the perp. He breaks our gaze, grabs the paper bag from the clerk, and takes off.

I was right—it's over in just about ninety seconds. None of us wants to stick around to give the cops a statement. Preppie, who might have gotten us all killed, helps Bethanie grab the stuff that fell out of her bag while I scan the store for cameras. There aren't any that I can tell. As the three of us leave the store, the clerk is picking up the phone to call either the owner or the police, depending on how good the owner is about obeying employment laws and paying his taxes. I manage not to puke until I reach the parking lot.

"Clean yourself up and let's get out of here," Bethanie says, handing me a fast-food napkin from her purse to wipe my mouth. It smells like a fish sandwich and perfume, which doesn't do a thing for my upset stomach.

"But we're witnesses," I say, though I have no intention of sticking around, either. But saying it makes me feel like I at least considered doing the right thing.

"Exactly. Get in the car and open your window. I don't want my car smelling like sick."

I do what she says and tell myself I have to leave because Bethanie is my ride, even though I'm only two blocks from home. She hustled me out of the store and to her car because she's hiding something and has been since I met her a little over a month ago. So far, I've figured out that she lied her way into Langdon Preparatory School, pretending to be poor so she could get in on a scholarship because the only remaining slots were for the underprivileged. Like me. Unlike Bethanie, I never wanted to be there. Lana—that's my mother—forced me to because she was worried that I'd get into trouble in my neighborhood school.

That's the real reason I don't stay around to talk to the cops. The minute I tell her I can identify that perp, Lana will take me down to the police department to pick him out of a lineup. That would be a problem because one, I am a total wuss and don't want some pissed-off bad guy after me for retaliation. And two, Lana will put me on lockdown immediately following the lineup, just when I'm beginning to have a life.

This is one of the many drawbacks to having a cop for a mother. She sees nothing but bad all day so she figures her number-one job is to shield me from it. That's a tough gig in our neighborhood, so she made me go way across town to this rich prep school, which turned out to have more bad guys than there are on my street. She made me quit working at the Tastee Treets because a couple of crackheads held it up one night during my shift. If she finds out about the robbery at the bodega, she'll make me identify the perp because she takes being a cop seriously, then she'll put me into her own version of a witness protection program because she takes being a mother seriously.

And I can't have that because, as I said, I am finally beginning to have a social life. It's sad to admit, but I am a high school junior who has never been kissed—I mean really kissed where you feel it in every part of you and you wonder how you were able to survive without it, as though oxygen and water and food will never be enough to sustain you ever again because of that kiss—until just two weeks ago. To my credit, I'm a year younger than the average junior, so the fact that I'm a late bloomer isn't all that weird. Now that I'm finally blooming, there is no way anyone can stop me from having that kind of kiss again.

Bethanie definitely won't tell anyone what happened today. That's a fact. She's been through something worse than what just went down. I know this not just because she didn't lose her lunch in the parking lot like I did, but because of something she said to me when I figured out she was really rich and she thought I might expose her: *You don't know nothing about me or where I come from. I can tell you now—I'm never going back.* She's running from something bad, and anytime someone's running, it's either from the cops or from someone who is being chased by the cops, which is probably worse.

I'm not sure why Preppie was in such a hurry to get out of here—maybe he doesn't want his friends to know he was slumming in Denver Heights—but he was gone by the time Bethanie and I got in her car.

I just hope the bodega didn't have a surveillance camera I missed when I made a quick scan of the store, that the clerk doesn't recognize me from the neighborhood (not a stretch since I've never seen him before), and that there were no witnesses who saw me go in or out. Then it would be as though I was never there. That's why I get into Bethanie's car even though I know it's wrong to run. I guess the owner minds all the laws because we can hear the sirens approaching as we drive away.